DESTINY AT THE DOOR

"I have been on a far journey," said the seer Oktav. "I have visited many worlds that were supposed to be dead, and have seen what strange horrors result when mere men use power befitting only a god. I must tell you all I know, so that you can judge how best to act."

He looked up quickly, and Clawly followed his glance. Once again Oktav's summoner stood in the doorway.

Clawly had time only for the barest glance— and Oktav had even less. A great tongue of softly bluish flame licked out from the summoner's hand and folded around Oktav like a shroud.

TORCH RIDER

D'mahl did not look back at the scoutship for a long time. When he did, his universe had neither back nor front nor sides nor top nor bottom. All around him was an infinite black hole dusted with meaningless stars, and every direction seemed to be down. His mind rejected the impossible sensory data. Polarities reversed, so that the entire universe of stars and nothingness seemed to be collapsing in on him.

He screamed. .

D1473976

BINARY STAR NO.1

DESTINY TIMES THREE

Fritz Leiber

RIDING THE TORCH

Norman Spinrad

A DELL BOOK

Published by
Dell Publishing Co., Inc.
1 Dag Hammarskjold Plaza
New York, New York 10017

DESTINY TIMES THREE originally appeared in
Astounding Stories.
Copyright © 1945 by Fritz Leiber
Copyright © renewed 1973 by Fritz Leiber
RIDING THE TORCH was originally published in
THREADS OF TIME,
an anthology edited by Robert Silverberg.
Copyright © 1974 by Norman Spinrad

Afterword to DESTINY TIMES THREE
copyright © 1978 by Norman Spinrad
Afterword to RIDING THE TORCH
copyright © 1978 by Fritz Leiber

Illustrations copyright © 1978 by Freff

All rights reserved. No part of this book may be
reproduced or transmitted in any form or by any
means, electronic or mechanical, including photo-
copying, recording or by any information storage
and retrieval system, without the written permission
of the Publisher, except where permitted by law.

Dell ® TM 681510, Dell Publishing Co., Inc.

ISBN: 0-440-10564-1

Printed in the United States of America
First printing—August 1978

DESTINY TIMES THREE

THREE

BY FRITZ LEIBER

The ash Yggdrasil great evil suffers,
Far more than men do know;

The hart bites its top, its trunk is rotting,
And Nidhogg gnaws beneath.

ELDER EDDA.

In ghostly, shivering streamers of green and blue, like northern lights, the closing hues of the fourth Hoderson synchromy, called "the Yggdrasil," shuddered down toward visual silence. Once more the ancient myth, antedating even the Dawn Civilization, had been told—of the tree of life with its roots in heaven and hell and the land of the frost giants, and serpents gnawing at those roots and the gods fighting to preserve it. Transmuted into significant color by Hoderson's genius, interpreted by the world's greatest color instrumentalists, the primeval legend of cosmic dread and rottenness and mystery, of wheels within cosmic wheels, had once more enthralled its beholders.

In the grip of an unearthly excitement, Thorn crouched forward, one hand jammed against the grassy earth beyond his outspread cloak. The lean wrist shook. It burst upon him, as never before, how the Yggdrasil legend paralleled the hypothesis which Clawly and he were going to present later this night to the World Executive Committee.

More roots of reality than one, all right, and worse than serpents gnawing, if that hypothesis were true.

And no gods to oppose them—only two fumbling, overmatched men.

Thorn stole a glance at the audience scattered across the hillside. The upturned faces of utopia's sane, healthy citizenry seemed bloodless and cruel and infinitely alien. Like masks. Thorn shuddered.

A dark, stooped figure slipped between him and Clawly. In the last dying upflare of the synchromy—the last wan lightning stroke as the storm called life departed from the universe—Thorn made out a majestic, ancient face shadowed by a black hood. Its age put him in mind of a fancy he had once heard someone advance, presumably in jest—that a few men of the Dawn Civilization's twentieth century had somehow secretly survived into the present. The stranger and Clawly seemed to be conversing in earnest, low-pitched whispers.

Thorn's inward excitement reached a peak. It was as if his mind had become a thin, taut membrane, against which, from the farthest reaches of infinity, beat unknown pulses. He seemed to sense the presence of stars beyond the stars, time-streams beyond time.

The synchromy closed. There began a long moment of complete blackness. Then—

Thorn sensed what could only be described as something from a region beyond the stars beyond the stars, from an existence beyond the time-streams beyond time. A blind but purposeful fumbling that for a moment closed on him and made him its agent.

No longer his to control, his hand stole sideways, touched some soft fabric, brushed along it with infinite delicacy, slipped beneath the layer of similar fabric, closed lightly on a round, hard, smooth something about as big as a hen's egg. Then his hand came swiftly back and thrust the something into his pocket.

Gentle groundlight flooded the hillside, though hardly touching the black false-sky above. The audience burst into applause. Cloaks were waved, making the hillside a crazy sea of color. Thorn blinked stupidly. Like a flimsy but brightly painted screen switched abruptly into place, the scene around him cut off his vision of many-layered infinities. And the groping power that a moment before had commanded his movements now vanished as suddenly as it had come, leaving him with the realization that he had just committed an utterly unmotivated, irrational theft.

He looked around. The old man in black was already striding toward the amphitheater's rim, threading his way between applauding groups. Thorn half-withdrew from his pocket the object he had stolen. It was about two inches in diameter and of a bafflingly gray texture, neither a gem, nor a metal, nor a stone, nor an egg, though faintly suggestive of all four.

It would be easy to run after the man, to say, "You dropped this." But he didn't.

The applause became patchy, erratic, surged up again as members of the orchestra began to emerge from the pit. There was a lot of confused activity in that direction. Shouts and laughter.

A familiar sardonic voice remarked, "Quite a gaudy show they put on. Though perhaps a bit too close for comfort to our business of the evening."

Thorn became aware that Clawly was studying him speculatively. He asked, "Who was that you were talking to?"

Clawly hesitated a moment. "A psychologist I consulted some months back when I had insomnia. You remember."

Thorn nodded vaguely, stood sunk in thought. Clawly prodded him out of it with, "It's late. There are quite a few arrangements to check, and we haven't much time."

Together they started up the hillside.

Especially as a pair, they presented a striking appearance—they were such a study in similarities and contrasts. Certainly they both seemed spiritually akin to some wilder and more troubled age than safe, satisfied, wholesome utopia. Clawly was a small man, but dapper and almost dancingly lithe, with gleamingly alert, subtle features. He might have been some Borgia or Medici from that dark, glittering, twisted core of the Dawn Civilization, when by modern standards mankind was more than half insane. He looked like a small, red-haired, devil-may-care Satan, harnessed for good purposes.

Thorn, on the other hand, seemed like a somewhat disheveled and reckless saint, lured by evil. His tall, gaunt frame increased the illusion. He, too, would have fitted into that history-twisted black dawn, perhaps as a Savonarola or da Vinci.

In that age they might have been the bitterest and most vindictive of enemies, but it was obvious that in this they were the most unshakably loyal of friends.

One also sensed that more than friendship linked them. Some secret, shared purpose that demanded the utmost of their abilities and put upon their shoulders crushing responsibilities.

They looked tired. Clawly's features were too nervously mobile, Thorn's eyes too darkly circled, even allowing for the shadows cast by the groundlight, which waned as the false-sky faded, became ragged, showed the stars.

They reached the amphitheater's grassy rim, walked along a row of neatly piled flying togs with distinctive luminescent monograms, spotted their own. Already members of the audience were lurching like bats into the summary darkness, filling it with the faint gusty hum of subtronic power, that basic force underlying electric, magnetic, and gravitational phenomena, that titan, potentially earth-destroying power, chained for human use.

As he climbed into his flying togs, Thorn kept looking around. False-sky and groundlight had both dissolved, opening a view to the far horizon, although a little weather, kept electronically at bay for the synchromy, was beginning to drift in—thin streamers of cloud. He felt as never before a poignancy in the beauty of utopia, because he knew as never before how near it might be to disaster, how closely it was pressed upon by alien infinities. There was something spectral about the grandeur of the lonely, softly glowing skylons, lofty and distant as mountains, thrusting up from the dark rolling countryside. Those vertical, one-building cities of his people, focuses of communal activity, gleaming pegs sparsely studding the whole earth—the Mauve Z peering over the next hill, seeming to top it but actually miles away; beyond it the Gray Twins, linked by a fantastically delicate aerial bridge; off to the left the pearly finger of the Opal Cross; last, farther left, thirty miles away but jutting boldly above the curve of the earth, the mountainous Blue Lorraine—all these majestic skylons seemed to Thorn like the last pinnacles of some fairy city engulfed by a rising black tide. And the streams of flying men and women, with their softly winking identification lights, no more than fireflies doomed to drown.

His fingers adjusted the last fastening of his togs, paused there. Clawly only said, "Well?" but there was in that one word the sense of a leave-taking from all this beauty and comfort and safety—an ultimate embarkation.

They pulled down their visors. From their feelings, it might have been Mars toward which they launched themselves—a sullen ember halfway up the sky, even now being tentatively probed by the First Interplanetary Expedition. But their actual destination was the Opal Cross.

Never before had the screams of nightmare been such a public problem; now the wise men almost wished they could forbid sleep in the small hours, that the shrieks of cities might less horribly disturb the pale, pitying moon as it glimmered on green waters.

Nyarlathotep, H. P. LOVECRAFT.

Suppressing the fatigue that surged up in him disconcertingly, Clawly rose to address the World Executive Committee. He found it less easy to suppress the feeling that had in part caused the surge of fatigue: the illusion that he was a charlatan seeking to persuade sane men of the truth of fabricated legends of the supernatural. His smile was characteristic of him—friendly, but faintly diabolic, mocking himself as well as others. Then the smile faded.

He summed up, "Well, gentlemen, you've heard the experts. And by now you've guessed why, with the exception of Thorn, they were asked to testify separately. Also, for better or worse"—he grimaced grayly—"you've guessed the astounding nature of the danger which Thorn and I believe overhangs the world. You know what we want—the means for continuing our research on a vastly extended and accelerated scale, along with a program of confidential detective investigation throughout the world's citizenry. So nothing remains but to ask your verdict. There are a few points, however, which perhaps will bear stressing."

There was noncommittal silence in the Sky Room of the Opal Cross. It was a huge chamber and seemed no less huge because the ceiling was at present opaque—a great gray span arching from the World Map on the south wall to the Space Map on the north. Yet the few men gathered in an uneven horseshoe of armchairs near the center in no way suggested political leaders seeking a prestige-enhancing background for their deliberations, but rather a group of ordinary men who for various practical reasons had chosen to meet in a ballroom. Any other group than the World Executive Committee might just as well have reserved the Sky Room. Indeed, others had danced here earlier this night, as was mutely testified by a scattering of lost gloves, scarves, and slippers, along with half-emptied glasses and other flotsam of gaiety.

Yet in the faces of the gathered few there was apparent a wisdom and a penetrating understanding and a leisurely efficiency in action that it would have been hard to find the equal of, in any similar group in earlier times. And a good thing, thought Clawly, for what he was trying to convince them of was something not calculated to appeal to the intelligence of practical administrators—it was doubtful if any earlier culture would have granted him and Thorn any hearing at all.

He surveyed the faces unobtrusively, his dark glance flitting like a shadow, and was relieved to note that only in Conjerly's and perhaps Tempelmar's was a completely unfavorable reaction apparent. Firemoor, on the contrary, registered feverish and unquestioning belief, but that was to be expected in the volatile, easily swayed chief of the Extraterrestrial Service—and a man who was Clawly's admiring friend. Firemoor was alone in this open expression of credulity. Chairman Shielding, whose opinion mattered most, looked on the whole skeptical and perhaps a shade disapproving; though that, fortunately, was the heavy-set man's normal expression.

The rest, reserving judgment, were watchful and attentive. With the unexpected exception of Thorn, who seemed scarcely to be listening, lost in some strange fatigued abstraction since he had finished making his report.

A still-wavering audience, Clawly decided. What he said now, and how he said it, would count heavily.

He touched a small box. Instantly some tens of thousands of pinpricks of green light twinkled from the World Map.

He said, "The nightmare-frequency for an average night a hundred years ago, as extrapolated from random samplings. Each dot—a bad dream. A dream bad enough to make the dreamer wake in fright."

Again he touched the box. The twinkling pattern changed slightly—there were different clusterings—but the total number of pinpricks seemed not to change.

"The same, for fifty years ago," he said. "Next—forty." Again there was merely a slight alteration in the grouping.

"And now—thirty." This time the total number of pinpricks seemed slightly to increase.

Clawly paused. He said, "I'd like to remind you, gentlemen, that Thorn proved conclusively that his method of sampling was not responsible for any changes in the frequency. He met all the objections you raised—that his subjects were reporting their dreams more fully, that he wasn't switching subjects often enough to avoid cultivating a nightmare-dreaming tendency, and so on."

Once more his hand moved toward the box. "Twenty-five." This time there was no arguing about the increase.

"Twenty."

"Fifteen."

"Ten."

"Five."

Each time the total greenness jumped, until now it was a general glow emanating from all the continental areas. Only the seas still showed widely scattered points, where men dreamed in supra- or sub-surface craft, and a few heavy clusters, where ocean-based skylons rose through the waves.

"And now, gentlemen, the present."

The evil radiance swamped the continents, reached out and touched the faces of the armchair observers.

"There you have it, gentlemen. A restful night in utopia," said Clawly quietly. The green glow unwholesomely emphasized his tired pallor and the creases of strain around eyes and mouth. He went on, "Of course it's obvious that if nightmares are as common as all that, you and yours can hardly have escaped. Each of you knows the answer to that question. As for myself—

my nightly experiences provide one more small confirmation of Thorn's report."

He switched off the map. The carefully noncommittal faces turned back to him.

Clawly noted that the faint, creeping dawn-line on the World Map was hardly two hours away from the Opal Cross. He said, "I pass over the corroborating evidence—the slight steady decrease in average sleeping time, the increase in day sleeping and nocturnal social activity, the unprecedented growth of art and fiction dealing with supernatural terror, and so on—in order to emphasize as strongly as possible Thorn's secondary discovery: the similarity between the nightmare landscapes of his dreamers. A similarity so astonishing that, to me, the wonder is that it wasn't noticed sooner, though of course Thorn wasn't looking for it and he tells me that most of his earlier subjects were unable, or disinclined, to describe in detail the landscapes of their nightmares." He looked around. "Frankly, that similarity is unbelievable. I don't think even Thorn did full justice to it in the time he had for his report—you'd have to visit his offices, see his charts and dream-sketches, inspect his monumental tables of correlation. Think: hundreds of dreamers, to take only Thorn's samples, thousands of miles apart, and all of them dreaming—not the *same* nightmare, which might be explained by assuming telepathy or some subtle form of mass suggestion—but nightmares with the same landscape, the same general landscape. As if each dreamer were looking through a different window at a consistently distorted version of our own world. A dream world so real that when I recently suggested to Thorn he try to make a map of it, he did *not* dismiss my notion as nonsensical."

The absence of a stir among his listeners was more impressive than any stir could have been. Clawly noted that Conjerly's frown had deepened, become almost angry. He seemed about to speak, when Tempelmar casually forestalled him.

"I don't think telepathy can be counted out as an

explanation," said the tall, long-featured, sleepy-eyed man. "It's still a purely hypothetical field—we don't know how it would operate. And there may have been contacts between Thorn's subjects that he didn't know about. They may have told each other their nightmares and so started a train of suggestion."

"I don't believe so," said Clawly slowly. "His precautions were thorough. Moreover, it wouldn't fit with the reluctance of the dreamers to describe their nightmares."

"Also," Tempelmar continued, "we still aren't a step nearer the underlying cause of the phenomenon. It might be anything—for instance, some unpredictable physiological effect of subtronic power, since it came into use about thirty years ago."

"Precisely," said Clawly. "And so for the present we'll leave it at that—vastly more frequent nightmares with strangely similar landscapes, cause unknown— while I—" he again gauged the position of the dawn-line "—while I hurry on to those matters which I consider the core of our case: the incidence of cryptic amnesia and delusions of nonrecognition. The latter first."

Again Conjerly seemed about to interrupt, and again something stopped him. Clawly got the impression it was a slight deterring movement from Tempelmar.

He touched the box. Some hundreds of yellow dots appeared on the World Map, a considerable portion of them in close clusters of two and three.

He said, "This time, remember, we can't go back any fifty years. These are such recent matters that there wasn't any hint of them even in last year's Report on the Psychological State of the World. As the experts agreed, we are dealing with an entirely new kind of mental disturbance. At least, no cases can be established prior to the last two years, which is the period covered by this projection."

He looked toward the map. "Each yellow dot is a case of delusions of nonrecognition. An otherwise nor-

DESTINY TIMES THREE 21

mal individual fails to recognize a family member or friend, maintains in the face of all evidence that he is an alien and impostor—a frequent accusation, quite baseless, is that his place has been taken by an unknown identical twin. This delusion persists, attended by emotional disturbances of such magnitude that the sufferer seeks the services of a psychiatrist—in those cases we *know* about. With the psychiatrist's assistance, one of two adjustments is achieved: the delusions fade and the avowed alien is accepted as the true individual, or they persist and there is a separation—where husband and wife are involved, a divorce. In either case, the sufferer recovers completely.

"And now—cryptic amnesia. For a reason that will soon become apparent, I'll first switch off the other projection."

The yellow dots vanished, and in their place glowed a somewhat smaller number of violet pinpoints. These showed no tendency to form clusters.

"It is called cryptic, I'll remind you, because the victim makes a very determined and intelligently executed effort to conceal his memory lapse—frequently shutting himself up for several days on some pretext and feverishly studying all materials and documents relating to himself he can lay hands on. Undoubtedly sometimes he succeeds. The cases we hear about are those in which he makes such major slips—as being mistaken as to what his business is, whom he is married to, who his friends are, what is going on in the world—that he is forced, against his will, to go to a psychiatrist. Whereupon, realizing that his efforts have failed, he generally confesses his amnesia, but is unable to offer any information as to its cause, or any convincing explanation of his attempt at concealment. Thereafter, readjustment is rapid."

He looked around. "And now, gentlemen, a matter which the experts didn't bring out, because I arranged it that way. I have saved it in order to impress it upon your minds as forcibly as possible—the correlation between cryptic amnesia and delusions of nonrecognition."

He paused with his hand near the box, aware that there was something of the conjurer about his movements and trying to minimize it. "I'm going to switch on both projections at once. Where cases of cryptic amnesia and delusions of nonrecognition coincide—I mean, where it is the cryptic amnesiac about whom the other person or persons had delusions of nonrecognition —the dots will likewise coincide; and you know what happens when violet and yellow light mix. I'll remind you that in ordinary cases of amnesia there are no delusions of nonrecognition—family and friends are aware of the victim's memory lapse, but they do not mistake him for a stranger."

His hand moved. Except for a sprinkling of yellow, the dots that glowed on the map were pure white.

"Complementary colors," said Clawly quietly. "The yellow has blanked out all the violet. In some cases one violet has accounted for a cluster of yellows— where more than one individual had delusions of nonrecognition about the same cryptic amnesiac. Except for the surplus cases of nonrecognition—which almost certainly correspond to cases of successfully concealed cryptic amnesia—the nonrecognitions and cryptic amnesias are shown to be dual manifestations of a single underlying phenomenon."

He paused. The tension in the Sky Room deepened. He leaned forward. "It is that underlying phenomenon, gentlemen, which I believe constitutes a threat to the security of the world, and demands the most immediate and thoroughgoing investigation. Though staggering, the implications are obvious."

The tautness continued, but slowly Conjerly got to his feet. His compact, stubby frame, bald bullethead, and uncompromisingly impassive features were in striking contrast with Clawly's mobile, half-haggard debonair visage.

Leashed anger deepened Conjerly's voice, enhanced its authority.

"We have come a long way from the Dawn Era, gentlemen. One might think we would never again have to grapple with civilization's old enemy superstition. But I am forced to that regretful conclusion when I hear this gentleman, to whom we have granted the privilege of an audience, advancing theories of demoniac possession to explain cases of amnesia and nonrecognition." He looked at Clawly. "Unless I wholly misunderstood?"

Clawly decisively shook his head. "You didn't. It is my contention—I might as well put it in plain words—that alien minds are displacing the minds of our citizens, that they are infiltrating Earth, seeking to gain a foothold here. As to what minds they are, where they come from—I can't answer that, except to remind you that Thorn's studies of dream landscapes hint at a world strangely like our own, though strangely distorted. But the secrecy of the invaders implies that their purpose is hostile—at best, suspect. And I need not remind you that, in this age of subtronic power, the presence of even a tiny hostile group could become a threat to Earth's very existence."

Slowly Conjerly clenched his stub fingers, unclenched them. When he spoke, it was as if he were reciting a creed.

"Materialism is our bedrock, gentlemen—the firm belief that every phenomenon must have a real existence and a real cause. It has made possible science technology, unbiased self-understanding. I am openminded. I will go as far as any in granting a hearing to new theories. But when those theories are a revival of the oldest and most ignorant superstitions, when this gentleman seeks to frighten us with nightmares and tales of evil spirits stealing human bodies, when he asks us on this evidence to institute a gigantic witchhunt, when he raises the old bogey of subtronic power breaking loose, when he brings in a colleague"—he glared at Thorn—"who takes seriously to the idea of surveying dream worlds with transit and theodolite—then I say, gentlemen, that if we yield to such suggestions, we might as well throw materialism over-board and, as for safeguarding the future of mankind, ask the advice of fortune-tellers!"

At the last word Clawly started, recovered himself. He dared not look around to see if anyone had no-ticed.

The anger in Conjerly's voice strained at its leash, threatened to break it.

"I presume, sir, that your confidential investigators will go out with wolfsbane to test for werewolves, garlic to uncover vampires, and cross and holy water to exorcise demons!"

"They will go out with nothing but open minds," Clawly answered quietly.

Conjerly breathed deeply, his face reddened slightly; he squared himself for a fresh and more uncompromis-ing assault. But just at that moment Tempelmar eased himself out of his chair. As if by accident, his elbow brushed Conjerly's.

"No need to quarrel," Tempelmar drawled pleas-antly, "though our visitor's suggestions do sound rather peculiar to minds tempered to a realistic mate-rialism. Nevertheless, it is our duty to safeguard the world from any real dangers, no matter how improb-able or remote. So, considering the evidence, we must not pass lightly over our visitor's theory that alien minds are usurping those of Earth—at least not until there has been an opportunity to advance alternate theories."

"Alternate theories *have* been advanced, tested, and discarded," said Clawly sharply.

"Of course," Tempelmar agreed smilingly. "But in science that's a process that never quite ends, isn't it?"

He sat down, Conjerly following suit as if drawn. Clawly was irascibly conscious of having got the worst of the interchange—and the lanky, sleepy-eyed Tem-pelmar's quiet skepticism had been more damaging than Conjerly's blunt opposition, though both had told. He felt, emanating from the two of them, a weight of personal hostility that bothered and oppressed him. For a moment they seemed like utter strangers.

He was conscious of standing too much alone. In every face he could suddenly see skepticism. Shielding was the worst—his expression had become that of a man who suddenly sees through the tricks of a sleight-of-hand artist masquerading as a true magician. And Thorn, who should have been mentally at his side, lending him support, was sunk in some strange reverie.

He realized that even in his own mind there was a growing doubt of the things he was saying.

Then, utterly unexpectedly, adding immeasurably to his dismay, Thorn got up, and, without even a muttered excuse to the men beside him, left the room. He moved a little stiffly, like a sleepwalker. Several glanced after him curiously. Conjerly nodded. Tempelmar smiled.

Clawly noted it. He rallied himself. He said, "Well, gentlemen?"

But who will reveal to our waking ken
The forms that swim and the shapes that creep
Under the waters of sleep?

> The Marshes of Glynn, SIDNEY LANIER.

Like a dreamer who falls headforemost for giddy miles and then is wafted to a stop as gently as a leaf, Thorn plunged down the main vertical levitator of the Opal Cross and swam out of it at ground level, before its descent into the half mile of basements. At this hour the great gravity-less tube was relatively empty, except for the ceaseless silent plunge and ascent of the graduated subtronic currents and the air they swept along. There were a few other down-and-up swimmers—distant leaflike swirls of color afloat in the contrasting white perspective of the tube—but, like a dreamer, Thorn did not seem to take note of them.

Another levitating current carried him along some hundred yards of mural-faced corridor to one of the pedestrian entrances of the Opal Cross. A group of revelers stopped their crazy, squealing dance in the current to watch him. They looked like figures swum out of the potently realistic murals—but with a more hectic, troubled gaiety on their faces. There was something about the way he plunged past them unseeing, his sleepwalker's eyes fixed on something a dozen yards ahead, that awakened unpleasant personal thoughts and spoiled their feverish fun-making.

The pedestrian entrance was really a city-limits. Here the one-building metropolis ended, and there began the horizontal miles of half-wild countryside, dark as the ancient past, trackless and roadless in the main, dotted in many areas with small private dwellings, but liberally brushed with forests.

A pair of lovers on the terrace, pausing for a kiss as they adjusted their flying togs, broke off to look curiously after Thorn as he hurried down the ramp and across the close-cropped lawn, following one of the palely glowing pathways. The up-slanting pathlight, throwing into gaunt relief his angular cheekbones and chin, made him resemble some ancient pilgrim or crusader in the grip of a religious compulsion.

Then the forest had swallowed him up.

A strange mixture of trance and willfulness, of dream and waking, of aimless wandering and purposeful tramping, gripped Thorn as he adventured down that black-fringed ghost-trail. Odd memories of childhood, of old hopes and desires, of student days with Clawly, of his work and the bewildering speculations it had led to, drifted across his mind, poignant but meaningless. Among these, but drained of significance, like the background of a dream, there was a lingering picture of the scene he had left behind him in the Sky Room. He was conscious of somehow having deserted a friend, abandoned a world, betrayed a great purpose—but it was a blurred consciousness and he had forgotten what the great purpose was.

Nothing seemed to matter any longer but the impulse pulling him forward, the sense of an unknown but definite destination.

He had the feeling that if he looked long enough at that receding, beckoning point a dozen yards ahead, something would grow there.

The forest path was narrow and twisting. Its faint glow silhouetted weeds and brambles partly overgrowing it. His hands pushed aside encroaching twigs.

He felt something tugging at his mind from ahead, as if there were other avenues leading to his subconscious than that which went through his consciousness. As if his subconscious were the core of two or more minds, of which his was only one.

Under the influence of that tugging, imagination awoke.

Instantly it began to re-create the world of his nightmares. The world which had obscurely dominated his life and turned him to dream-research, where he had found similar nightmares. The world where danger lay. The blue-litten world in which a mushroom growth of ugly squat buildings, like the factories and tenements and barracks of ancient times, blotched the utopian countryside, and along whose sluicelike avenues great crowds of people ceaselessly drifted, unhappy but unable to rest—among them that other, dream Thorn, who hated and envied him, deluged him with an almost unbearable sense of guilt.

For almost as long as he could remember, that dream Thorn had tainted his life—the specter at his feasts, the suppliant at his gates, the eternal accuser in the courts of inmost thought—drifting phantomwise across his days, rising up starkly real and terrible in his nights. During the long, busy holiday of youth, when every day had been a new adventure and every thought a revelation, that dream Thorn had been painfully discovering the meaning of oppression and fear, had seen security swept away and parents exiled, had attended schools in which knowledge was forbidden and all a man learned was his place. When he was discovering happiness and love, that dream Thorn had been rebelliously grieving for a young wife snatched away from him forever because of some autocratic government's arbitrary decrees. And while he was accomplishing his life's work, building new knowledge stone by stone, that dream Thorn had toiled monotonously at meaningless jobs, slunk away to brood and plot with others of his kind, been harried by a fiendishly efficient secret police, become a hater and a killer.

Day by day, month by month, year by year, the dark-stranded dream life had paralleled his own.

He knew the other Thorn's emotions almost better than his own, but the actual conditions and specific details of the dream Thorn's life were blurred and confused in a characteristically dreamlike fashion. It was as if he were dreaming that other Thorn's dreams—while, by some devilish exchange, that other Thorn dreamed his dreams and hated him for his good fortune.

A sense of guilt toward his dream-twin was the dominant fact in Thorn's inner life.

And now, pushing through the forest, he began to fancy that he could see something at the receding focus of his vision a dozen yards ahead, something that kept flickering and fading, so that he could scarcely be sure that he saw it, and that yet seemed an embodiment of all the unseen forces dragging him along—a pale, wraithlike face, horribly like his own.

The sense of a destination grew stronger and more urgent. The mile wall of the Opal Cross, a pale cataract of stone glimpsed now and then through overhanging branches, still seemed to rise almost at his heels, creating the maddening illusion that he was making no progress. The wraith-face blacked out. He began to run.

Twigs lashed him. A root caught at his foot. He stumbled, checked himself, and went on more slowly, relieved to find that he could at least govern the rate of his progress.

The forces tugging at him were both like and infinitely unlike those which had for a moment controlled his movements at the synchromy. Whereas those had seemed to have a wholly alien source, these seemed to have come from a single human mind.

He felt in his pocket for the object he had stolen from Clawly's mysterious confidant. He could not see much of its color now, but that made its baffling texture stand out. It seemed to have a little more inertia than its weight would account for. He was certain he had never touched anything quite like it before.

He couldn't say where the notion came from, but he suddenly found himself wondering if the thing could be a single molecule. Fantastic! And yet, was there anything to absolutely prevent atoms from assembling, or being assembled, in such a giant structure?

Such a molecule would have more atoms than the universe had suns.

Oversize molecules were the keys of life—the hormones, the activators, the carriers of heredity. What doors might not a supergiant molecule unlock?

The merest fancy—yet frightening. He started to throw the thing away, but instead tucked it back in his pocket.

There was a rush in the leaves. A large cat paused for an instant in the pathlight to snarl and stare at him. Such cats were common pets, for centuries bred for intelligence and for centuries tame. Yet now, on the prowl, it seemed all wild—with an added, evil insight gained from long association with man.

The path branched. He took a sharp turn, picking his way over bulbous roots. The pathlight grew dim and diffuse, its substance dissolved and spread by erosion. At places the vegetation had absorbed some of the luminescence. Leaves and stems glowed faintly.

But beyond, on either side, the forest was a black, choked infinity.

It had come inscrutably alive.

The sense of a thousand infinities pressing upon him, experienced briefly at the Yggdrasil, now returned with redoubled force.

The Yggdrasil was true. Reality was not what it seemed on the surface. It had many roots, some strong and true, some twisted and gnarled, nourished in many worlds.

He quickened his pace. Again something seemed to be growing at the focus of his vision—a flitting, pulsating, bluish glow. It was like the Yggdrasil's Nidhogg motif. Nidhogg, the worm gnawing ceaselessly at the root of the tree of life that goes down to hell. It droned against his vision—an unshakable color-tune.

Then, gradually, it became a face. His own face, but seared by unfamiliar emotions, haggard with unknown miseries, hard, vengeful, accusing—the face of the dream Thorn, beckoning, commanding, luring him toward some unknown destination in the maze of unknown, unseen worlds.

With a sob of courage and fear, he plunged toward it.

He must come to grips with that other Thorn, settle accounts with him, even the balance of pleasure and pain between them, right the wrong of their unequal lives. For in some sense he must *be* that other Thorn, and that other Thorn must be he. And a man could not be untrue to himself.

The wraithlike face receded as swiftly as he advanced.

His progress through the forest became a nightmarish running of the gauntlet, through a double row of giant black trees that slashed him with their branches.

The face kept always a few yards ahead.

Fear came, but too late—he could not stop.

The dreamy veils that had been drawn across his thoughts and memories during the first stages of his flight from the Opal Cross were torn away. He realized that that was the same thing that had happened to countless other individuals. He realized that an alien mind was displacing his own, that another invader and potential cryptic amnesiac was gaining a foothold on Earth.

The thought hit him hard that he was deserting Clawly, leaving the whole world in the lurch.

But he was only a will-less thing that ran with outclutched hands.

Once he crossed a bare hilltop and for a moment caught a glimpse of the lonely glowing skylons—the Blue Lorraine, the Gray Twins, the Myrtle Y—but distant beyond reach, like a farewell.

He was near the end of his strength.

The sense of a destination grew overpoweringly strong.

Now it was something just around the next turn in the path.

He plunged through a giddy stretch of darkness thick as ink—and came to a desperate halt, digging in his heels, flailing his arms.

From somewhere, perhaps from deep within his own mind, came a faint echo of mocking laughter.

IV

If you can look into the seeds of time,
And say which grain will grow and which will not—

MACBETH.

Like a mote in the grip of an intangible whirlwind, Clawly whipped through the gray dawn on a steady surge of subtronic power toward the upper levels of the Blue Lorraine. The brighter stars, and Mars, were winking out. Through the visor of his flying togs the rushing air sent a chill to which his blood could not quite respond. He should be home, recuperating from defeat, planning new lines of attack. He should be letting fatigue poisons drain normally from his plasma, instead of knocking them out with stimulol. He should be giving his thoughts a chance to unwind. Or he should have given way to lurking apprehensions and be making a frantic search for Thorn. But the itch of a larger worry was upon him, and until he had done a certain thing, he could not pursue personal interests, or rest.

With Thorn gone, his rebuff in the Sky Room loomed as a black and paralyzingly insurmountable obstacle that grew momently higher. They were lucky, he told himself, not to have had their present research funds curtailed—let alone having them increased, or being given a large staff of assistants, or being granted access to the closely guarded files of confidential information on cryptic amnesiacs and other citizens. Any earlier culture would probably have forbidden their research entirely, as a menace to the mental stability of the public. Only an almost fetishlike reverence for individual liberty and the inviolability of personal pursuits had saved him.

The Committee's adverse decision had even shaken his own beliefs. He felt himself a puny little man, beset by uncertainties and doubts, quite incompetent to protect the world from dangers as shadowy, vast, and inscrutable as the gloom-drenched woodlands a mile below.

Why the devil had Thorn left the meeting like that, of necessity creating a bad impression? Surely he couldn't have given way to any luring hypnotic impulse—he of all men ought to know the danger of that. Still, there had been that unpleasant suggestion of sleepwalking in his departure—an impression that Clawly's memory kept magnifying. And Thorn was a strange fellow. After all these years, Clawly still found him unpredictable. Thorn had a spiritual recklessness, an urge to plumb all mental deeps. And God knows there were deeps enough for plumbing these days, if one were foolish. Clawly felt them in himself—the faint touch of a darker, less pleasant version of his own personality, against which he must keep constantly on guard.

If he had let something happen to Thorn—!

A variation in the terrestrial magnetic field, not responded to soon enough, sent him spinning sideways a dozen yards, forced his attention back on his trip.

He wondered if he had managed to slip away as unobtrusively as he had thought. A few of the committee members had wanted to talk. Firemoor, who had voted against the others and supported Clawly's views rather too excitedly, had been particularly insistent. But he had managed to put them off. Still, what if he were followed? Surely Conjerly's reference to "fortune-tellers" had been mere chance, although it had given him a nasty turn. But if Conjerly and Tempelmar should find out where he was going now—what a handle that would give them against him!

It would be wiser to drop the whole business, at least for a time.

No use! The vice of the thing—if vice it be—was in his blood. The Blue Lorraine drew him as a magnet flicks up a grain of iron.

A host of images fought for possession of his tired mind, as he plunged through thin streamers of paling cloud. Green dots on the World Map. The greens and blues of the Yggdrasil—and in what nightmare worlds had Hoderson found his inspiration? The blue-tinted sketches one of Thorn's dreamers had made of the world of his nightmares. A sallow image of Thorn's face altered and drawn by pain, such an image as might float into the mind of one who watches too long by a sickbed. The looks on the faces of Conjerly and Tempelmar—that fleeting impression of a hostile strangeness. The hint of a dark alien presence in the depths of his own mind.

The Blue Lorraine grew gigantic, loomed as a vast, shadow-girt cliff, its pinnacles white with frost although the night below had been summery. There were already signs of a new day beginning. Here and there freighters clung like beetles to the wall, discharging or receiving cargo through unseen ports. Some distance below, a stream of foodstuffs for the great dining halls, partly packaged, partly not, was coming in on a subtronic current. Off to one side an attendant shepherded a small swarm of arriving schoolchildren, although it was too early yet for the big crowds.

Clawly swooped to a landing stage, hovered for a moment like a bird, then dropped. In the anteroom he and another early arriver helped each other remove and check their flying togs.

He was breathing hard, there was a deafness and a ringing in his ears, he rubbed his chilled fingers. He should not have made such a steep and swift ascent. It would have been easier to land at a lower stage and come up by levitator. But this way was more satisfying to his impatience. And there was less chance of someone following him unseen.

A levitating current wafted him down a quarter mile of mainstem corridor to the district of the psychologists. From there he walked.

He looked around uneasily. Only now did real doubt hit him. What if Conjerly were right? What if he were merely dragging up ancient superstitions, foisting them on a group of overspecialized experts, Thorn included? What if the world-threat he had

tried to sell to the World Executive Committee were
just so much morbid nonsense, elaborately bastioned
by a vast array of misinterpreted evidence? What if the
darker, crueler, deviltry-loving side of his mind were
more in control than he realized? He felt uncomfortably like a charlatan, a mountebank trying to pipe the
whole world down a sinister side street, a chaos-loving
jester seeking to perpetuate a vast and unpleasant
hoax. It was all such a crazy business, with origins far
more dubious than he had dared reveal even to
Thorn, from whom he had no other secrets. Best back
down now, at least quit stirring up any more dark currents.

But the other urge was irresistible. There were
things he had to know, no matter the way of knowing.

Steeling himself, he paraphrased Conjerly. "If the
evidence seems to point that way, if the safety of mankind seems to demand it, then I *will* throw materialism overboard and ask the advice of fortune-tellers!"

He stopped. A door faced him. Abruptly it was a
doorway. He went in, approached the desk and the
motionless, black-robed figure behind it.

As always, there was in Oktav's face that overpowering suggestion of age—age far greater than could be
accounted for by filmy white hair, sunken cheeks, skin
tight-drawn and wrinkle-etched. Unwilled, Clawly's
thoughts turned toward the Dawn Civilization with its
knights in armor and aircraft winged like birds, its
whispered tales of elixirs of eternal life—and toward
that oddly long-lived superstition, rumor, hallucina-
tion, that men clad in the antique garments of the
Late Middle Dawn Civilization occasionally appeared
on Earth for brief periods at remote places.

Oktav's garb, at any rate, was just an ordinary houserobe. But in their wrinkle-meshed orbits, his eyes
seemed to burn with the hopes and fears and sorrows
of centuries. They took no note of Clawly as he edged
into a chair.

"I see suspense and controversy," intoned the seer
abruptly. "All night it has surged around you. It re-

gards that matter whereof we spoke at the Yggdrasil. I see others doubting and you seeking to persuade them. I see two in particular in grim opposition
to you, but I cannot see their minds or motives. I see
you in the end losing your grip, partly because of a
friend's seeming desertion, and going down in defeat."

Of course, thought Clawly, he could learn all this by
fairly simple spying. Still, it impressed him, as it always had since he first chanced—but was it wholly
chance?—to contact Oktav in the guise of an ordinary
psychologist.

Not looking at the seer, with a shyness he showed
toward no one else, Clawly asked, "What about the
world's future? Do you see anything more there?"

There was a faint drumming in the seer's voice.
"Only thickening dreams, more alien spirits stalking
the world in human mask, doom overhanging, great
claws readying to pounce—but whence or when I cannot tell, only that your recent effort to convince others
of the danger has brought the danger closer."

Clawly shivered. Then he sat straighter. He was no
longer shy. Docketing the question about Thorn that
was pushing at his lips, he said, "Look, Oktav, I've got
to know more. It's obvious that you're hiding things
from me. If I map the best course I can from the hints
you give me, and then you tell me that it is the wrong
course, you tie my hands. For the good of mankind,
you've got to describe the overhanging danger more
definitely."

"And bring down upon us forces that will destroy us
both?" The seer's eyes stabbed at him. "There are
worlds within worlds, wheels within wheels. Already I
have told you too much for our safety. Moreover,
there are things I honestly do not know, things hidden
even from the Great Experimenters—and my guesses
might be worse than yours."

Taut with a sense of feverish unreality, Clawly's
mind wandered. What was Oktav—what lay behind
that ancient mask? Were all faces only masks? What
lay behind Conjerly's and Tempelmar's? Thorn's? His

own? Could your own mind be a mask, too, hiding things from your own consciousness? What was the world—this brief masquerade of inexplicable events, flaring up from the future to be instantly extinguished in the past?

"But then what am I to do, Oktav?" he heard his tired voice ask.

The seer replied, "I have told you before. Prepare your world for any eventuality. Arm it. Mobilize it. Do not let it wait supine for the hunter."

"But how can I, Oktav? My request for a mere program of investigation was balked. How can I ask the world to arm—for no reason?"

The seer paused. When he finally answered there drummed in his voice, stronger than ever, the bitter wisdom of centuries.

"Then you must give it a reason. Always governments have provided appropriate motives for action, when the real motives would be unpalatable to the many, or beyond their belief. You must extemporize a danger that fits the trend of their short-range thinking. Now let me see—Mars—"

There was a slight sound. The seer wheeled around with a serpentine rapidity, one skinny hand plunged in the breast of his robe. It fumbled wildly, agitating the black, weightless fabric, then came out empty. A look of extreme consternation contorted his features.

Clawly's eyes shifted with his to the inner doorway.

The figure stayed there peering at Oktav for only a moment. Then, with an impatient, peremptory flirt of its head, it turned and moved out of sight. But it was indelibly etched down to the very last detail, on Clawly's panic-shaken vision.

Most immediately frightening was the impression of age—age greater than Oktav's, although, or perhaps because, the man's physical appearance was that of thirty-odd, with dark hair, low forehead, vigorous jaw. But in the eyes, in the general expression—centuries of knowledge. Yet knowledge without wisdom, or with only a narrow-minded, puritanic, unsympathetic, overweening simulacrum of wisdom. A disturbing blend of unconscious ignorance and consciousness of power. The animal man turned god, without transfiguration.

But the most lingering impression, oddly repellent, was of its clothing. Crampingly unwieldy upper and nether garments of tight-woven, compressed, tortured animal-hair, fastened by bits of bone or horn. The upper garment had an underduplicate of some sort of bleached vegetable fiber, confined at the throat by two devices—one a tightly knotted scarf of crudely woven and colored insect spinnings, the other a high and unyielding white neckband, either of the same fiber as the shirt, glazed and stiffened, or some primitive plastic.

It gave Clawly an added, anticlimactic start to realize that the clothing of the nineteenth and twentieth centuries, which he had seen pictured in history albums, would have just this appearance, if actually prepared according to the ancient processes and worn by a human being.

Without explanation, Oktav rose and moved toward the inner doorway. His hand fumbled again in his robe, but it was merely an idle repetition of the earlier gesture. In the last glimpse he had of his face, Clawly saw continued consternation, frantic memory-searching, and the frozen intentness of a competent mind scanning every possible avenue of escape from a deadly trap.

Oktav went through the doorway.

There was no sound.

Clawly waited.

Time spun on. Clawly shifted his position, caught himself, coughed, waited, coughed again, got up, moved toward the inner doorway, came back, and sat down.

There was time, too much time. Time to think again and again of that odd superstition about fleeting appearances of men in Dawn-Civilization garb.

Time to make a thousand nightmarish deductions from the age of Oktav's, and that other's, eyes.

Finally he got up and walked to the inner doorway.

There was a tiny unfurnished room, without windows or another door, the typical secondary compartment of offices like this. Its walls were bare and seamless.

There was no one.

V

. . . and still remoter spaces where only a stirring in vague blackness had told of the presence of consciousness and will.

The Hunter of the Dark, H. P. LOVECRAFT.

With a sickening ultimate plunge that seemed to plumb in instants distances greater than the diameter of the cosmos—a plunge in which more than flesh and bones were stripped away, transformed—Oktav followed his summoner into a region of not only visual night.

Here in the Zone, outside the bubble of space-time, on the borders of eternity, even the atoms were still. Only thought moved—but thought powered beyond description or belief, thought that could make or mar universes, thought not unbefitting gods.

Most strange, then, to realize that it was human thought, with all its homely biases and foibles. Like finding, on another planet in another universe, a peasant's cottage with smoke wreathing above the thatched roof and an ax wedged in a half-chopped log.

Mice scurrying at midnight in a vast cathedral—and the faint suggestion that the cathedral might not be otherwise wholly empty.

Oktav, or that which had been Oktav, oriented itself—himself—making use of the sole means of perception that functioned in the Zone. It was most akin to touch, but touch strangely extended and sensitive only to projected thought or processes akin to thought.

Groping like a man shut in an infinite closet, Oktav felt the eternal hum of the Probability Engine, the lesser hum of the seven unlocked talismans. He felt the seven human minds in their stations around the engine, felt six of them stiffen with cold disapproval as Ters made report. Then he took his own station, the last and eighth.

Ters concluded.

Prim thought, "We summoned you, Oktav, to hear your explanation of certain highly questionable activities in which you have recently indulged—only to learn that you have additionally committed an act of unprecedented negligence. Never before has a talisman been lost. And only twice has it been necessary to make an expedition to recover one—when its possessor met accidental death in a space-time world. How can you have permitted this to happen, since a talisman gives infallible warning if it is in any way spacially or temporarily parted from its owner?"

"I am myself deeply puzzled," Oktav admitted. "Some obscure influence must have been operative, inhibiting the warning or closing my mind to it. I did not become aware of the loss until I was summoned. However, casting my mind back across the last Earth-day's events, I believe I can now discern the identity of the individual into whose hands it fell—or who stole it."

"Was the talisman inert at the time?" thought Prim quickly.

"Yes," thought Oktav. "A Key-idea known only to myself would be necessary to unlock its powers."

"That is one small point in your favor," thought Prim.

"I am gravely at fault," thought Oktav, "but it can easily be mended. Lend me another talisman and I will return to the world and recover it."

"It will not be permitted," thought Prim. "You have already spent too much time in the world, Oktav. Although you are the youngest of us, your body is senile."

Before he could check himself, or at least avoid projection, Oktav thought, "Yes, and by so doing I have learned much that you, in your snug retreat, would do well to become aware of."

"The world and its emotions have corrupted you," thought Prim. "And that brings me to the second and major point of our complaint."

Oktav felt the seven minds converge hostilely upon him. Careful to mask his ideational processes, Oktav probed the others for possible sympathy or weakness.

Lack of a talisman put him at a great disadvantage. His hopes fell.

Prim thought, "It has come to our attention that you have been telling secrets. Moved by some corrupt emotionality, and under the astounding primitive guise of fortune-telling, you have been disbursing forbidden knowledge—cloudily perhaps, but none the less unequivocally—to Earthlings of the main-trunk world."

"I do not deny it," thought Oktav, crossing his Rubicon. "The main-trunk world *needs* to know more. It has been your spoiled brat. And as often happens to a spoiled brat, you now push it, unprepared and unaided, into a dubious future."

Prim's answering thought, amplified by his talisman, thundered in the measureless dark. "*We* are the best judges of what is good for the world. Our minds are dedicated far more selflessly than yours to the world's welfare, and we have chosen the only sound scientific method for insuring its continued and ultimate happiness. One of the unalterable conditions of that method is that no Earthling have the slightest concrete hint of our activities. Has your mind departed so far from scientific clarity—influenced perhaps by bodily decay due to injudicious exposure to space-time—that I must recount to you our purpose and our rules?"

The darkness pulsed. Oktav projected no answering thought. Prim continued, thinking in a careful step-by-step way, as if for a child.

"No scientific experiment is possible without controls—setups in which the conditions are unaltered, as a comparison, in order to gauge the exact effects of the alteration. There is, under natural conditions, only one world. Hence no experiments can be performed upon it. One can never test scientifically which form of social organization, government, and so forth, is best for it. But the creation of alternate worlds by the Probability Engine changes all that."

Prim's thought beat at Oktav.

"Can it be that the underlying logic of our procedure has somehow always escaped you? From our vantage point we observe the world as it rides into the cone of the future—a cone that always narrows toward the present, because in the remote future there are many major possibilities still realizable, in the near future only a relative few. We note the approach of crucial epochs, when the world must make some great choice, as between democracy and totalitarianism, managerialism and servicism, benevolent elitism and enforced equalism, and so on. Then, carefully choosing the right moment and focusing the Probability Engine chiefly upon the minds of the world's leaders, we widen the cone of the future. Two or more major possibilities are then realized instead of just one. Time is bifurcated, or trifurcated. We have alternate worlds, at first containing many objects and people in common, but diverging more and more—bifurcating more and more completely—as the consequences of the alternate decisions make themselves felt."

"I criticize," thought Oktav, plunging into uncharted waters. "You are thinking in generalities. You are personifying the world, and forgetting that major possibilities are merely an accumulation of minor ones. I do not believe that the distinction between the two major alternate possibilities in a bifurcation is at all clear-cut."

The idea was too novel to make any immediate impression, except that Oktav's mind was indeed being hazy and disordered. As if Oktav had not thought, Prim continued, "For example, we last split the time-stream thirty Earth-years ago. Discovery of subtronic power had provided the world with a practically unlimited source of space-time energy. The benevolent elite governing the world was faced with three clearcut alternatives: It could suppress the discovery completely, killing its inventors. It could keep it a Party secret, make it a Party asset. I could impart it to the world at large, which would destroy the authority of the Party and be tantamount to dissolving it, since it would put into the hands of any person, or at least any small group of persons, the power to destroy the world. In a natural state, only one of these possibilities could be realized. Earth would only have one chance in three of guessing right. As we arranged it, all three possibilities were realized. A few years' continued observation sufficed to show us that the third alternative—that of making subtronic power common property—was the right one. The other two had already resulted in untold unendurable miseries and horrors."

"Yes, the botched worlds," Oktav interrupted bitterly. "How many of them have there been, Prim? How many, since the beginning?"

"In creating the best of all possible worlds, we of necessity also created the worst," Prim replied with a strained patience.

"Yes—worlds of horror that might have never been, had you not insisted on materializing all the possibilities, good and evil lurking in men's minds. If you had not interfered, man still might have achieved that best world—suppressing the evil possibilities."

"Do you suggest that we should leave all to chance?" Prim exploded angrily. "Become fatalists? We, who are masters of fate?"

"And then," Oktav continued, brushing aside the interruption, "having created those worst of near-worlds—but still human, living ones, with happiness as well as horror in them, populated by individuals honestly striving to make the best of bad guesses—you destroy them."

"Of course!" Prim thought back in righteous indignation. "As soon as we were sure they were the less desirable alternatives, we put them out of their misery."

"Yes." Oktav's bitterness was like an acid drench. "Drowning the unwanted kittens. While you lavish affection on one, putting the rest in the sack."

"It was the most merciful thing to do," Prim retorted. "There was no pain—only instantaneous obliteration."

Oktav reacted. All his earlier doubts and flashes of rebellion were suddenly consolidated into a burning desire to shake the complacency of the others. He gave his ironic thoughts their head, sent them whipping through the dark.

"Who are you to tell whether or not there's pain in instantaneous obliteration? Oh yes, the botched worlds, the controls, the experiments that failed—they don't matter, let's put them out of their misery, let's get rid of the evidence of our mistakes, let's obliterate them because we can't stand their mute accusations. As if the Earthlings of the botched worlds didn't have as much right to their future, no matter how sorry and troubled, as the Earthlings of the main trunk. What crime have they committed save that of guessing wrong, when, by your admission, all was guesswork? What difference is there between the main trunk and the lopped branches, except your judgment that the former seems happier, more successful? Let me tell you something. You've coddled the main-trunk world for so long, you've tied your limited human affections to it so tightly, that you've gotten to believing that it's the only real world, the only world that counts—that the others are merely ghosts, object lessons, hypothetics. But in actuality they're just as throbbingly alive, just as deserving of consideration, just as real."

"They no longer exist," thought Prim crushingly. "It is obvious that your mind, tainted by Earthbound emotions, has become hopelessly disordered. You are pleading the cause of that which no longer is."

"Are you so sure?" Oktav could feel his questioning thought hang in the dark, like a great black bubble, coercing attention. "What if the botched worlds still live? What if, in thinking to obliterate them, you have merely put them beyond the reach of your observation, cut them loose from the main-trunk time-stream, set them adrift in the oceans of eternity? I've told you that you ought to visit the world more often in the flesh. You'd find out that your beloved main-trunkers are becoming conscious of a shadowy, overhanging

danger, that they're uncovering evidences of an infil-
tration, a silent and mystery-shrouded invasion across
mental boundaries. Here and there in your main-
trunk world, minds are being displaced by minds from
somewhere else. What if that invasion comes from one
of the botched worlds—say from one of the worlds of
the last trifurcation? That split occurred so recently
that the alternate worlds would still contain many duplicate individuals, and between duplicate individuals
there may be subtle bonds that reach even across the
intertime void—on your admission, time-splits are
never at first complete, and there may be unchanging
shared deeps in the subconscious minds of duplicate
individuals, opening the way for forced interchanges
of consciousness. What if the botched worlds have continued to develop in the everlasting dark, outside the
range of your knowledge, spawning who knows what
abnormalities and horrors, like mutant monsters confined in caves? What if, with a tortured genius resulting from their misery, they've discovered things about
time that even you do not know? What if they're out
there—waiting, watching, devoured by resentment, preparing to leap upon your pet?"

Oktav paused and probed the darkness. Faint, but
unmistakable, came the pulse of fear. He had shaken
their complacency all right—but not to his advantage.

"You're thinking nonsense," Prim thundered at him
coldly, in thought-tones in which there was no longer
any hope of mercy or reprieve. "It is laughable even to
consider that we could be guilty of such a glaring error
as you suggest. We know every crevice of space-time,
every twig and leaflet. We are the masters of the Probability Engine."

"Are you?" Reckless now of all consequences, Oktav
asked the unprecedented, forbidden, ultimate question. "I know when I was initiated, and presumably
when the rest of you were initiated, it was always assumed and strongly suggested, though never stated
with absolute definiteness, that Prim, the first of us, a
mental mutant and supergenius of the nineteenth cen-

tury, invented the Probability Engine. I, an awestruck neophyte, accepted this attitude. But now I know that I never really believed it. No human mind could ever have conceived the Probability Engine. Prim did not invent it. He merely found it, probably by chancing on a lost talisman. Thereafter some peculiarity of the Engine permitted him to take it out of reach of its True Owners, hide it from them. Then he took us in with him, one by one, because a single mind was insufficient to operate the engine in all its phases and potentialities. But Prim never invented it. He stole it."

With a sense of exultation, Oktav realized that he had touched their primal vulnerability—though at the same time ensuring his own doom. He felt the seven resentful, frightened minds converge upon him suffocatingly. He probed now for one thing only—any relaxing of watchfulness, any faltering of awareness, on the part of any of them. And as he probed, he kept choking out additional insults against the resistance.

"Is there any one of you, Prim included, who even understands the Probability Engine, let alone having the capacity to devise it?

"You prate of science, but do you understand even the science of modern Earthlings? Can any one of you outline to me the theoretic background of subtronic physics? Even your puppets have outstripped you. You're atavisms, relics of the Dawn Civilization, mental mummies, apes crept into a factory at night and monkeying with the machinery.

"You're sorcerer's apprentices—and what will happen when the sorcerer comes back? What if I should stop this eternal whispering and send a call winging clear and unhampered through eternity: 'Oh sorcerer, True Owners, here is your stolen Engine'?"

They pressed on him frantically, frightenedly, as if by sheer mental weight to prevent any such call being sent. He felt that he would go down under the pressure, cease to be. But at the same time his probing uncovered a certain muddiness in Kart's thinking, a certain wandering due to doubt and fear, and he clutched at it, desperately but subtly.

Prim finished reading the sentence. "—so Ters and Septem will escort Oktav back to the world, and when he is in the flesh, make disposition of him." He paused, continued, "Meanwhile, Sikst will make an expedition to recover the lost talisman, calling for aid if not immediately successful. At the same time, since the functioning of the Probability Engine is seriously hampered so long as there is an empty station, Sekond, Kart, and Kent will visit the world in order to select a suitable successor for Oktav. I will remain here and—"

He was interrupted by a flurry of startled thought from Kart, which rose swiftly to a peak of dismay.

"My talisman! Oktav has stolen it! He is gone!"

VI

By her battened hatch I leaned and caught
  Sounds from the noisome hold—
Cursing and sighing of souls distraught
  and cries too sad to be told.

Gloucester Moors, WILLIAM VAUGHN MOODY.

Thorn teetered on the dark edge. His footgear made sudden grating noises against it as he fought for balance. He was vaguely conscious of shouts and of a needle of green light swinging down at him.

Unavailingly he wrenched the muscles of his calves, flailed the air with his arms.

Yet as he lurched over, as the edge receded upward—so slowly at first—he became glad that he had fallen, for the down-chopping green needle made a red-hot splash of the place where he had been standing.

He plummeted, frantically squeezing the controls of flying togs he was not wearing.

There was time for a futile, spasmodic effort to get clear in his mind how, plunging through the forest, he should find himself on that dark edge.

Indistinct funnel-mouths shot past, so close he almost brushed them. Then he was into something tangly that impeded his fall—slowly at first, then swiftly, as pressures ahead were built up. His motion was sickeningly reversed. He was flung upward and to one side, and came down with a bone-shaking jolt.

He was knee-deep in the stuff that had broken his fall. It made a rustling, faintly skirring noise as he ploughed his way out of it.

He stumbled around what must have been a corner of the dark building from whose roof he had fallen. The shouts from above were shut off.

He dazedly headed for one of the bluish glows. It faintly outlined scrawny trees and rubbish-littered ground between him and it.

He was conscious of something strange about his body. Through the twinges of numbness caused by his fall, it obtruded itself—a feeling of pervasive ill-health and at the same time a sense of light, lean toughness of muscular fiber—both disturbingly unfamiliar.

He picked his way through the last of the rubbish and came out at the top of a terrace. The bluish glow was very strong now. It came from the nearest of a line of illuminators set on poles along a broad avenue at the foot of the terrace. A crowd of people were moving along the avenue, but a straggly hedge obscured his view.

He started down, then hesitated. The tangly stuff was still clinging to him. He automatically started to brush it off, and noted that it consisted of thin, springy spirals of plastic and metal—identical with the shavings from an old-style, presubtronic hyperlathe. Presumably a huge heap of the stuff had been vented from the funnel-mouths he had passed in his fall. Though it bewildered him to think how many hyperlathes must be in the dark building he was skirting, to produce so much scrap. Hyperlathes were obsolete, almost a curiosity. And to gather so many engines of any sort into one building was unthought of.

His mind was jarred off this problem by sight of his hands and clothing. They seemed strange—the former pallid, thin, heavy-jointed, almost clawlike.

Sharp, but far away, as if viewed through a reducing glass, came memories of the evening's events. Clawly, the synchromy, the old man in black, the conference in the Sky Room, his plunge through the forest.

There was something clenched in his left hand—so tightly that the fingers opened with difficulty. It was the small gray sphere he had stolen at the Yggdrasil. He looked at it disturbedly. Surely, if he still had that thing with him, it meant that he couldn't have changed. And yet—

His mind filled with a formless but mounting foreboding.

Under the compulsion of that foreboding, he thrust the sphere into his pocket—a pocket that wasn't quite where it should be and that contained a metallic cylinder of unfamiliar feel. Then he ran down the terrace, pushed through the straggly hedge, and joined the crowd surging along the blue-litten avenue.

The foreboding became a tightening ball of fear, exploded into realization.

That other Thorn had changed places with him. He was wearing that other Thorn's clothing—drab, servile, workaday. He was inhabiting that other Thorn's body—his own but strangely altered and ill-cared-for, aquiver with unfamiliar tensions and emotions.

He was in the world of his nightmares.

He stood stock-still, staring, the crowd flowing around him, jostling him wearily.

His first reaction, after a giant buffet of amazement and awe that left him intoxicatedly weak, was one of deep-seated moral satisfaction. The balance had at last been righted. Now that other Thorn could enjoy the good fortunes of utopia, while he endured that other Thorn's lot. There was no longer the stifling sense of being dominated by another personality, to whom misfortune and suffering had given the whip-hand.

He was filled with an almost demoniac exhilaration—a desire to explore and familiarize himself with this world which he had long studied through the slits of nightmare, to drag from the drifting crowd around him an explanation as to its whys and wherefores.

But that would not be so easy.

An atmosphere of weary secrecy and suspicion pervaded the avenue. The voices of the people who jostled him dropped to mumbles as they went by. Heads were bowed or averted—but eyes glanced sharply.

He let himself move forward with the crowd, meanwhile studying it closely.

The misery and boredom and thwarted yearning for escape bluely shadowed in almost all the faces was so much like that he remembered from his nightmares that he could easily pretend that he was dreaming—but only pretend.

There was a distorted familiarity about some of the faces that provided undiminishing twinges of horror.

Those must be individuals whose duplicates in his own world he vaguely knew, or had glimpsed under different circumstances.

It was as if the people of his own world were engaged in acting out some strange pageant—perhaps a symbolic presentation dedicated to all the drab, monotonous, futile lives swallowed up in the muck of history.

They were dressed, both men and women, in tunic and trousers of some pale color that the blue light made it impossible to determine. There was no individuality—their clothes were all alike, although some seemed more like work clothes, others more like military uniforms.

Some seemed to be keeping watch on the others. These were treated with a mingled deference and hostility—way was made for them, but they were not spoken to. And they were spied on in turn—indeed, Thorn got the impression of an almost intolerably complex web of spying and counterspying.

Even more deference was shown to occasional individuals in dark clothing, but for a time Thorn did not get a close glimpse of any of these.

Everyone seemed on guard, wearily apprehensive.

Everywhere was the suggestion of an elaborate hierarchy of authority.

There was a steady drone of whispered or mumbled conversation.

One thing became fairly certain to Thorn before long. These people were going nowhere. All their uneasy drifting had no purpose except to fill up an empty period between work and sleep—a period in which some unseen, higher authority allowed them freedom, but forbade them from doing anything with it.

As he drifted along Thorn became more a part of the current, took on its coloring, ceased to arouse special suspicion. He began to overhear words, phrases, then whole fragments of dialogue. All of these had one thing in common: some mention of, or allusion to, the activities of a certain "they." Whatever the subject matter, this pronoun kept cropping up. It was given a score of different inflections, none of them free from haunting anxiety and veiled resentment. There grew in Thorn's mind the image of an authority that was at once tyrannical, fatherly, arbitrary, austere, possessed of overpowering prestige, yet so familiar that it was never referred to in any more definite way.

"They've put our department on a twelve-hour shift."

The speaker was evidently a machinist. Anyway, a few hyperlathe shavings stuck to his creased garments.

His companion nodded. "I wonder what the new parts that are coming through are for."

"Something big."

"Must be. I wonder what they're planning."

"Something big."

"I guess so. But I wish we at least knew the name of what we're building."

No answer, except a tired, mirthless chuckle.

The crowd changed formation. Thorn found himself trailing behind another group, this time mostly elderly women.

"Our work-group has turned out over seven hundred thousand identical parts since the speedup started. I've kept count."

"That won't tell you anything."

"No, but they must be getting ready for something. Look at how many are being drafted. All the forty-one-year-olds, and the thirty-seven-year-old women."

"They came through twice tonight, looking for Recalcitrants. They took Jon."

"Have you had the new kind of inspection? They line you up and ask you a lot of questions about who you are and what you're doing. Very simple questions—but if you don't answer them right, they take you away."

"That wouldn't help them catch Recalcitrants. I wonder who they're trying to catch now."

"Let's go back to the dormitory."

"Not for a while yet."

Another meaningless shift put Thorn next to a group containing a girl.

She said, "I'm going into the army tomorrow."

"Yes."

"I wish there were something different we could do tonight."

"Yes?"

"They won't let us do anything." A weak, whining note of rebellion entered her voice. "They have everything—powers like magic—they can fly—they live in the clouds, away from this horrible light. Oh, I wish—"

"*Sh!* They'll think you're a Recalcitrant. Besides, all this is temporary—they've told us so. There'll be happiness for everyone, as soon as the danger is over."

"I know—but why won't they tell us what the danger is?"

"There are military reasons. *Sh!*"

Someone who smiled maliciously had stolen up behind them, but Thorn did not learn the sequence to this interlude, if it had one, for yet another shift carried him to the other side of the avenue and put him near two individuals, a man and a woman, whose drab clothing was of the more soldierly cut.

"They say we may be going on maneuvers again next week. They've put a lot of new recruits in with us. There must be millions of us. I wish I knew what they were planning to do with us, when there's no enemy."

"Maybe things from another planet—"

"Yes, but that's just a rumor."

"Still, there's talk of marching orders coming any day now—complete mobilization."

"Yes, but against what?" The woman's voice had a faint overtone of hysteria. "That's what I keep asking myself at practice whenever I look through the slit and depress the trigger of the new gun—not knowing what it is that the gun will shoot or how it really works. I keep asking myself, over and over, what's going to be out there instead of the neat little target—what it is

I'm going to kill. Until sometimes I think I'm going crazy. Oh Burk, there's something I've got to tell you, though I promised not to. I heard it yesterday—I mustn't tell who told me. It's that there's really a way of escape to that happier world we all dream of, if only you know how to concentrate your mind—"

"Sh!"

This time it was Thorn's eavesdropping that precipitated the warning.

He managed to listen in on many similar, smaller fragments of talk.

Gradually a change came over his mood—a complete change. His curiosity was not satisfied, but it was quenched. Oh, he had guessed several things from what he had heard, all right—in particular, that the "new kind of inspection" was designed to uncover displaced minds like his own, and that the "way of escape" was the one the other Thorn had taken—but this knowledge no longer lured him on. The fever of demoniac excitement had waned as swiftly as drunkenness, and left as sickening a depression in its wake. Normal human emotions were reasserting themselves—a shrinking from the ominous strangeness of the distorted world, and an aching, unreasoning, mountingly frantic desire to get back to familiar faces and scenes.

Bitter regret began to torture him for having deserted Clawly and his home-world because of the pressure of a purely personal moral problem. No knowing what confusions and dangers the other Thorn might weave for an unsuspecting Clawly. And upon Clawly alone, now that he was gone, the safety of the home-world depended. True, if most of the displaced minds from this world were only those of oppressed individuals seeking escape, they would constitute no immediate unified danger. But if the shadowy, autocratic "they" were contemplating an invasion—that would be a very different matter.

The avenue, now skirting some sort of barren hillside, had become hateful to him. It was like a treadmill, and the glaring lights prevented any extended glimpse of the surrounding landscape. He would probably have left it soon in any case, even without sight of the jam-up ahead, where some sort of inspection of all walkers seemed to be going on. As it was, that sight decided him. He edged over to the side, waited for what he thought was a good opportunity, and ducked through the hedge.

Some minutes later, panting from concentrated exertion, his clothes muddied and grass-stained, he came out on the hilltop. The darkness and the familiar stars were a relief. He looked around.

His first impression was reassuring. For a moment it even roused in him the hope that, in his scramble up the hillside, the world had come right again. There, where it should be, was the Opal Cross. There were the Gray Twins. Concentrating on them, he could ignore the unpleasant suggestion of darker, squatter buildings bulging like slugs or beetles from the intervening countryside, could ignore even the meshwork of blue-litten, crawling avenues.

But the aerial bridge connecting the Twins must be darked out. Still, in that case the reflected light from the two towers ought to enable him to catch the outlines of either end of it.

And where was the Blue Lorraine? It didn't seem a hazy enough night to blot out that vast skylon.

Where, between him and the Twins, was the Mauve Z?

Shakingly he turned around. For a moment again his hope surged up. The countryside seemed clearer this way, and in the distance the Myrtle Y and the Gray H were like signposts of home.

But between him and them, rearing up from that very hillside where this evening he had watched the Yggdrasil, as if built in a night by jinn, was a great dark skylon, higher than any he had ever seen, higher even than the Blue Lorraine. It had an ebon shimmer. The main elements of its structure were five tapering wings radiating at equal intervals from a central tower. It looked like some symbol of pride and power conceived in the dreams of primeval kings.

A name came to him. The Black Star.

"Who are you up there? Come down!"

Thorn whirled around. The blue glare from the avenue silhouetted two men halfway up the hillside. Their heads were craned upward. The position of their arms suggested that they held weapons of some sort trained upon him.

He stood stock-still, conscious that the blue glow extended far enough to make him conspicuous. His senses were suddenly very keen. The present instant seemed to widen out infinitely, as if he and his two challengers were frozen men. It burst on him, with a dreadful certainty, that those men shouting on the roof had been trying to kill him. Save for the luck of overbalancing, he would this moment be a mangled cinder. The body he was in was one which other men were trying to kill.

"Come down at once!"

He threw himself flat. There was no needle of green, but something hissed faintly through the grass at his heels. He wriggled desperately for a few feet, then came up in a crouch and ran recklessly down the hillside away from the avenue.

Luck was with him. He kept footing in his crazy, breathless plunge through the semidark.

He entered thin forest, had to go more slowly. Leaves and fallen branches crackled under his feet. Straggly trees half blotted the stars.

All at once he became aware of shouting ahead. He turned, following a dry gravelly watercourse. But after a while there was shouting in that direction, too. Then something big swooped into the sky overhead and hung, and from it exploded blinding light, illuminating the forest with a steady white glare crueler than day's.

He dove to cover in thick underbrush.

For a long time the hunt beat around him, now receding a little, now coming close. Once footsteps crunched in the gravel a dozen feet away.

The underbrush, shot through with the relentless white glare, seemed a most inadequate screen. But any attempt to change position would be very risky.

He hitched himself up a little to peer through the gaps in the leaves, and found that his right hand was clutching the metal cylinder he had felt in his pocket earlier. He must have snatched it out at some stage in his flight—perhaps an automatic response of his alien muscles.

He examined the thing, wondering if it was a weapon. He noted two controlling levers, but their function was unclear. As a last resort, he could try pointing the thing and pushing them.

A rustle of leaves snapped his attention to one of the leafy gaps. A figure had emerged on the opposite bank of the dried watercourse. It was turned away, but from the first there was something breathlessly familiar about the self-assured posture, the cock of the close-cropped, red-haired head.

The theatric glare struck an ebon shimmer from the uniform it was wearing, and outlined on one shoulder, of a more somber blackness than the uniform, a black star.

Thorn leaned forward, parting with his hand the brambly wall of his retreat.

The figure turned and the face became visible.

In a strangled voice—his first words since he had found himself on the roof-edge—Thorn cried out, "Clawly!" and rushed forward.

For a moment there was no change in Clawly's expression. Then, with feline agility, he sprang to one side. Thorn stumbled in the pitted streambed, dropped the metal cylinder. Clawly whipped out something and pointed it. Thorn started up toward him. Then—there was no sound save a faint hissing, no sight, but agonizing pain shot through Thorn's right shoulder.

And stayed. Lesser waves of it rippled through the

rest of his body. He was grotesquely frozen in the act of scrambling upward. It was as if an invisible red-hot needle in Clawly's hand transfixed his shoulder and held him helpless.

Staring up in shocked, tortured dismay, the first glimmerings of the truth came to Thorn.

Clawly—*this* Clawly—smiled.

VII

There was the Door to which I found no Key;
There was the Veil through which I might not see:

The Rubaiyat.

Clawly quit his nervous prowling and perched on Oktav's desk. His satanic face was set in tight, thwarted lines. Except for his rummaging everything in the room was just as it had been when he had stolen out early this morning. The outer door aslit, Oktav's black cloak thrown over the back of his chair, the door to the empty inner chamber open. As if the seer had been called away on some brief, minor errand.

Clawly was irked at the impulse which had drawn him back to this place. True, his rummaging had uncovered some suggestive and disquieting things—in particular, an assortment of small objects and implements that seemed to extend back without a break to the Late Middle Dawn Civilization, including a maddeningly random collection of notes that began in faded stain on sheets of bleached and compressed vegetable fiber, shifted to typed characters on similar sheets, kept on through engraving stylus and plastic film to memoranda ribbon and recording wire, and finally ended in multilevel writing tape.

But what Clawly wanted was something that would enable him to get a hook into the problem that hung before him like a vast, slippery, ungraspable sphere.

He still had, strong as ever, the conviction that this room was the center of a web, the key to the whole thing—but it was a key he did not know how to use.

Thorn? That was a whole problem in itself, only a few hours old, but full of the most nerve-wracking possibilities. He took from his pouch and nervously fingered the fragment of tape with its scrawlingly recorded message which he had found earlier today on Thorn's desk at their office—that message which no one had seen Thorn leave.

A matter of the greatest importance has arisen. I must handle it alone. Will be back in a few days. Cancel or postpone all activities until my return.

Thorn.

Although the general style of recording was characteristically Thorn's, it had a subtly different swing to it, an alien undercurrent, as if some other mind were using Thorn's habitual patterns of muscular action. And the message itself, which might refer to anything, was alarmingly suggestive of a cryptic amnesiac's play for time.

On the other hand, it would be just like Thorn to play the lone wolf if he saw fit.

If he followed his simplest impulses, Clawly would resume the search for Thorn he had begun on finding the message. But he had already put that search into the hands of agencies more competent than any single individual could possibly be. They would find Thorn if anyone could, and for him to try to help them would merely be a concession to his anxiety.

His heels beat a sharper tattoo.

The research program? But that was crippled by the Committee's adverse decision, and by Thorn's absence. He couldn't do much there. Besides, he had the feeling that any research program was becoming too slow and remote a measure for dealing with the present situation.

The Committee itself? But what single, definite thing could he tell them that he had not told them last night?

His own mind, then? How about that as an avenue of attack? Stronger than ever before, the conviction came that there were dark avenues leading down from his consciousness—one of them to a frighteningly devilish, chaos-loving version of himself—and that if he concentrated his mind in a certain peculiar way he might be able to slip down one of them.

There was a devil-may-care lure to those dark avenues—the promise of a world better suiting the darker, Dawn phases of his personality. And, if Thorn *had* been displaced, that would be the only way of getting to him.

But that wasn't grappling with the problem. That was letting go, plunging with indefensible recklessness into the unknown—a crazy last resort.

To grapple with a problem, you had to have firm footing—and grab.

The tattoo ended with a sudden slam of heels. Was this room getting on his nerves? This silent room, with its feel of tangible linkages with future and past, its sense of standing on the edge of a timeless, unchanging center of things, in which action had no place—sapping his willpower, rendering him incapable of making a decision, now that there was no longer a seer to interpret for him.

The problem was in one sense so clear-cut. Earth threatened by invasion from across a new kind of frontier.

But to get a grip on that problem.

He leaned across the desk and flipped the televisor, riffling through various local scenes in the Blue Lorraine. The Great Rotunda, with its aerial promenade, where a slow subtronic current carried chatting, smiling throngs in an upward spiral past displays of arts and wares. The Floral Rotunda, where pedestrians strolled along gently rolling paths under arches of exotic greenery. The other formal social centers. The endless corridors of individual enterprises, where one might come upon anything from a puppet-carver's to a specialized subtronic lab, a mood-creator's to a cat-fancier's. The busy schools. The production areas, where keen-eyed machine tenders governed and artistically varied the flow of processing. The maintenance and replacement centers. The vast kitchens, where subtle cooks ruled to a hairbreadth the mixing of foodstuffs and their exposure to heat and moisture and other influences. The entertainment and games centers, where swirling gaiety and high-pitched excitement were the rule.

Everywhere happiness—or, rather, creative freedom. A great rich surging world, unaware, save for nightmare glimpses, of the abyss-edge on which it danced.

Maddeningly unaware.

Clawly's features writhed. Thus, he thought, the Dawn gods must have felt when looking down upon mankind the evening before Ragnarok.

To be able to shake those people out of their complacency, make them aware of danger!

The seer's words returned to him: "Arm it. Mobilize it. Do not let it wait supine for the hunter—You must give it a reason . . . extemporize a danger—Mars."

Mars! The seer's disappearance had caused Clawly to miss the idea behind the word, but now, remembering, he grasped it in a flash. A faked Martian invasion. Doctored reports from the First Interplanetary Expedition—mysterious disappearance of spaceships—unknown craft approaching Earth—rumor of a vast fleet—running fights in the stratosphere—

Firemoor of the Extraterrestrial Service was his friend, and believed in his theories. Moreover, Firemoor was daring—even reckless. Many of the young men under him were of similar temperament. The thing could be done!

Abruptly Clawly shook his head, scowled. Any such invasion scare would be a criminal hoax. It was a notion that must have been forced upon him by the darker, more wantonly mischievous side of his nature—or by some lingering hypnotic influence of Oktav.

And yet—

No! He must forget the notion. Find another way.

He slid from the desk, began to pace. Opposition. That was what he needed. Something concrete to fight against. Something, some person, some group, that was opposed to him, that was trying to thwart him at every turn.

He stopped, wondering why he had not thought of it before.

There were two men who were trying to thwart him, who had shrewdly undermined his and Thorn's theories, two men who had shown an odd personality reversal in the past months, who had impressed him with a fleeting sense of strangeness and alienage.

Two members of the World Executive Committee. Conjerly and Tempelmar.

Brushing the treetops, swooping through leaf-framed gaps, startling a squirrel that had been dozing on an upper branch, Clawly glided into the open and made a running landing on the olive-floored sundeck of Conjerly's home.

It was very quiet. There was only the humming of some bees in the flower garden, up from which sweet, heavy odors drifted sluggishly and curled across the deck. The sun beat down. On all sides without a break, the trees—solid masses of burnished leaves—pressed in.

Clawly crossed quietly to the dilated doorway in the cream-colored wall. He did not remove his flying togs. His visor he had thrown open during flight.

Raising his hand, he twice broke the invisible beam spanning the doorway. A low musical drone sounded, was repeated.

There was no answering sound, no footsteps. Clawly waited.

The general quiet, the feeling of lifelessness, made his abused nerves twitch. Forest homes like this, reached only by flying, were devilishly lonely and isolated.

Then he became aware of another faint, rhythmic sound, which the humming of the bees had masked. It came from inside the house. Throaty breathing. The intervals between breaths seemed abnormally long.

Clawly hesitated. Then he smoothly ducked under the beam.

He walked softly down a dark, cool corridor. The breathing grew steadily louder, though there was no change in its labored, sighing monotony. Opposite the third doorway the increase in volume was abrupt.

As his eyes became accustomed to the semidarkness, he made out a low couch and the figure of a man sprawled on it, on his back, arms dropped to either side, pale blob of bald head thrown limply back. At intervals the vague face quivered with the slow-paced breathing.

Clawly fumbled sideways, switched on a window, went over to the couch.

On the floor, under Conjerly's hand, was a deflated elastoid bag. Clawly picked it up, sniffed, quickly averted his head from the faintly pungent soporific odor.

He shook the bulky sleeper, less gently after a moment.

It did not interrupt the measured snores.

The first impression of Conjerly's face was one of utter emptiness, the deep-grooved wrinkles of character and emotion a network of disused roads. But on closer examination, hints of personality became dimly apparent, as if glimpsed at the bottom of a smudgy pool.

The longer Clawly studied them, the surer he became that the suspicions he had clutched at so eagerly in Oktav's office were groundless. This was the Conjerly he had known. Unimaginative perhaps, stubborn and blunt, a little too inclined to conservatism, a little too fond of curling down those deep furrows at the corners of the mouth—but nothing alien, nothing malign.

The rhythm of the breathing changed. The sleeper stirred. One hand came slowly up, brushing blindly at the chest.

Clawly watched motionless. From all sides the heavy summery silence pressed in.

The rhythm of the breathing continued to change. The sleeper tossed. The hand fumbled restlessly at the neck of the loose houserobe.

And something else changed. It seemed to Clawly as if the face of the Conjerly he knew were sinking downward into a narrow bottomless pit, becoming tiny as a cameo, vanishing utterly, leaving only a hollow mask. And then, as if another face were rising to fill the mask—and in this second face, if not malignity, at least grim and unswervingly hostile purpose.

The sleeper mumbled, murmured. Clawly bent low, caught words. Words with a shuddery, unplaceable quality of distance to them, as if they came from another cosmos.

" . . . transtime machine . . . invasion . . . three days . . . we . . . prevent action . . . until—"

Then, from the silence behind him, a different sound—a faint crunch.

Clawly whirled. Standing in the doorway, filling half its width and all its height, was Tempelmar.

And in Tempelmar's lean, horselike face the vanishing flicker of a look in which suspicion, alarm, and a more active emotion were blended—a lethal look.

But by the time Clawly was looking straight at him, it had been replaced by an urbane, condescending, eyebrow-raising "Well?"

Again a sound from behind. Turning, backing a little so that he could take in both men at once, Clawly saw that Conjerly was sitting up, rubbing his face. He took away his hands and his small eyes stared at Clawly—blankly at first. Then his expression changed too, became a "Well?"—though more angry, indignant, less urbane. It was an expression that did not belong to the man who had lain there drugged.

The words Clawly had barely caught were still humming in his ears.

Even as he phrased his excuse—". . . came to talk with you about the program . . . heard sounds of distressed breathing . . . alarmed . . . walked in . . ." —even as he considered the possibility of immediate physical attack and the best way to meet it, he came to a decision.

He would see Firemoor.

VIII

In what a shadow, or deep pit of darkness,
Doth womanish and fearful mankind live!

The Duchess of Malfi, JOHN WEBSTER.

With bent shoulders, sunken head, paralyzed arm still dangling at his side, Thorn crouched uncomfortably in his lightless cell, as if the whole actual weight of the Black Star—up to the cold, cloud-piercing pinnacle where "they" held council—were upon him. His mind was tried to the breaking point, oppressed by the twisted, tyrannous world into which he had blundered, by the aching body not his own, by the brain which refused to think his thoughts in the way he wanted to think them.

And yet, in a sense, the human mind is tireless—an instrument built for weary decades of uninterrupted thinking and dreaming. And so Thorn continued to work on, revolving miseries, regrets, and fears, striving to unlock the stubborn memory chambers of the unfamiliar brain, turning from that to equally hopeless efforts to make plans. Mostly it struggled nightmarishly with the problem of escape back to his own world, and with the paradoxical riddles which that problem involved. He must, Thorn told himself, still be making partial use of his brain back in World I—to give it a name—just as Thorn II—to give him a name—must be making use of these locked memory chambers. All thought had to be based on a physical brain; it couldn't go on in emptiness. Also, since Universes I and II—to give them names—were independent, self-contained space-time setups, they couldn't have an ordinary spatial relationship—they couldn't be far from or near to each other. The only linkage between them seemed to be the mental ones between quasiduplicate brains, and such linkages would not involve distance in any common sense of the term. His transition into World II had seemed to take place instantaneously; hence, pragmatically speaking, the two universes could be considered as superimposed on each other. Whether he was in one or the other was just a matter of viewpoint.

So near and yet so far. So diabolically similar to attempts to wake from a nightmare—and the blackness of his cell increased the similarity. All he had to do was summon up enough mental energy, find sufficient impetus, to force a re-exchange of viewpoints between himself and Thorn II. And yet as he struggled and strained through seeming eternities in the dark, as he strove to sink, to plunge, down the dark channels of the subconscious and found them closed, as he felt out the iron resistances of that other Thorn, he began to think the effort impossible—even began to wonder if World I were not just the wishful dream of a scarred, hunted, memoryless man in a world where invisible tyrants plotted un-understandable invasions, commanded the building of inexplicable machines, and bent millions to their wholly cryptic will.

At least, whatever the sufficient impetus was, he could not find it.

A vertical slit of light appeared, widened to a square, revealing a long corridor. And in it, flanked by two black-uniformed guards, the other Clawly.

So similar was the dapper figure to the Clawly he knew—rigged out in a strange costume and acting in a play—that it was all he could do not to spring up with a friendly greeting.

And then, to think that this Clawly's mind was linked to the other's, that somewhere, just across its subconscious, his friend's thoughts moved— Dizzying. He stared at the trim, ironic face with a terrible fascination.

Clawly II spoke, "Consider yourself flattered. I'm going to deliver you personally to the Servants of the People. They'll want to be the ones to decide, in your case, between immediate self-sacrifice, assisted confession, or what not." He chuckled without personal malice. "The Servants have devised quite amusing euphemisms for Death and Torture, haven't they? The odd thing is, they seem to take them seriously—the euphemisms, I mean."

The uniformed guards, in whose stolid faces were written years of unquestioning obedience to incomprehensible orders, did not laugh. If anything, they looked shocked.

Thorn staggered up and stepped slowly forward, feeling that by that action he was accepting a destiny not of his own making but as inescapable as all destinies are, that he was making his entrance, on an unknown stage, into an unknown play. They started down the corridor, the guards bringing up the rear.

"You make rather a poorer assassin than I'd have imagined, if you'll pardon the criticism," Clawly II remarked after a moment. "That screaming my name to get me off guard—a very ill-advised dodge. And then dropping your weapon in the streambed. No—you can't exactly call it competent. I'm afraid you didn't live up to your reputation of being the most dangerous of the Recalcitrants. But then, of course, you were fagged."

Thorn sensed something more in the remarks than courteous knife-twisting. Undeniably, Clawly II was vaguely aware of something off-key, and was probing for it. Thorn tightened his guard, for he had decided on at least one thing in the dark—that he would not reveal that he was a displaced mind, except to escape some immediate doom. It might be all right if they would consider him insane. But he was reasonably certain they would not.

Clawly II looked up at him curiously. "Rather silent, aren't you? Last time we met, as I recall, you denounced me—or was it the things I stood for?—in the most bitter language, though with admirable restraint. Can it be that you're beginning to reconsider the wisdom of recalcitrance? Rather late for that, I'm afraid."

He waited a while. Then, "It's you that hate me, you know. I hate no one." He caught Thorn's involuntary grimace, the twitch of the shoulder from which hung the paralyzed right arm. "Oh, I sometimes hurt people, but that's mainly adjustment to circumstances—quite another thing. My ideal, which I've pretty well achieved, is to become so perfectly adjusted to circumstances that I float freely on the stream of life, unannoyed by any tugs of hate, love, fear, caution, guilt, responsibility, and so forth—all the while enjoying the spectacle and occasionally poking in a finger."

Thorn winced—Clawly II's remarks were so similar to those which Clawly I sometimes made when he was in a banteringly bitter mood. Certainly the man must have some sort of suspicions and be trying to draw him out—he'd never talk so revealingly otherwise. Beyond that, there was the suggestion that Clawly II was bothered by certain unaccustomed feelings of sympathy and was trying to get to the bottom of them. Perhaps the independence of quasiduplicate minds wasn't as complete as it had at first appeared. Perhaps Clawly I's emotions were obscurely filtering through to Clawly II. It was all very confusing, unnervingly so, and Thorn was relieved when their entry into a large room postponed the moment when he would have to decide on a line of answers.

It was an arresting room, chiefly because it was divided into two areas in which two separate ways of life held sway, as clearly as if there had been a broad white line extending across the middle, with the notice "Thou shalt not pass." On this side was quite a crowd of people, most of them sitting around on benches, a few in black uniforms, the rest in servile gray. They were all obviously waiting—for orders, permissions, judgments, interviews. They displayed, to an exaggerated degree, that mixture of uneasiness and boredom characteristic of people who must wait. Four words sprang to Thorn's mind, summing them up. *They did not know.*

On the other side were fewer people—a bare half dozen, seated at various desks. Their superiority was not obviously displayed. Their clothing was, if anything, drabber and more severe, and the furnishings they used were in no way luxurious. But something in

their manner, something in the way they glanced speculatively up from their work, put gulfs between them
and those who uneasily waited. This time only two
words were needed. *They knew.*

Clawly II's arrival seemed to cause an increase in
the uneasiness. At least, Thorn caught several frightened glances, and sensed a general relaxing of tension
when it became obvious that Clawly II's mission did
not concern anyone here. He also noted that the two
guards seemed relieved when Clawly dismissed them.

One other glance he thought he caught was of a per-
plexingly different sort. It was directed at him rather
than Clawly II. It came from an elderly gray-clad
man, whose face awoke no sense of recognition either
in this world or his own. It conveyed, if he was not
mistaken, sympathy, anxiety, and—strangest of all—
loyalty. Still, if Thorn II had been some sort of rebel
leader, the incident was understandable. Thorn
quailed, wondering if he had put himself into the position of betraying a worthy movement in this world as
well as his own.

Clawly II seemed to be a person of reputation on
the other side of the room as well, for his clipped "To
the Servants' Hall, with a person for the Servants"
passed them through without a question.

They entered another corridor, and their surroundings began to change very rapidly. A few paces
brought them to a subtronic tube. Thorn was glad
that he was startled into moving jerkily when the
upward-surging current gripped them, for a glance at
Clawly II warned him that it would not be well to
show much familiarity with this form of transportation.

And now, for the first time since his plunge into
World II, Thorn's mind began to work with clarity. It
may have been the soothing familiarity of the current.

Obviously, in World II subtronic power was the
closely guarded possession of a ruling elite. There had
been no evidence at all of its employment on the other
side of the dividing line. Moreover, that would explain

why the workers and soldiers on the other side were kept ignorant of the true nature and theory of at least some of the instruments they constructed or used. It would also explain the need for the vast amount of work—there were two ways of life, based on entirely different power-systems, to be maintained.

Then as to the relationship between Worlds I and II. For closely related they must be—it was unthinkable that two eternally independent universes could have produced two near-identical Opal Crosses, Gray Twins, Clawlys, Thorns, and an uncounted host of other similars; if one granted that possibility, one would have to grant anything. No—Worlds I and II must be the results of a split in that time-stream, however caused, and a fairly recent split at that, for the two worlds contained duplicate individuals and it was again unthinkable that, if the split had occurred as much as a hundred years ago, the same individuals would have been born in the two worlds—the same gametes, under different circumstances, still uniting to form the same zygotes.

The split must—of course!—have occurred when the nightmare-increase began in World I. About thirty years ago.

But—Thorn's credulity almost rebelled—would it have been possible for two worlds to become so different in a short time? Freedom in one, tyranny in the other. Decent people in one, emotional monsters and cringing, embittered underlings in the other. It was horrible to think that human nature, especially the nature of people you loved and respected, could be so much the toy of circumstance.

And yet—the modern world was keyed for change. Wars could, had, come overnight. Sweeping technological changes had been accomplished in a few months. And granting such an immense initial difference as the decision to keep subtronic power a government secret in World II, to make it public property in World I—

Moreover, there was a way of testing. Without pausing to consider, Thorn said, "Remember when we were children? We used to play together. Once we swore an oath of undying friendship."

Clawly II twisted toward him in the current, which was now taking them up past winking corridor entries.

"You *are* breaking," he remarked in surprise. "I never expected a play for sympathy. Yes, of course I remember."

"And then about two years later," Thorn plunged on, "when our glider dropped in the lake and I was knocked out, you towed me ashore."

Clawly II laughed, but the puzzled look around his eyes deepened. "Did you really believe I saved you? It hardly fits with your behavior toward me afterwards. No, as I think you know, I swam ashore. That was the day on which I first realized that I was I, and that everything and everybody else was circumstances."

Thorn shivered, as much in horror of this changeling beside him as in satisfaction at having checked the date of the time-split. Then he felt revulsion rising in him, more from the body he occupied than from his own thoughts.

"There isn't room in the world for even two people with that attitude," he heard himself challenge bitterly.

"Yes, but there is room for one," Clawly II replied laughingly. Then he frowned and continued hesitatingly, as if against his better judgment. "Look, why don't you try the same thing? Your only chance with the Servants is to make yourself useful to them. Remember, they too are just something to be adjusted to."

For a moment it seemed to Thorn as if Clawly I were striving to look through the eyes of Clawly II. As he tried to gain control of the baffling jumble of emotions this sensation produced, Clawly II took him by the arm and steered them into the slower periphery of the current, then into a dead-current area before the mouth of a short pedestrian corridor.

"No talk from here on," he warned Thorn. "But remember my advice."

There were calculatingly eyed guards inside the corridor mouth, but again a mere "With a person for the Servants" passed them in.

A low, gray door, without numeral or insignia, blocked the end of the corridor. Some yards short of it was a narrow side-door. Clawly II touched something and the side-door opened. Thorn followed him through it. After a few paces down a dim, curving passageway, they came to a large room, but Clawly II stopped them just short of it. Again he touched something. A door slid silently out of the wall behind them, changing the end of the passageway into a dark niche in the room ahead. Signing to Thorn that they were to wait and watch, Clawly II leaned back with a slow speculative smile.

IX

Black Star, would I were steadfast as thou art—
JOHN KEATS *(with an ironic alteration).*

It was a notably bare room, smaller and lower-ceilinged than he had expected. It was furnished with ostentatious simplicity, and nothing broke the gray monotony of the walls.

Around the longer side of the kidney-shaped table, eleven men sat on stools. Their gray tunics, though clean, were like those of beggars. They were all old, some bald, some capped with close-cropped white or gray. They all sat very erect.

The first thing that struck Thorn—with surprise, he realized—was that the Servants of the People looked in no way malignant, villainous, or evil.

But looking at them a second time, Thorn began to wonder if there was not something worse. A puritanic grimness that knew no humor. A suffocating consciousness of responsibility, as if all the troubles of the world rested on their shoulders alone. A paternal aloofness, as if everyone else were an irresponsible child. A selflessness swollen to such bounds as to become supreme selfishness. An intolerable sense of personal importance that their beggarly clothes and surroundings only emphasized.

But Thorn had barely gleaned this impression, had had no time to survey the faces in detail, except to note that one or two seemed vaguely familiar, when his attention became riveted on the man who was standing on the other side of the table, the focus of their converging eyes.

That man was obviously one of them. His manner and general appearance were the same.

But that man was also Conjerly.

He was speaking. "I must return at once. The soporific I inhaled into my other body will wear off shortly, and if the other mind becomes conscious, exchange will be difficult. True, Tempelmar is on guard there and could administer another dose. But that is dangerous. Understand, we will attempt no further exchanges unless it becomes necessary to transmit to you information of vital importance. The process is too risky. There is always the possibility of the mental channels being blocked, and one or both of us being marooned here."

"You are wise," observed the midmost of the Servants, apparently their chairman, a tall thin man with wrinkle-puckered lips. "No further exchanges should be necessary. I anticipate no emergencies."

"And so I take my leave," Conjerly continued, "assured that the trans-time machine is ready and that the invasion will begin in three days, at the hour agreed. We will prevent the World Executive Committee from taking any significant action until then."

Thorn leaned forward, half guessing what was coming. Clawly II's hand touched his sleeve.

Conjerly bowed his head, stood there rigid. Two black-uniformed guards appeared and took up positions close to him, one on either side.

For a full half minute nothing happened.

Then a great shiver went through Conjerly. He slumped forward, would have fallen except for the two guards. He hung in their arms, breathing heavily.

When he raised his face, Thorn saw that it had a different expression, was that of a different man. A man who looked dazed and sick.

"Where—? Who—?" he mumbled thickly. The guards began to lead him out. Then his eyes cleared. He seemed to recognize the situation. "Don't lock me up. Let me explain," he cried out, his voice racked by a desperate yet hopeless urgency. "My name's Conjerly. I'm a member of the World Executive Committee." His face, twisted back over his shoulder, was a white, uncomprehending mask. "Who are you? What do you want out of me? Why am I drugged? What have you done to my body? What are you trying to do to my mind? What—"

The guards dragged him out.

The wrinkle-lipped chairman lowered his eyes. "A distressing occurrence. But, of course, strictly necessary. It is good to think that, when we have things under control in the other world, no such confinements and withholdings of permissible information will have to be practiced—except, of course, in the case of hopeless Recalcitrants."

The others nodded silently. Then Thorn started, for from beside him came an amused, incredulous snicker—not a polite or pleasant sound, and certainly unexpected.

All eyes were turned in their direction.

Clawly II strode out leisurely.

"What did your laughter signify?" the chairman asked sharply, without preliminaries, a look of displeasure settling on his face. "And who is that you have smuggled into our council, without informing us? Let me tell you, some day you will go too far in your disregard of regulations."

Clawly II ignored the second question—and the comment. He swaggered up to the table, planted his hands on it, looked them over, and said, "I laughed to think of how sincerely you will voice your distress when you discover all inhabitants of the other world to be hopeless Recalcitrants—and take appropriate measures. Come, face circumstances. You will be forced to destroy most of the inhabitants of the other world, and you know it."

"We know nothing of the sort," replied the chairman coldly. "Take care that your impudent and foolish opinions do not make us lose confidence in you. In these critical times your shrewdness and ingenuity are valuable to us. You are a useful tool, and only imprudent men destroy a tool because its mannerisms annoy them. But if in your foolhardy opinionatedness you cease to be useful—that is another matter. As regards the misguided inhabitants of the other world, you very well know that our intentions are the best."

"Of course," agreed Clawly II, smiling broadly, "but

just consider what's actually going to happen. In three days the trans-time machine will subtronically isolate and annihilate a spatio-temporal patch in this world, setting up stresses which cannot be relieved by any redistribution of material in this world; accordingly the lacuna will bind with the corresponding patch from the other world, thereby creating an area common to both worlds. Through this common area your armed forces will pour. They will come as invaders, awakening horror and fear. They will have the element of surprise on their side, but there will inevitably be resistance—organized in desperate haste, but using improved subtronic weapons. Most important, that resistance will not come, as it would in this world, from a small elite directing an ignorant multitude, but from a people of uniformly high education—a people used to freedom and adverse to submitting to any autocratic government, no matter how well-intentioned. That resistance will not cease until the other world has been destroyed in subtronic battle, or you are forced to destroy it subtronically yourselves and retire through the gap. All that is painfully clear."

"It is nothing of the sort," replied the chairman in measured and dispassionate tones. "Our invasion will be well-nigh bloodless, though we must prepare for all eventualities. At the proper moment Conjerly and Tempelmar will seize control of the so-called World Executive Committee, thereby preventing any organized resistance at the fountainhead. The majority of inhabitants of the other world have no technical knowledge of subtronic power and will therefore constitute no danger. Ultimately they will be grateful to us for insuring the safety of their world and protecting them from their irresponsible leaders. It will only be necessary for us to capture and confine all technicians and scientists having a knowledge of subtronic physics. To do this, we must admittedly be ready to take any and all necessary steps, no matter how unpleasant. For our main purpose, of which we never lose sight, is always to keep the knowledge of subtronic power—

which now imperils two worlds—in the possession of a small, responsible, and benevolent elite."

Thorn shivered. The horrible thing was that these Servants actually believed that they were acting for the best, that they had the good of mankind—of two mankinds—at heart.

"Exactly," said Clawly II, continuing to smile. "The only thing you don't see, or pretend not to see, is the inevitable consequences of that main purpose. Even now your secrets are gravely endangered. Mind-exchange is putting more and more Recalcitrants and Escapists into the other world. It is only a matter of time before some of them begin to realize that the inhabitants of that world are their potential allies rather than their foes, and join forces with them. Similarly it is only a matter of time until the mind of a subtronic technician is displaced into this world and contacted by the Recalcitrants here—then you will have to fight subtronic wars in two worlds. Your only chance, as I'm glad you recognize in part, is to strike hard and fast, destroy the other world, along with all the Recalcitrants and Escapists who have entered it, then seek out and eliminate all displaced minds in this world. Your weakness is in not admitting this at the start. Everything would be much easier if you would leave out pseudobenevolent intentions and recognize that you are up against an equation in destruction, which you must solve in the only logical way possible—by a general canceling out."

And he rocked back on his heels a little, again surveying the eleven old faces. It struck Thorn that thus legendary Loke must have mocked the Dawn Gods and flayed their high-sounding pretenses, confident that his cunning and proven usefulness would protect him from their wrath. As for the Servants, their paternalism was unpleasantly apparent in their attitude toward Clawly II. They treated him like a brilliantly mischievous favorite child—always indulged, often threatened, seldom punished.

Certainly there was a germ of greatness about this

Clawly II. If only he had Clawly I's sane attitude toward life, so that his critical thinking would come to something more than mere sardonic jibing!

One thing was certain, Clawly II's claim that he wanted to float on the stream of life was a gross understatement. What he really wanted was to dance along a precipice—and this time, apparently, he had taken one heedless step too many.

For the chairman looked at him and said, "The question arises whether your insistence on destruction has not assumed the proportions of a mania. We will at once reconsider your usefulness as a tool."

Clawly II bowed. He said smoothly, "First it would be well to interview the person I have brought you. You will be pleased when I tell you who he is." And he motioned to Thorn.

All eyes turned on the niche.

Abruptly, painfully, Thorn woke from his impersonal absorption in the scene unrolling before him. Again it came to him, like a hammer blow, that he was not watching from the safety of a spy-hole, but was himself immediately and fatally involved. Again the urge to escape racked him—with redoubled force, because of the warning that he must now at all costs take back to World I. It was such a simple thing. Just a change of viewpoints. He had seen Conjerly accomplish it. Surely, if he concentrated his mind in the right way, it would be that other Thorn who walked forward to face the Servants and the destiny of that other Thorn's own making, while he sank back. Surely his need to warn a world would give him sufficient impetus.

But all the time he was walking toward the table. It was *his* dragging feet that scuffed the gray flooring, *his* dry throat that swallowed, *his* cold hands that clenched and unclenched. The eleven old faces wavered, blurred, came clear again, seemed to swell, grow gray and monstrous, become the merciless masks of judges of some fabled underworld, where he must answer for another man's crimes.

The table stopped his forward progress. He heard Clawly II say, "I am afraid that I am still very useful to you. Here is your chief enemy, brought to book by my efforts alone. He was part of our bag when we raided the local Recalcitrant headquarters last night. He escaped and took to the hills, where I personally recaptured him—the Recalcitrant leader Thorn 37-P-82."

But the Servants' reaction could not have been the one Clawly was expecting, for the old faces registered anger and alarm. "Irresponsible child!" the chairman rapped out. "Didn't you hear what Conjerly reported—that he is certain there has occurred a mind-exchange between the Thorns? This man is not the Recalcitrant, but a displaced mind come to spy on us. You have provided him with what he wanted—an opportunity to learn our plans."

Thorn felt their converging hostility—a palpable force. His mind shrank back from the windows of his eyes, but, chained there, continued to peer through them.

The chairman's wrinkled hand dropped below the table. He said, "There is only one course of action." His hand came up, and in it a slim gleaming cone. "To eliminate the displaced mind before a re-exchange can be—"

Thorn was dimly conscious of Clawly II leaping forward. He heard him begin, "No! Wait! Don't you see—"

But although that was all he heard, he knew what Clawly II was going to say and why he was going to say it. He also knew why Thorn II had been able to exchange with him when Thorn II thought he was trapped and facing death on the rooftop. He knew that the chairman's action was the very thing that would nullify the chairman's purpose. At last he had found the sufficient impetus—it was staring at him down the slim, gleaming cone, leering at him even as the chains broke and his mind dropped back from the windows of his eyes into a black, dimensionless pit.

The fear of death.

Three roots there are that three ways run
'Neath the ash-tree Yggdrasil;
'Neath the first lives Hel, 'neath the second the frost giants,
'Neath the last are the lands of men.

ELDER EDDA.

Thorn did not ask himself why his resting place was dark and stuffy, rocky and dry, or where the stale, sour smell of woodsmoke came from. He was content to lie there and let his mind snuggle down into his body, lull itself with simple sensations, forget the reverberations of its terrible journey. World II still clung to him sluggishly. But like a nightmare from which one has wakened, it could be disregarded.

In a moment he would rouse himself and do what must be done. In a moment, he knew, he would know no peace until the warning had been given and all essential steps taken, until the invasion had been met and decisively thrown back. He would be a creature of tension, of duty, of war.

But for the moment nothing mattered, nothing could break his sense of peace.

Odd, though, that the heavy woodsmoke did not make him cough, and that his body was not aching from its cramped position and rocky crouch.

Muffledly, as if its source were underground, came a distant howling, melancholy and long-drawn-out, ending on a low note of menace.

He started up. His shielding hand encountered a low ceiling of rock, hurriedly traced it to jagged, sloping walls on either side.

It was he that was underground, not the howling.

What the devil had Thorn II been doing in a cave in World I? Why was he wearing this odd jumble of heavy clothing that seemed to include thick, stiff boots and furs? Where had he gotten the long knife that was stuck in his belt?

The cramping darkness was suddenly full of threats. In panicky haste he continued his feeling-out of the walls, found that he was in a small domed chamber, high enough in the center so that he could almost stand upright. On three sides the walls extended down to the uneven floor, or to the mouths of horizontal crevices too narrow to stick more than an arm in.

On the fourth side was a low opening. By getting down on hands and knees he could wriggle in.

It led slightly upward. The smell of woodsmoke grew heavier. After two sharp turns, where jagged edges caught but did not tear his heavy clothing, he began to see the gray gleam of daylight.

The roof of the passageway grew higher, so that he could almost walk upright. Then it suddenly opened into a larger chamber, the other end of which was completely open to a gloomy landscape.

This landscape consisted of a steep hillside of granite boulders and wind-warped pines, all patched with snow. At a middle distance, as if across a ravine.

But Thorn did not inspect it closely, for he was looking chiefly at the fire blocking the mouth of the narrow passageway, sending up smoke that billowed back from the ceiling, making the day even more gloomy and dim.

It immediately struck him as being a very remarkable fire, though he couldn't say why. After a while he decided that it was because it had been very cleverly constructed to burn steadily for a long time, some of the logs and branches being so placed that they would not fall into the fire until others had been consumed. Whoever had built that fire must have painstakingly visualized just how it was going to burn over a period of several hours.

But why should he waste time admiring a fire? He kicked it aside with the clumsy boots Thorn II had dug up God knows where, and strode to the mouth of the cave.

Claws skirred on rock, and he had the impression of a lithe furry animal whisking off to one side.

The cave opened on a hillside, similar to the one opposite and slanting down to a twisting, ice-choked stream. Overhead a gray, dreary sky seemed to be trending toward nightfall. The walls of the ravine shut off any more distant horizon. It was very cold.

The scene was hauntingly familiar.

Had Thorn II been insane, or gone insane? Why else should he have hidden himself in a cave in a near-arctic wildlife reserve? For that certainly seemed to be what he had done, despite the difficulty in picturing just how he had managed to do it in so short a time.

A fine thing if, after getting back to his rightful world, he should starve to death in a reserve, or be killed by some of the formidable animals with which they were stocked.

He must climb the hill behind him. Wherever he was, he'd be able to sight a beacon or skylon from its top.

It suddenly occurred to him that this ravine was devilishly like one in the woodland near the synchromy amphitheater, a ravine in which he and Clawly used to go exploring when they were boys. There was something unforgettably distinctive about the pattern of the streambed.

But that couldn't be. The weather was all wrong. And that ravine was much more thickly wooded. Besides, erosion patterns were always repeating themselves.

He started to examine the queer, bulky clothing Thorn II had been wearing. In doing so, he got one good look at his hands—and stopped.

He stood for a long moment with his eyes closed. Even when soft paws pattered warily somewhere over his head and a bit of gravel came trickling down, he did not jerk.

Rapidly the determination grew in his mind that he must get to the hilltop and establish his position before he did anything else, before he thought anything else, certainly before he examined his hands or his face more closely. It was more a terror-inspired compulsion than a determination. He stepped to the rocky lip in front of the cave, and looked back. Again there was the impression of a gray, furry animal streaking for cover.

Something about the size of a cat. He hurriedly surveyed the routes leading upward, picked one that seemed to slope more gradually and avoid the steeper barren stretches, and immediately started up it at a scrambling trot, his eyes fixed resolutely ahead.

But after he had gone a little way, he saw something that made him stop and stare despite the compulsion driving him.

On a pine-framed boulder about a dozen yards ahead, to one side of the route he was taking, three cats sat watching him.

They were cats, all right, house cats, though they seemed to be of a particularly thick-furred breed.

But one wouldn't normally find house cats on a wildlife reserve. Their presence argued the nearness of human habitation. Moreover, they were eyeing him with a poised intentness that indicated some kind of familiarity, and did not fit with their earlier racing for cover—if those had been the same animals.

He called, "Kitty!" His voice cracked a little. "Kitty!"

The sound drifted thinly across the hillside, as if congealed by the cold.

And then the sound was answered, or rather echoed, by the cat to the right, a black-and-gray.

It was not exactly the word "Kitty" that the cat miauled, but it was a sound so like it, so faithful to his exact intonations, that his flesh crawled.

"Kii . . . eee." Again the eerily mocking, mimicking challenge rang out.

He was afraid.

He started forward again. At the first scrape of his boots on gravel, the cats vanished.

For some time he made fast, steady progress, although the going was by no means easy, sometimes leading along the rims of landslides, sometimes forcing him to fight his way through thick clumps of scrub trees. The last "Kii . . . eee" stuck in his ears, and at times he was pretty sure he glimpsed furry bodies slipping along to one side, paralleling his progress. His thoughts went off on unpleasant tacks, chiefly about the degree to which careful breeding had increased the intelligence of house cats, the way in which they had always maintained their aloof and independent life in the midst of man's civilization, and other less concrete speculations.

Once he heard another sound, a repetition of the melancholy howling that had first startled him in the cave. It might have been wolves, or dogs, and seemed to come from somewhere low in the ravine and quite a distance away.

The sky was growing darker.

The rapid ascent was taking less out of him than he would have imagined. He was panting, but in a steady, easy way. He felt he could keep up this pace for a considerable distance.

The pines began to thin on the uphill side. He emerged onto a long, wide slope that stretched, ever-steepening, boulder-strewn but almost barren of vegetation, to the ravine's horizon. His easiest way lay along its base, past tangled underbrush.

A little distance ahead and up the slope, a large chunk of granite jutted out. On its rim sat three cats, again regarding him. Something about the way they were turned toward each other, the little movements they made, suggested that they were holding a conference and that the topic of the conference was—he.

From behind and below the howling came again. The cats pricked up their ears. There were more movements, more glances in his direction. Then as he began jogging along again, one of the cats—the tiger—leaped down and streaked away past him, downhill. While the black-and-gray and the black dropped off the granite rim more leisurely and began to trot along in the direction he was taking, with frequent sidewise glances.

He quickened his pace, grateful for the reserve energy.

The going was good. There were no eroded chutes to be edged around, no pines to fight.

Once the howling was repeated faintly.

The shadowy bodies of the cats slipped between the boulders, in and out. Gradually he began to draw ahead of them.

For some reason everything felt very natural, as if he had been created for this running through the dusk.

He sprinted up the last stretch, came out on top.

For a long time he just looked and turned, and turned and looked. Everything else—emotions, thought—was subordinated to the act of seeing.

Up here it was still pretty light. And there were no hills to shut out the view. It stretched, snow-streaked, lightless, lifeless, achingly drear, to black horizons in three directions and a distant glittering icewall in the fourth.

The only suggestion of habitation was a thin pencil of smoke rising some distance across the plateau he faced.

For as long as he could, he pretended not to recognize the ruins sparsely dotting the landscape—vast mountainous stumps of structures, buckled and tortured things, blackened and ice-streaked, surrounded by strange formations of rock that suggested lava ridges, as if the very ground had melted and churned and boiled when those ruins were made.

A ruined world, from which the last rays of a setting sun, piercing for a moment the smoky ruins, struck dismal yellow highlights.

But recognition could only be held at bay for a few minutes. His guess about the ravine had been correct. The snow-shrouded, mile-long mound ahead of him was the grave of the Opal Cross. That dark monolith far to the left was the stump of the Gray H. Those two lopped towers, crazily buckled and leaning toward each other as if for support, were the Gray Twins. That split and jagged mass the other side of the ravine, black against the encroaching ice, upthrust like the hand of a buried man, was the Rusty T.

It could hardly be World I, no matter after what

catastrophe or lapse of years. For there was no sign, not even a suggestive hump, of the Blue Lorraine, the Mauve Z, or the Myrtle Y. Nor World II, for the Black Star's ruins would have bulked monstrously on the immediate left.

He looked at his hands.

They were thickened and calloused, ridged and darkened by scars of wounds and frostbite, the nails grained and uneven. And yet they were Thorn's hands.

He lifted them and touched his chapped, scaly face, with its high-growing, uncombed beard and long hair matted against his neck under the fur hood.

His clothes were a miscellany of stiff, inexpertly trimmed furs, portions of a worn and dirty suit of flying togs, and improvised bits of stuff, such as the hacked-out sections of elastoid flooring constituting the soles of his boots.

His heavy belt, which was reinforced with reading tape, supported two pouches, besides the knife, which seemed to be a crudely hilted cutter from a hyperlathe.

One of the pouches contained a slingshot powered by strips of elastoid, several large pebbles, and three dark, dubious chunks of meat.

In the other were two small containers of nutriment-concentrate with packaging-insignia of twenty-five years ago, a stimuloid canister with one pellet left, two bits of sharp metal, a jagged fragment of flint, three more pieces of elastoid, more reading tape, a cord made of sinew, a plastic lens, a wood-carver's handsaw, a small, dismantled heat-projector showing signs of much readaptive tinkering, several unidentifiable objects, and—the smooth gray sphere he had stolen at the Yggdrasil.

Even as he was telling himself it could not be the same one, his blunt fingers were recognizing its unforgettable smoothness, its oblate form, its queerly exaggerated inertia. His mind was remembering he had fancied it a single supergiant molecule, a key—if one knew how to use it—to the doors of unseen worlds.

But there was only time to guess that the thing must

be linked to his mind rather than to any of the bodies his mind had occupied, and to wonder how it had escaped the thorough search to which he had been subjected in the Black Star, when his attention was diverted by a faint eager yapping that burst out suddenly and was as suddenly choked off.

He turned around. Up the boulder-studded slope he had just ascended, streaming out of the underbrush at its base, came a pack of wolves, or dogs—at least thirty of them. They took the same sloping course that he had taken. There was a strange suggestion of discipline about their silent running. He could not be sure—the light was very bad—but he fancied he saw smaller furry shapes clinging to the backs of one or two of them.

He knew now why he had spent time admiring a fire.

But the pack was between him and that fire, so he turned and ran across the plateau toward where he had glimpsed the rising wisp of smoke.

As he ran he broke and chewed the lone stimulol pellet, breathing thanks to that Thorn—he would call him Thorn III—who had hoarded the pellet for so many years, against some ultimate emergency.

He ran well. His clumsily booted feet avoided rocks and ruts, hit firmly on icy patches, with a sureness that made him wonder if they did not know the route. And when the stimulol hit his bloodstream, he was able to increase speed slightly. But risking a look back, he saw the pack pouring up over the crest. A steady baying began, eager and mournful.

In the growing darkness ahead a low, ruddy, winking light showed. He studied its slow increase in size, intent on gauging the exact moment when he would dare to sprint.

The way became rougher. It was a marvel how his feet carried him. The ruddy light became a patch, illumining a semicircular opening behind it. The baying drew near. He could hear the scuff of clawed feet. He started to sprint.

And just in time. There was a great brown hound springing higher than his shoulder, snapping in at his neck, splashing it with slaver, as he jumped the fire, turned with his whipped-out knife, and took his stand beside the gnarled man with the spear, in front of the doorless doorway of the half-buried room, or large crate, of weathered plastoid.

Then for a moment it was chaotic battle—gaunt-bellied forms rearing above the flames—red eyes and clashing yellow fangs—spear and cutter licking out—reek of singed hair—snarls, squeals, grunts, gasps—and, dominating it all, making it hellish, those three spitting, mewing cat-faces peering over the shoulders of three dogs that hung in the rear.

Then, as if at a note of command, the dogs all retreated and it was suddenly over. Without a word, Thorn and the other man began to repair and restock with fuel the scattered fire. When it was finished, the other man asked, "Did they get you anywhere? I may be crazy, but I think the devils are starting to poison the teeth of some of the hounds."

Thorn said, "I don't think so," and began to examine his hands and arms.

The other man nodded. "What food you got?" he asked suddenly.

Thorn told him. The other man seemed impressed by the nutriment-concentrate. He said, "We could hunt together for a while, I guess. Ought to work out good—having one watching while the other sleeps." He spoke rapidly, jumbling the words together. His voice sounded disused. He studied Thorn uneasily.

Thorn studied him. He was smaller and moved with a limp, but beard, skin, and clothing were like Thorn's. The screwed-up face was not familiar. The darting, red-rimmed eyes below the jutting brows were not altogether sane. Thorn's presence seemed to put him on edge, to shake his emotions to the core. Every time he snapped shut his cracked, nervous lips, Thorn felt that he dammed up a torrent of babblingly eager talk.

He asked Thorn, "Where did you come from?"

"A cave in the ravine," Thorn replied, wondering how much to tell. "What's your story?"

The man looked at him queerly. He trembled. Then the cracked lips opened.

To Thorn, squatting there behind the crackling fence of flame, staring out into a night that was black except for the occasional red hint of eyes, it seemed that what he heard was what he had always known.

"My name was Darkington. I was a geology student. What saved me was that I was in the mountains when the power broke loose. I guess we all knew about the power, didn't we? It was in the air. We'd always known that some day someone would find out what it was behind gravity and electricity and magnetism"—he stumbled over the long words—"and the more they tried to hush it up, the surer we were that someone had found out. I guess they shouldn't have tried to hush it up. I guess intelligent creatures can't back out of their destiny like that.

"But anyway I was in the mountains when the power broke loose and ate up all the metal it could reach. Our party was laid up by the fumes, and two of them died. Afterwards some of us started out to try to contact other survivors, but the fumes were worse where we went and some more died and the rest broke up. I got in with a gang that was trying to make a go of farming just north of the volcano belt, but we made a lot of mistakes and then came the first of the long winters and finished off all our plans and made us realize that the weather had all gone different, what with the exposed raw rock taking all the carbon dioxide out of the air, and not enough green stuff left to replace it. After that I drifted around and took up with different scavenging gangs, but when the cannibalism started and the cats and dogs began to get really dangerous, I headed north and made it to the glaciers. Since then I've just hung on, like you see."

He turned to Thorn. Already his voice was hoarse.

Like nervous hunger, his eagerness to talk had not carried him far.

Thorn shook his head, peering beyond the fire. "There must be a way," he said slowly. "Admittedly it would be difficult and we'd risk our lives, but still there must be a way."

"A way?" the other asked blankly.

"Yes, back to wherever men are beginning to band together and rebuild. South, I suppose. We might have to hunt for a long time, but we'd find it."

There was a long silence. A curious look of sympathy came into the other man's face.

"You've got the dreams," he told Thorn, making his croaking voice gentle. "I get them myself, so strong that I can make myself believe for a while that everything's the way it was. But it's just the dreams. Nobody's banding together. Nobody's going to rebuild civilization, unless"—his hand indicated something beyond the fire—"unless it's those devils out there."

XI

He who lets fortunetellers shape his decisions, follows a chartless course.

ARTEMIDORUS OF CILICIA.

Alternate waves of guilt and almost unbearable excitement washed Clawly I as he hurried through the deserted corridors of the Blue Lorraine toward the office of Oktav. In grimmest seriousness he wondered whether his own fancied role of mad Pied Piper had not come true, whether his mind—and those of Firemoor and his other accomplices in the Martian hoax—were not already more than half usurped by diabolically mischievous mentalities whose only purpose, or pleasure, was to see a sane world reduced to chaos.

For the faked threat of a Martian invasion was producing all the effects he could ever have anticipated, and more, as the scenes he had just been witnessing proved. They stuck in his mind, those scenes. The air around the Blue Lorraine aswarm with fliers from bullet-swift couriers to meddlesome schoolchildren. Streams of machine-units and various materials and supplies going out on subtronic currents for distribution to selected points in the surrounding countryside, for it had early become apparent that the skylons were exceedingly vulnerable to attack from space—all Earth's eggs in a few thousand baskets. Engineers busy around the Blue Lorraine's frosty summit, setting up energy-projectors and other improvised subtronic artillery—for although the skylons were vulnerable, they were the proud symbols and beloved homes of civilization and would be defended to the last. All eyes craned apprehensively upward as a thundering spaceship burst through the blue sky, then lowered in ruefully humorous relief as it became obvious that it was, of course, no alien invader, but one of Earth's own ships headed for the nearby yards to be fitted with subtronic weapons. All eyes turned momentarily to the west, where defensive screens were being tried out, to watch a vast iridescent dome leap momentarily into being and a circle of woodland puff into smoke. Excited eyes, all of them, as ready to flash with humor as to betray shock, anxiety, or fear. Eyes that were seven-eighths "There probably won't be any invasion" and one-eighth "There will be." Eyes that made Clawly proud of mankind, but that also awakened sickening doubts as to the wisdom of his trickery.

And to think that this sort of thing was going on all over the world. The use of subtronic power in transport and fabrication made possible a swiftness in preparation never before known in Earth's history. Organization was a weak point, the Earth being geared for the leisurely existence of peace and individual freedom, but various local agencies were taking over while the World Executive Committee created the framework of a centralized military authority. Confusedly perhaps, and a little bunglingly, but eagerly, wholeheartedly, and above all swiftly, Earth was arming to meet the threat.

It was all so much *bigger* than anyone could have anticipated, Clawly told himself for the hundredth time, unconsciously increasing his already rapid pace as he neared Oktav's office. He had started it all, but now it was out of his hands. He could only wait and hope that, when the real invasion came, across time rather than space, the present preparations would prove useful to Earth's bewildered defenders. In any case, a few hours would tell the story, for this was the third day.

But what if the trans-time invasion did not come in three days? The hoax might be uncovered at any moment now—Firemoor was already regretting the whole business, on the verge of a funk—and during the period of angry reaction no invasion reports of any sort would be believed. Then he would be in the position of having cried wolf to the world.

Or what if the trans-time invasion did not come at all? All his actions had been based on such insubstantial evidence—Thorn's dream-studies, certain suggestive psychological aberrations, the drugged Conjerly's murmur of ". . . invasion . . . three days . . ." He was becoming increasingly convinced that he would soon wake, as if from a nightmare, and find himself accused as a madman or charlatan.

Certainly his nerves were getting out of hand. He needed Thorn. Never before had he realized the degree to which he and Thorn were each other's balance wheel. But Thorn was still missing, and the inquiry agencies had no progress to report. Despite the larger anxieties in which his mind was engulfed, Thorn's absence preyed upon it to such a degree that he had twice fancied he spotted Thorn among the swirling crowd outside the Blue Lorraine.

But even more than he needed Thorn, he needed Oktav. Now that the crisis had come, he could see to what an extent the seer's advice had determined all his actions, from his first serious belief in the possibility of trans-time invasion to his engineering of the Martian hoax. Call it superstition, ignorant credulity, hypnotism, the fact remained that he believed in Oktav, was convinced that Oktav had access to fields of knowledge undreamed of by ordinary men. And now that Oktav was gone, he felt an increasing helplessness and desperation, so that he could not resist the impulse driving him back once more to the cryptically empty office.

As he raised his hand to activate the door, memories came stealing eerily back—of former sessions in the room beyond, of the last session, of Oktav's strange summoner clad in the garments of Dawn Civilization, of the inexplicable disappearance of summoner and summoned in the exitless inner chamber.

But before his hand could activate the door, it opened.

Clad in his customary black robe, Oktav was sitting at his desk.

As if into a dream within a dream, Clawly entered.

Although the seer had always seemed supernaturally ancient, Clawly's first impression was that Oktav had vastly aged in the past three days. Something had happened to drain his small remaining store of life forces almost to the last drop. The hands were folded white claws. The face was wrinkle-puckered skin drawn tight over a fragile skull. But in the sunken, droopingly lidded eyes, knowledge burned more fiercely than ever. And not knowledge alone, but also something new—a reckless determination to use that knowledge. It was a look that made Clawly shiver—and thrill.

All the questions that had pounded at his brain so long, waiting for this interview, were suddenly mute.

"I have been on a far journey," said the seer. "I have visited many worlds that were supposed to be dead, and have seen what strange horrors can result when mere men seek to make wise use of a power befitting only a god or creatures like gods. I have gone in constant danger, for there are those against whom I have rebelled and who therefore seek my life, but I am safe from them for a time. Sit down, and I will tell you what is in my mind."

Clawly complied. Oktav leaned forward, tapping the desk with one bone-thin finger.

He continued, "For a long time I have spoken to you in riddles, dealt with you vaguely, because I was trying to play a double game—impart essential information to you, and yet not impart it. That time is past. From now on I speak clearly. In a little while I shall depart on a desperate venture. If it succeeds, I do not think you will have to fear the invasion threatening your world. But it may fail, and therefore I must first put at your disposal all the information I possess, so that you can judge how best to act in that event."

He looked up quickly. Clawly heard movement in the corridor. But it was from the inner chamber that the sudden interruption came.

Once again Oktav's summoner stood in the inner doorway. Once again that young-old, ignorant-wise, animal-god face was turned on Oktav. The muscles of the clamped jaw stood out like knobs. One arm in its cylinderlike sleeve of stiff, ancient fabric was rigidly extended toward the seer.

But Clawly had only time for the barest glance, and Oktav had even less—he was just starting to turn and his eyes were only on the verge of being lighted with a flicker of recognition—when a great tongue of softly bluish flame licked out from the summoner's hand and, not dying as flames should, folded around Oktav like a shroud.

Before Clawly's eyes, Oktav's robe burst into flame. His body shriveled, blackened, contorted in agony, curling like a leaf. Then it was still.

The soft flame returned to the summoner's hand.

Incapable of motion or connected thought or any feeling but a sick dismay, Clawly watched. The summoner walked over to Oktav's desk—clumsily, as if he were not used to dealing with three-dimensional worlds, but also contemptuously, as if worlds of three or any other number of dimensions were very trivial affairs to him. He extracted from the charred remains of Oktav's robe a small gray sphere, which Clawly now saw was similar to one which the summoner had been holding in his outstretched hand. Then, with an equal clumsiness and contempt, with a sweeping glance that saw Clawly and ignored him, the summoner walked back through the inner doorway.

Clawly's body felt like a sack of water. He could not take his eyes off the thing behind the desk. It looked more like a burnt mummy than a burnt man. By some chance the blue flame had spared the high forehead, giving the face a grotesque splotched appearance.

The outer door was opened, but Clawly did not turn or otherwise move. He heard a hissing inhalation—presumably when the newcomer saw the hideous corpse—but the newcomer had to come round in front before Clawly saw and recognized—or rather, partly recognized—him. And even then Clawly felt no reaction of astonishment or relief, or any reaction he might have expected to feel. The incredible scene he had just witnessed lingered like an after-image, and other thoughts and feelings refused to come into focus. The dead body of Oktav dominated his vision and his mind, as if emanating a palpable aura that blurred everything else.

The newcomer noted the incompleteness of Clawly's recognition, for he said, "Yes, I'm Thorn, but, I think you know, not the Thorn who was your friend, although I am inhabiting his body." To Clawly the words seemed to come from a great distance; he had to fight an insidious lethargy to hear them at all. They continued, "That Thorn is taking my place in the world—and three days ago I rejoiced to think of the suffering he would undergo there. Fact is, I was your enemy—his and yours—but now I'm not so sure. I'm even beginning to think we may be able to help each other a great deal. But I'm responsible for more lives than just my own, so until I'm sure of you, I daren't take any chances. That's the reason for this."

And he indicated the small tubular object in his hand, which seemed to be the dismantled main propulsion unit of a suit of flying togs—a crude but effective short-range blaster.

Clawly began to take him in, though it was still hard for him to see anything but the thing behind the desk. Yes, it was Thorn's face, all right, but with a very uncharacteristic expression of stubborn and practical determination.

The newcomer continued, "I've been following you because Thorn's memoranda tapes showed that you and he were working together in what seemed to be an effort to warn this world of its danger. But lately things have been happening that make me doubt that—things I want explained. What's this Martian invasion? Is it real? Or an attempt to rouse your world into a state of preparedness? Or a piece of misdirection designed to confuse the issue and make the Servants' invasion easier? Then, why did you come here, and who is this creature, and how did he die?" With a gesture of repugnance, he indicated the body of Oktav. "What I overheard reawakened my old suspicion that there's somebody behind this business of duplicate worlds, somebody who's making a profit from it, somebody—"

His voice went dead. In an instant, all the frowning concentration blanked out of his face. Very slowly, like a man who suddenly becomes aware that there is a monster behind him, he began to turn around.

At the same time, Clawly felt himself begin to shake—and for the same reason.

It was a very small and ordinary thing—just a small cough, a dry clearing of the throat. But it came from behind the desk.

The shriveled, scorched body was swaying a little; the charred hands were pushing across the desk, leaving black smears; a tremor was apparent in the blackened jaw.

For a moment they only watched in horror. Then, drawn by the same irresistible impulse, they slowly approached the desk.

The blind, ghastly movements continued. Then the burnt lips parted, and they heard the whisper—a whisper that was in every syllable a hard-won victory over seared tissues.

"I should be dead, but strange vitalities linger in him who has possessed a talisman. My eyes are embers, but I can dimly see you. Come closer, that I may say what must be said. I have a testament to make, and little time in which to make it, and no choice as to whom it is to be made. Draw nearer, that I may tell you what must be done for the sake of all worlds."

They obeyed, sweat starting from their foreheads, in awe of the inhumanly sustained vitality that permitted this charred mummy to speak.

"Purely by chance, a man of the Dawn Civilization discovered a talisman—a small nonmechanical engine controlled by thought—giving him the power of traveling in time, and across time, and into the regions beyond time. There it led him to seven other talismans, and to a similar but larger engine of even greater power, which he named the Probability Engine. He took in with him seven accomplices, I being one, and together we used the Probability Engine to split time and make actual all possible worlds, preserving only the best of them, and—so we thought—destroying the rest."

The whisper slowly began to diminish in strength. Clawly and the other leaned in closer to the black, white-foreheaded face.

"But I discovered that those destroyed worlds still exist, and I know too well what mad tinkering the others will be prompted to, when they make the same discovery. You must prevent them, as I intended to. In particular, you must find the Probability Engine and summon its True Owners, whatever creatures they may be, who built it and who lost the first talisman. They're the only ones fitted to deal with the tangle of problems we have created. But to find the Probability Engine, you must have a talisman. Ters, who destroyed me, took mine, but that was one which I had stolen. My own original talisman is in the possession of Thorn, the Thorn of this world, who stole it from me, I now believe, because of some unconscious prompting from the True Owners, groping through many-layered reality in an effort to find their lost engine. That Thorn is worlds away from here, more worlds than you suspect. But you"—his fingers fumbled sideways, touching those of the other Thorn, who did not withdraw his hand—"can get into touch . . . with him . . . through your linked . . . subconscious minds." The whisper was barely audible. It was obvious that even the talisman-vitalized strength was drawing to an end. "That talisman . . . which he has . . . is inert. It takes a key-thought . . . to unlock its powers. You must transmit . . . the key-thought . . . to him. The key-thought . . . is . . . 'Three botched . . . worlds—'"

The whisper trailed off into a dry rattle, then silence. The jaw fell open. The head slumped forward. Clawly caught it, palm to white forehead, and let it gently down onto the desk, where the groping fingers had traced a black, crisscross pattern.

Over it, Clawly's eyes, and those of the other Thorn, met.

XII

The coup d'état may appear in a thousand different guises.
The prudent ruler suspects even his own shadow.

DE ETIENNE.

The Sky Room of the Opal Cross was so altered it was hard to believe it had been a festivities center only three days ago. The World Map and Space Map still held their dominating positions, but the one was dotted with colored pictorial symbols indicating the location of spaceports and spaceyards, defense installations, armament fabrication and conversion centers, regular and emergency power stations, field headquarters, and like military information; while the Space Map, in which a system of perspective realistically conveyed three-dimensional depth, was similarly dotted in the Marsward sector to indicate the real or hypothetic location of spacecraft. This latter map emphasized with chilling clarity the fact that Earth had nothing at all in the unarmed or lightly armed exploratory craft that now, by stretching a point, could be counted as scouts. While fanning out from Mars in a great hemisphere, hypothetic but nonetheless impressive, loomed a vast armada.

The rest of the Sky Room was filled with terraced banks of televisor panels, transmission boards, plotting tables, and various calculating machines, all visible from the central control table around which they crowded. One whole sector was devoted to other military installations and specialized headquarters in the Opal Cross. Other sectors linked the control table with field headquarters, observation centers, spacecraft, and so on.

But now all the boards and tables, save the central one, were unoccupied. The calculating machines were untended and inoperative. And the massed rows of televisor panels were all blank gray—as pointless as a museum with empty cases.

A similar effect of bewildered deflation was apparent in most of the faces of the World Executive Committee around the control table. The exceptions included Chairman Shielding, who looked very angry, though it was a grave anger and well under control; Conjerly and Tempelmar, completely and utterly impassive; Clawly, also impassive, but with the suggestion that it would only take a hairtrigger touch to release swift speech or action; and Firemoor, who, sitting beside Clawly, was plainly ill at ease—pale, nervous, and sweating.

Shielding, on his feet, was explaining why the Sky Room had been cleared of its myriad operators and clerks. His voice was as cuttingly realistic as a spray of ice water.

". . . and then," he continued, "when astronomic photographs incontrovertibly proved that there were no alien craft of any sort near Mars—certainly none of the size reported and nothing remotely resembling a fleet, not even any faintly suspicious asteroids or cometary bodies—I hesitated no longer. On my own responsibility I sent out orders countermanding any and all defense preparations. That was half an hour ago."

One of the gray panels high in the Opal Cross sector came to life. As if through a window, a young man with a square face and crisply cropped blond hair peered out. The emptiness of the Sky Room seemed to startle him. He looked around for a moment, then switched to high amplification and called down to Shielding:

"Physical Research Headquarters reporting. A slight variation in spatio-temporal constants has been noted in this immediate locality. The variation is of a highly technical nature, but the influence of unknown spy-beams or range-finding emanations is a possible, though unlikely, explanation."

Shielding called sharply, "Didn't you receive the order countermanding all activities?"

"Yes, but I thought—"

"Sorry," called Shielding, "but the order applies to Research Headquarters as much as any others."

"I see," said the young man and, with a vague nod, blanked out.

There was no particular reaction to this dialogue, except that the studied composure of Conjerly and Tempelmar became, if anything, more marked—almost complacent.

Shielding turned back. "We now come to the question of who engineered this criminally irresponsible hoax, which," he added somberly, "has already cost the lives of more than a hundred individuals, victims of defense-preparation accidents." Firemoor winced and went a shade paler. "Unquestionably a number of persons must have been in on it, mainly members of the Extraterrestrial Service. It couldn't have been done otherwise. But we are more interested in the identity of the main instigators. I am sorry to say that there can be no question as to the identity of at least two of these. The confession of three of the accomplices make it—"

"Co-ordination Center 3 reporting." Another of the Opal Cross panels had flashed on, and its perplexed occupant, like the other, was using high amplification to call his message down to Shielding. "Local Power Station 4 has just cut me off, in the midst of a message describing an inexplicable drain on their power supply. Also, the presence of an unknown vehicle has been reported from the main rotunda."

"We are not receiving reports," Shielding shouted back. "Please consult your immediate superior for instructions."

"Right," the other replied sharply, immediately switching off.

"There you see, gentlemen," Shielding commented bitterly, "just how difficult it is to halt a hoax of this sort. In spite of all our efforts, there undoubtedly will be more tragic accidents before minds get back to normal." He paused, turned. "Clawly and Firemoor, what do you have to say for yourselves in justification of your actions, beyond a confession of wanton mischievousness, or—I must mention this possibility too—an attempt to create confusion for the furtherance of some treasonable plot? Remember it is not a matter of accomplices' confessions alone, who might conceivably perpetrate a hoax and then attempt to shift the blame onto blindly gullible and negligent superiors. There is also a testimony of two members of our own committee, who can for the moment remain anonymous—"

"I see no reason for that," drawled Tempelmar.

"Thank you." Shielding nodded to him. "Very well, then. The testimony of Conjerly and Tempelmar." And he turned again toward the accused.

Firemoor looked down at the table and twisted miserably. Clawly returned Shielding's gaze squarely. But before either of them could reply—

"Co-ordinator Center IV! Reporting the presence of a group of armed individuals in black garments of an unfamiliar pattern proceeding—"

"Please do not bother us!" Shielding shouted irritably. "Consult your superior! Tell him to refer all communications to Co-ordination Center I!"

This time the offending panel blanked out without reply.

Shielding turned to a master control board behind him and rapidly flipped off all the beams, insuring against future interruption.

Clawly stood up. His face had the frozenness of pent tension, an odd mixture of grim seriousness and mocking exasperation at men's blindness, suggestive of a gargoyle.

"It was a hoax," he said coolly, "and I alone planned it. But it was a hoax that was absolutely necessary to prepare the world for that other invasion, against which I tried to warn you three days ago. The invasion whose vanguard is already in our midst. Of course Conjerly and Tempelmar testified against me— for they are part of the vanguard!"

"You're psychotic," said Shielding flatly, lowering his head a little, like a bull. "Paranoid. The only wonder is how it escaped the psychiatrists. Watch him,

some of you"—he indicated those nearest Clawly—
"while I call the attendants."

"Stay where you are, all of you! And you, Shielding,
don't flip that beam!" Clawly had danced back a step,
and a metal tube gleamed in his hand. "Since you believe I planned the Martian hoax—and I did—perhaps
you'll believe that I won't stop at a few more deaths,
not accidental this time, in order to make you see the
truth. Idiots! Can't you see what's happening under
your very noses? Don't you see what those reports may
have meant? Call Co-ordination Center I, Shielding.
Go on, I mean it, call them!"

But at that instant Firemoor spun round in his
chair and dove at Clawly, pinioning his arms, hurling
them both down, wrenching the metal tube from his
hand, sending it spinning to one side. A moment later
he had dragged Clawly to his feet, still holding him pinioned.

"I'm sorry," he gasped miserably. "But I had to do
it for your own sake. We were wrong—wrong to the
point of being crazy. And now we've got to admit it.
Looking back, I can't see how I ever—"

But Clawly did not even look at him. He stared
grimly at Shielding.

"Thank you, Firemoor," said Shielding, a certain relief apparent in his voice. "You still have a great deal
to answer for. That can't be minimized—but this last
action of yours will certainly count in your favor."

This information did not seem to make Firemoor
particularly happy. The pinioned Clawly continued to
ignore him and to stare at Shielding.

"Call Communications Center I," he said deliberately.

Shielding dismissed the interruption with a glance.
He sat down.

"The attendants will remove him shortly. Well, gentlemen," he said, "it's time we considered how best to
repair the general dislocations caused by this panic.
Also there's the matter of our position with regard to

the trial of the accomplices." There was a general pulling-in of chairs.

"Call Communications Center I," Clawly repeated.

Shielding did not even look up.

But someone else said, "Yes. I think now you'd better call them."

Shielding had started automatically to comply, before he realized just who it was that was speaking—and the particular tone that was being used.

It was Conjerly and the tone was one of command.

Conjerly and Tempelmar had risen, and were standing there as soldierly as two obelisks—and indeed there was something unpleasantly monumental in their intensified, self-satisfied composure. Before anyone realized it, the center of attention of the meeting had shifted from Clawly and Firemoor to these new figures—or rather to these old and familiar figures suddenly seen in a new and formidable guise.

Shielding blinked at them a moment, as if he didn't know who they were. Then, with a haste that was almost that of fear, he swung around and flipped a beam on the board behind him.

Halfway up the terraced banks of gray squares, a panel came to life.

A man in a black uniform looked down from it.

"Communications Center I seized for the Servants," he announced crisply in a queerly accented though perfectly intelligent voice.

Shielding stood stock-still for a moment, then flipped another beam.

"The soldiers of the Servants are in control at this point," said the second black-uniformed individual, speaking with equal crispness.

With a stifled, incredulous gasp, Shielding ran his hand down the board, flipping on all the panels in the Opal Cross sector.

Most of them showed black-uniformed figures. Of the remainder, the majority were empty.

And then it became apparent that not all the black-uniformed figures were merely televised images. Some of them were standing between the panels, in the Sky Room itself, holding weapons trained.

By a psychological illusion, the figures of Conjerly and Tempelmar seemed to grow taller.

"Yes," Conjerly said soberly, almost kindly, "your government—or, rather, that absence of all sane control which you call a government—is now in the capable hands of the Servants of the People. Clawly's assertions were all quite correct, though fortunately we were able to keep you from believing them—a necessary deception. There *is* an invasion that is in the best interests of all worlds, and one from which yours will benefit greatly. It is being made across time, through a region that has become common to both our worlds. That region is our trans-time bridgehead. And, as is plain to see, our bridgehead coincided with your headquarters."

Clawly was not listening. He was watching a figure that was striding down the paneled terraces, its smilingly curious eyes fixed upon him. And as he watched, Firemoor and Shielding and some others began to watch too, slack-faced, dully amazed at this secondary impossibility.

The approaching figure was clad in black military flying togs whose sleek cut and suavely gleaming texture marked them as those of an individual of rank. But so far as physique and appearance were concerned, down to the last detail of facial structure, including even a similarity of expression—a certain latent sardonic mockery—he was Clawly's duplicate.

There was something very distinctive about the way the two eyed each other. No one could have said just when it started, but by the time they were facing each other across the control table, it was very plain: the look of two men come to fight a duel.

Clawly's face hardened. His gaze seemed to concentrate. His duplicate started, as if at a slight unexpected blow. For an instant he grinned unpleasantly, then his face grew likewise grim.

Neither moved. There was only that intense staring,

accompanied by a silent straining of muscles and a breathing that grew heavy. But none of those who watched doubted but that an intangible duel was being fought.

Conjerly, frowning, stepped forward. But just then there grew a look of sudden desperate terror in the contorted face of Clawly's black-clad duplicate. He staggered back a step, as if to avoid falling into a pit. An unintelligible cry was wrenched out of him, and he snatched at his holster.

But even as he raised the weapon, there flashed across the first Clawly's features a triumphant, oddly *departing* smile.

XIII

Yggdrasil shakes, and shiver on high
  The ancient limbs, and the giant is loose;

ELDER EDDA.

In the black, cramping tunnel Thorn could only swing his knife in a narrow arc, and the snarl of the attacking dog was concentrated into a grating roar that hurt his eardrums. Nevertheless, knife took effect before fangs, and with an angry whimper the dog backed away—there was no room to turn.

From the receding scuffle of its claws Thorn could tell that it had retreated almost to the beginning of the tunnel. He relaxed from the crouch that had put his back against the rocky roof, sprawled in a position calculated to rest elbows and knees, and considered his situation.

Of course, as he could see now, it had been an inexcusable blunder to enter the tunnel without first building a fire to insure his being able to get back to a place from which he could use his slingshot. But coming down the ravine he hadn't seen a sign of the devils, and there was no denying it had been necessary to revisit the cave to see if Thorn III had any extra food, weapons, or clothing stored there. The need for food was imperative, and yesterday he and Darkington had completely failed in their hunting.

He wondered if Darkington would attempt a rescue. Hardly, since it would be late afternoon before the gnarled little man returned from his own hunting circuit. With night coming on, it was unlikely that he would risk his life venturing down into the ravine for the sake of a man whom he believed to be half-crazy. For Thorn had tried to tell him altogether too much about alternate worlds in which civilization had not perished. Darkington had dismissed all this as "the dreams," and Thorn had shut up, but not until he realized he was forfeiting all Darkington's confidence in him as a hard-bitten and realistic neosavage.

Besides, Darkington was a little crazy himself. Long years of solitary living had developed fixed habit patterns. His hunger for comradeship had become largely a subjective fantasy, and the unexpected appearance of an actual comrade seemed to make him uncomfortable and uneasy rather than anything else, since it demanded readaptation. A man marooned in a wilderness and trying to get back to civilization is one thing. But a man who knows that civilization is dead and that before him stretch only dark savage eons, in which other creatures will have the center of the stage, is quite a different animal.

Something was digging into Thorn's side. Twisting his left hand back at an uncomfortable angle—his right still held the knife or cutter—he worked the pouch from under him and took out the offending article. It was the puzzling sphere that had stayed with him during all his passages between the worlds. Irritably he tossed it away. He had wasted enough time trying to figure out the significance or purpose of the thing. It was as useless as . . . as that graveyard of skylons up there.

He heard it bound up the tunnel, roll back a way, come to rest.

Evidently his captors heard it too, for there came a sharp mewing and growling, which did not break off sharply, but sank into a confused palaver of similar sounds, strongly suggestive of some kind of speech. Once or twice he thought he recognized human words, oddly telescoped and slurred to fit feline and canine palates. It was not pleasant to be cramped up in a tunnel and wondering what cats and dogs were saying about you in a half-borrowed, quasi-intelligent jargon.

And then very softly, Thorn thought he heard someone calling his name.

His almost immediate reaction was a sardonic grimace at the vast number of unlikely sounds a miserable man will twist into a resemblance of his name. But gradually the fancied sound began to exert a subtle pull on his thoughts, dragging them away toward speculations which his present predicament did not justify.

But who is to say what thoughts a trapped and doomed man shall think? As Thorn told himself with some calmness, this was probably his last stretch of reflective thinking. Of course, when death came sufficiently close, the fear of it might enable him to escape into another body. But that was by no means certain or even probable. He reflected that every exchange he had made had been into a worse world. And now, presumably, he was at the bottom, and like energy that has reached the nadir of its cycle of degradation, unable to rise except with outside help.

Besides, he did not like the idea of dooming any other Thorn to this predicament, although he was afraid he would do it if given the chance.

Again he dreamily fancied he heard his name called.

He wondered what was happening to those other Thorns, in their hodgepodged destinies. Thorn III in World II—had he died in the instant of his arrival there, or had the Servants noted the personality-change in time and perhaps spared him? Thorn II in World I. Thorn I in World III. It was like some crazy game—some game devised by a mad, cruel god.

And yet what was the whole universe, so far as it had been revealed to him, but a mad, cruel pageantry? The Dawn myth was right—there were serpents gnawing at every root of the cosmic ash Yggdrasil. In three days he had seen three worlds, and none of them were good. World III, wrecked by subtronic power, cold battlefield for a hopeless last stand. World II, warped by paternalistic tyranny, smoldering with hate and boredom. World I, a utopia in appearance, but lacking real stamina or inward worth, not better than the others—only luckier.

Three botched worlds.

He started. It was as if, with that last thought, something altogether outside his mind had attached itself to his mind in the most intimate way imaginable. He had the queerest feeling that his thoughts had gained power, that they were no longer locked-in and helpless except for their ability to control a puny lever-assembly of bones and contractile tissue, that they could reach out of his mind like tentacles and move things, that they had direct control of a vastly more competent engine.

A faint sound up the tunnel recalled his altered mind to his present predicament. It might have been a tiny scrape of claws on rock. It was not repeated. He gripped his knife. Perhaps one of the beasts was attempting a surprise attack. If only there were some light—

A yellowish flame, the color of the woodfire he had been visualizing, flared up without warning a few feet ahead, casting shafts of ruddy glare and shadow along the irregular tunnel. It lit up the muzzles of a gaunt gray dog and a scarred black cat that had been creeping toward him, side by side. For an instant surprise froze them. Then the dog backed off frantically, with a yelp of panic. The cat snarled menacingly and stared wildly at the flame, as if desperately trying to figure out its *modus operandi.*

But, with Thorn's thought, the flame advanced and the cat gave ground before it. At first it only backed, continuing to snarl and stare. Then it turned tail, and answering in a great screech the questioning mews and growls that had been coming down the tunnel, fled as if from death.

The flame continued to advance, changing color when Thorn thought of daylight. And as Thorn edged and squirmed along, it seemed to him that somehow his way was made easier.

The tunnel heightened, widened. He emerged in the outer chamber in time to hear a receding rattle of gravel.

The flame, white now, had come to rest in the middle of the rocky floor. Even as he stooped, it rose to meet him, winking out—and there rested lightly on his palm the gray sphere, cool and unsmirched, that he had tossed away a few minutes before.

But it was no longer a detached, external object. It was part of him, responsive to his every mood and thought, linked to his mind by tracts that were invisible but as real as the nerves connecting mind with muscle and sense organ. It was not a machine, telepathically controlled. It was a second body.

Relief, stark wonder, and exulting awareness of power made him weak. For a moment everything swam and darkened, but only for a moment—he seemed to suck limitless vitality from the thing.

He felt a surge of creativeness, so intense as to be painful, like a flame in the brain. He could do anything he wanted to, go anywhere he wanted to, make anything he wanted to, create life, change the world, destroy it if he so willed—

And then—fear. Fear that, since the thing obeyed his thoughts, it would also obey his foolish, ignorant, or destructive ones. People can't control their thoughts for very long. Even sane individuals often think of murder, or catastrophies, of suicide—

Suddenly the sphere had become a gray globe of menace.

And then—after all, he couldn't do *anything*. Besides any other limitations the thing might have, it was certainly limited by his thoughts. It couldn't do things he didn't really understand—like building a subtronic engine—

Or—

For the first time since he had emerged from the tunnel, he tried to think collectively, with more than the surface of his mind.

He found that the depths of his mind were strangely altered. His subconscious was no longer an opaque and impenetrable screen. He could see through it, as through a shadowy corridor, sink into it, hear the thoughts on the other side, the thoughts of the other Thorns.

One of them, he realized, was instructing him, laying a duty upon him.

The message dealt with such matters as to make the

imagination shiver. It seemed to engulf his personality, his consciousness.

His last glimpse of World III was a gray one of dark, snow-streaked pines wavering in a rocky frame. Then that had clouded over, vanished, and he was in a limitless blackness where none of the senses worked and where only thought—itself become a sense—had power.

It was an utterly alien darkness without real up or down, or this way or that, or any normal spatial properties. It seemed that every point was adjacent to every other point, and so infinity was everywhere, and all paths led everywhere, and only thought could impose order or differentiate. And the darkness was not that of lightlessness, but of thought itself—fluttering with ghostly visions, aflash with insight.

And then, without surprise or any consciousness of alteration, he realized that he was no longer one Thorn, but three. A Thorn who had lived three lives— and whether memory pictured them as having been lived simultaneously or in sequence seemed to matter not at all. A Thorn who had learned patience and endurance and self-sufficiency from harsh World III, who had had ground into the bedrock of his mind the knowledge that man is an animal in competition with other animals, that all human aspirations are but small and vaunting and doomed things—but not necessarily worthless therefore—in a blind and unfeeling cosmos, and that even death and the extinguishing of all racial hopes are ills that can be smiled at while you struggle against them. A Thorn who had seen and experienced in World II the worst of man's cruelty to man, who had gained a terrible familiarity with human nature's weaknesses, its cowardly submissiveness to social pressure, its capacity for self-delusion, its selfishness, its horrible adaptability, who had plumbed to their seething, poisoning depths the emotion of hate and resentment and envy and fear, but who in part had risen superior to all this and learned humility, and sympathy, and sacrifice, and devotion to a cause.

A Thorn who, in too-easy World I, had learned how to use the dangerous gift of freedom, how to fight human nature's tendency to do evil and foul itself when it is not being disciplined by hardship and adversity, how to endure happiness and success without souring, how to create goals and purposes in an environment that does not supply them ready-made.

All these experiences were now those of one mind. They did not contradict or clash with each other. Between them there was no friction or envy or guilt. Each contributed a fund of understanding, carrying equal weight in the making of future decisions. And yet there was no sense of three minds bargaining together or talking together or even thinking together. There was only one Thorn, who, except for that period of childhood before the split took place, had lived three lives.

This composite Thorn, sustained by the talisman, poised in the dimensionless dark beyond space and time, felt that his personality had suddenly been immeasurably enriched and deepened, that heretofore he had been going around two-thirds blind and only now begun to appreciate the many-sidedness of life and the real significance of all that he had experienced.

And without hesitation or inward argument, without any sense of responding to the urgings of Thorn II, since there was no longer a separate Thorn II, he remembered what the death-resisting Oktav had whispered to him in the Blue Lorraine, syllable by agonized syllable, and he recalled the duty laid upon him by the seer.

He thought of the first step—the finding of the Probability Engine—and felt the answering surge of the talisman, and submitted to its guidance.

There was a dizzying sense of almost instantaneous passage over an infinite distance—and also a sense that there had been no movement at all, but only a becoming aware of something right at hand. And then—

The darkness pulsed and throbbed with power, a power that it seemed must rack to pieces many-branched time and shake down the worlds like rotten fruit. The thought-choked void quivered with a terri-fying creativity, as if this were the growing-point of all reality.

Thorn became aware of seven minds crowded around the source of the pulsations and throbbing and quivering. Homely human minds like his own, but lacking even his own mind's tripled insight, narrower and more paternalistic than even the minds of World II's Servants of the People. Minds festooned with er-ror, barnacled with bias, swollen with delusions of godhead. Minds altogether horrible in their power, and in their ignorance—which their power protected.

Then he became aware of vast pictures flaring up in the void in swift succession—visions shared by the seven minds and absorbing them to such a degree that they were unconscious of his presence.

Like river-borne wreckage after an eon-long jam has broken, the torrent of visions flowed past.

World II loomed up. First the drab Servants Hall, where eleven old men nodded in dour satisfaction as they assured themselves, by report and trans-time tele-visor, that the invasion was proceeding on schedule. Then the picture broadened, to show great streams of subtronically mechanized soldiers and weapons mov-ing in toward the trans-time bridgehead of the Opal Cross. Individual faces flashed by—wry-lipped, uninter-ested, obedient, afraid.

For a moment World I was glimpsed—the interior of the Opal Cross shown in section like an anthill, aswarm with black uniforms. Quickly, as if the seven masters hated to look at their pet world so misused, this gave way to a panoramic vision of World III, in which hundreds of miles were swept over without showing anything but fallen or fire-tortured skylons, seared and scurb-grown wasteland, and—cheek by jowl—glacier walls and smoke-belching volcanoes.

But that was only the beginning. Fruits of earlier time-splits were shown. There was a world in which tele-pathic mutants fought with jealous nontelepaths,

who had found a way of screening their thoughts.
There was a world in which a scarlet-robed hierarchy
administered a science-powered religion that held millions in Dawn Age servitude. A world in which a tiny
clique of hypnotic telepaths broadcast thoughts which
all men believed in and lived by, doubtfully, as if in a
half-dream. A world where civilization, still atom-
powered, was split into tiny feudalistic domains, forever at war, and the memory of law and brotherhood
and research kept alive only in a few poor and unar-
mored monasteries. A world similarly powered and
even more divided, in which each family or friends-
group was an economically self-sustaining microcosm,
and civilization consisted only of the social intercourse
and knowledge-exchange of these microcosms. A world
where men lived in idle parasitism on the labor of submen they had artificially created—and another world
in which the relationship was reversed and the submen
lived on men.

A world where two great nations, absorbing all the
rest, carried on an endless bitter war, unable to defeat
or be defeated, forever spurred to new efforts by the
fear that past sacrifices might have been in vain. A
world that was absorbed in the conquest of space, and
where the discontented turned their eyes upward toward the new frontier. A world in which a great new
religion gripped men's thoughts, and strange cere-mo-
nies were performed on hilltops and in spacecraft and
converts laughed at hate and misery and fear, and un-
believers wonderingly shook their heads. A world in
which there were no cities and little obvious machinery, and simply clad men led unostentatious lives.
A sparsely populated world of small cities, whose inhabitants had the grave smiling look of those who make
a new start. A world that was only a second asteroid
belt—a scattering of exploded rocky fragments ringing
the sun.

"We've seen enough!"

Thorn sensed the trapped horror and the torturing
sense of unadmitted guilt in Prim's thought.

The visions flickered out, giving way to the blackness of unactualized thought. On this blackness Prim's next thought showed fiercely, grimly, monstrously. It was obvious that the interval had restored his power-bolstered egotism.

"Our mistake is evident but capable of correction. Our thoughts—or the thoughts of *some* of us—did not make it sufficiently clear to the Probability Engine that absolute destruction, rather than a mere veiling or blacking out, was intended, with regard to the botched worlds. There is no question as to our next step. Sekond?"

"Destroy! All of them, except the main trunk," instantly pulsed the answering thought.

"Ters?"

"Destroy!"

"Kart?"

"The invading world first. But all the others too. Swiftly!"

"Kent?"

"It might be well to . . . No! Destroy!"

With a fresh surge of horror and revulsion, Thorn realized that these minds were absolutely incapable of the slightest approach to unbiased reasoning. They were so frantically convinced of the correctness of all their past decisions as to the undesirability of the alternate worlds, that they were even completely blind to the apparent success of some of those worlds—or to the fact that the destruction of a lifeless asteroid belt was a meaningless gesture. They could only see the other worlds as horrible deviations from the cherished main trunk. Their reactions were as unweighed and hysterical as those of a murderer, who, taking a last look around after an hour spent in obliterating possible clues, sees his victim feebly stir.

Thorn gathered his willpower for what he knew he must do.

"Sikst?"

"Yes, destroy!"

"Septem?"

"Destroy!"

"Okt—"

But even as Prim remembered that there no longer was an Oktav and joined with the others in thinking destruction, even as the darkness began to rack and heave with a new violence, Thorn sent out the call.

"Whoever you may be, whatever you may be, Oh you who created it, here is the Divider of Time, here is the Probability Engine!"

His thought deafened him, like a great shout. He had not realized the degree to which the others had been thinking in the equivalent of muted whispers.

Instantly Prim and the rest were around him, choking his thoughts, strangling his mind, thinking his destruction along with that of the worlds.

The throbbing of the darkness became that of a great storm, in which even the Probability Engine seemed on the verge of breaking from its moorings. Like a many-branched lightning-flash came a vision of time-streams lashed and shaken—Worlds I and II torn apart—the invasion bridge snapped—

But through it Thorn kept sending the call. And he seemed to feel the eight talismans and the central Engine take it up and echo it.

His mind began to suffocate. His consciousness to darken.

All reality seemed to tremble on the edge between being and not being.

Then without warning, the storm was over and there was only a great quiet and a great silence present that might have come from the end of eternity and might have been here always.

Awe froze their thoughts. They were like boys scuffling in a cathedral who look up and see the priest.

What they faced gave no sign of its identity. But they knew.

Then it began to think. Great broad thoughts of which they could only comprehend an edge or corner. But what they did comprehend was simple and clear.

XIV

And many a Knot unraveled by the Road
But not the Master-knot of Human Fate.

The Rubaiyat.

Our quest for our Probability Engine and its talismans has occupied many major units even of our own time. We have prosecuted it with diligence, because we were aware of the dangers that might arise if the Engine were misused. We built several similar engines to aid us in the search, but it turned out that the catastrophe in our cosmos which swept away the Engine and cast one of the talismans up on your time-stream and planet was of an unknown sort, making the route of the talisman an untraceably random one. We would have attempted a canvass of reality, except that a canvass of an infinitude of infinities is impossible. Now our quest is at an end.

I will not attempt to picture ourselves to you, except to state that we are one of the dominant mentalities in a civilized cosmos of a different curvature and energy-content than your own.

Regarding the Probability Engine—it was never intended to be used in the way in which you have used it. It is in essence a calculating machine, designed to forecast the results of any given act, weighing all factors. It is set outside space-time, in order that it may consider all the factors in space-time without itself becoming one of them. When we are faced with a multiple-choice problem, we feed each choice into the Engine successively, note the results, and act accordingly. We use it to save mental labor on simple decision-making routines, and also for the most profound purposes, such as the determination of possible ultimate fates of our cosmos.

All this, understand, only involves forecasting— never the actualization of those forecasts.

But no machine is foolproof. Just because the Probability Engine was not made to create, does not mean that it cannot create, given sufficient mental tinkering. How shall I make it clear to you? I see from your minds that most of you are familiar with a type of wheeled vehicle, propelled by the internal combustion of gases, similar to vehicles used by some of the lower orders in our own cosmos. *You* would see in it only a means of transportation. But suppose one of your savages—someone possessing less knowledge than even yourselves—should come upon it. *He* might see it as a weapon—a ram, a source of lethal fumes, or an explosive mine. No safety devices you might install could ever absolutely prevent it from being used in that fashion.

You, discovering the Probability Engine, were in the same position as that hypothetic savage. Unfortunately, the Engine was swept away from our cosmos with all its controls open—ready for tinkering. You poked and pried, used it, as I can see, in many ways, some close to the true one, some outlandishly improbable. Finally you worked off the guards that inhibit the Engine's inherent reactivity. You began to actualize alternate worlds.

In doing this, you completely reversed the function of the Probability Engine. We built it in order to avoid making unfavorable decisions. You used it to insure that unfavorable decisions would be made. You actualized worlds which for the most part would never have had a remote chance of existing, if you had left the decision up to the people inhabiting your world. Normally, even individuals of your caliber will show considerable shrewdness in weighing the consequences of their actions and in avoiding any choice that seems apt to result in unpleasant consequences. You, however, forced the unwise choices to be made as well as the wise ones—and you continued to do this after your own race had acquired more real wisdom than you yourselves possessed.

For the Probability Engine in no way increased your mental stature. Indeed, it had just the opposite effect, for it gave you powers which enabled you to escape the consequences of your bad judgments—and it truckled to your delusions by only showing you what you wanted to see. Understand, it is just a machine. A perfect servant—not an educator. And perfect servants are the worst educators. True, you could have used it to educate yourselves. But you preferred to play at being gods, under the guise of performing scientific experiments on a world that you didn't faintly understand. Godlike, you presumed to judge and bless and damn. Finally, in trying to make good on your damnations, you came perilously close to destroying much more than you intended to—there might even have been unpleasant repercussions in our own cosmos.

And now, small things, what shall we do with you and your worlds? Obviously we cannot permit you to retain the Probability Engine or any of the powers that go with it or the talismans. Also, we cannot for a moment consider destroying any of the alternate worlds, with a view to simplification. That which has been given life must be allowed to use life, and that which has been faced with problems must be given an opportunity of solving them. If the time-splits were of more recent origin, we might consider healing them; but deviation has proceeded so far that that is out of the question.

We might stay here and supervise your worlds, delivering judgments, preventing destructive conflicts, and gradually lifting you to a higher mental and spiritual level. But we do not relish playing god. All our experiences in that direction have been unpleasant, making us conclude that, just as with an individual, no species can achieve a full and satisfactory maturity except by its own efforts.

Again, we might remain here and perform various experiments, using the setups which you have created. But that would be abhorrent.

So, small things, there being no better alternative, we will take away our Engine, leaving the situation you have created to develop as it will—with trans-time invasions and interworld wars no longer an immediate prospect, though looming as a strong future possibility. With such sufferings and miseries and misunderstandings as exist, but with the future wide open and no unnatural constraints put on individuals sufficiently clear-headed and strong-willed to seek to avoid unpleasant consequences. And with the promise of rich and unusual developments lying ahead, since, so far as we know, your many-branched time-stream is unique among the cosmoses. We will watch your future with interest, hoping some day to welcome you into the commonwealth of mature beings.

You may say that we are at fault for allowing the Probability Engine to fall into your hands—and, indeed, we shall make even stronger efforts to safeguard it from accident or tinkering in the future. But remember this. Young and primitive as you are, you are not children, but responsible and awakened beings, holding in your hands the key to your future, with yourselves to blame if you go astray.

As for you individuals who are responsible for all this botchwork, I sympathize with your ignorance and am willing to admit that your intentions were in part good. But you chose to play at being gods, and even ignorant and well-intentioned gods must suffer the consequences of their creations. And that shall be your fate.

With regard to you, Thorn, your case is of course very different. You responded to our blindly broadcast influencings, stole a talisman, and finally summoned us in time to prevent a catastrophe. We are grateful. But there is no reward we can give you. To remove you from your environment to ours would be a meaningless gesture, and one which you would regret in the end. We cannot permit you to retain any talismanic powers, for in the long run you would be no better able to use them wisely than these others. We would like to continue your satisfying state of triplicated personality—it presents many interesting features—but even that may not be, since you have three destinies to fulfill in three worlds. However, a certain compromise

solution, retaining some of the best features of the trip-
lication, is possible.

And so, small things, we leave you.

From hastily chosen places of concealment and half-
scooped foxholes around the Opal Cross, a little improvised army stood up. A few scattered fliers swooped
down and silently joined them. The only uniforms
were those of a few members of the Extraterrestrial
Service. Among the civilians were perhaps a score of
Recalcitrant Infiltrants from World II, won over to
last-minute co-operation by Thorn II.

The air still reeked acridly. White smoke and fumes
came from a dozen areas where earth and vegetation
had been blasted by subtronic weapons. And there
were those who did not stand up, whose bodies lay
charred or had vanished in disintegration.

The ground between them and the Opal Cross was
still freshly scored by the tracks of great vehicles.
There were still wide swathes of crushed vegetation.
At one point a group of low buildings had been mashed
flat. And it seemed that the air above still shook with
the aftermath of the passage of mighty warcraft.

But of the great mechanized army that had been
fanning out toward and above them, not one black-
uniformed soldier remained.

They continued to stare.

In the Sky Room of the Opal Cross, the members of
the World Executive Committee looked around at a
similar emptiness. Only the tatters of Clawly's body remained as concrete evidence of what had happened. It
was blown almost in two, but the face was untouched.
This no longer showed the triumphant smile which
had been apparent a moment before death. Instead,
there was a look of horrified surprise.

Clawly's duplicate had vanished with the other
black-uniformed figures.

The first to recover a little from the frozenness of
shock was Shielding. He turned toward Conjerly and
Tempelmar.

But the expression on the faces of those two was no longer that of conquerors, even thwarted and trapped conquerors. Instead there was a dawning, dazed amazement, and a long-missed familiarity that told Shielding that the masquerading minds were gone and the old Conjerly and Tempelmar returned.

Firemoor began to laugh hysterically.

Shielding sat down.

At the World II end of the broken trans-time bridgehead, where moments before the Opal Cross had risen, now yawned a vast smoking pit, half-filled with an indescribable wreckage of war machines and men, into which others were still falling from the vanished skylon—like some vision of Hell. To one side, hung even in comparison with that pit, loomed the fantastically twisted metal of the trans-time machine. Ear-splitting sounds still echoed. Hurricane gusts still blew.

Above it all, like an escaping black hawk above an erupting volcano, Clawly flew. Not even the titanic confusion around him, nor the shock of the time-streams' split, nor his horror at his own predicament, could restrain his ironic mirth at the thought of how that other Clawly, in trying to kill him, had insured the change of minds and his own death.

Now he was forever marooned on World II, in Clawly II's body. But the memory chambers of Clawly II's brain were open to him, since Clawly II's mind no longer existed to keep them closed, and so at one bound he had become a half-inhabitant of World II. He knew where he stood. He knew what he must do. He had no time for regrets.

A few minutes' flying time brought him to the Opal Cross and it was not long before he was admitted to the Servants Hall. There eleven shaken old men looked up vengefully at him from reports of disaster. Their chairman's puckered lips writhed as he accused: "Clawly, I have warned you before that your lack of care and caution would be your finish. We hold you to a considerable degree responsible for this calamity.

It is possible that your inexcusable lax handling of the prisoner Thorn was what permitted word of our invasion to slip through to the enemy. We have decided to eliminate you." He paused, then added, a little haltingly, "Before sentence is carried out, however, do you have anything to say in extenuation of your actions?"

Clawly almost laughed. He knew this scene—from myth. The Dawn Gods blaming Loke for their failures, trying to frighten him—in hopes that he would think up a way to get them out of their predicament. The Servants were bluffing. They weren't even looking for a scapegoat. They were looking for help.

This was *his* world, he realized. The dangerous, treacherous world of which he had always dreamed. The world for which his character had been shaped. The world in which he could play the traitor's role as secret ally of the Recalcitrants in the Servants' camp, and prevent or wreck future invasions of World I. The world in which his fingers could twitch the cords of destiny.

Confidently, a gargoyle's smile upon his lips, he stepped forward to answer the Servants.

Briefly Thorn lingered in the extra-cosmic dark, before his tripled personality and consciousness should again be split. He knew that the True Owners of the Probability Engine had granted him this respite in order that he would be able to hit upon the best solution of his problem. And he had found that solution.

Henceforward, the three Thorns would exchange bodies at intervals, thus distributing the fortunes and misfortunes of their lives. It was the strangest of existences to look forward to—for each, a week of the freedoms and pleasures of World I, a week of the tyrannies and hates of World II, a week of the hardships and dangers of World III.

Difficulties might arise. Now, being one, the Thorns agreed. Separate, they might rebel and try to hog good fortune. But each of them would have the memory of this moment and its pledge.

The strangest of existences, he thought again, hazily,

as he felt his mind beginning to dissolve, felt a three-way tug. But was it really stranger than any life? One week in heaven—one week in hell—one week in a frosty ghost-world—

And in seven different worlds of shockingly different cultures, seven men clad in the awkward and antique garments of the Late Middle Dawn Civilization began to look around, in horror and dismay, at the consequences of their creations.

Afterword by Norman Spinrad

Less than a handful of writers have spanned the five-decade history of modern science fiction from the Campbellian Golden Age of the late 1930s to the post-New Wave 1970s with significant works. Heinlein. Theodore Sturgeon. Murray Leinster. Perhaps one or two more of lesser stature. A. E. Van Vogt. And Fritz Leiber.

Of these, with perhaps the exception of Heinlein, Fritz Leiber has produced most steadily and measuredly over this long period, turning out major works of science fiction in each decade, from the award-winning *The Big Time* way back when, on through to the award-winning *The Wanderer*, to the award-winning "Gonna Roll the Bones" in *Dangerous Visions* near the apogee of the revolutionary 1960s, to the award-winning "Catch That Zeppelin" of the mid-1970s. During most of this same period, Leiber has also been a major figure in heroic fantasy with the long-running Fafhrd and the Grey Mouser series, and one of his best-known novels, *Conjure Wife*, has been made into at least two films.

Although perhaps never generally considered *the* single most important science fiction writer in any of these periods, Leiber has been regarded as one of the most significant writers in *all* of them.

In a field where such long-term major production seems like an anomaly, where so many fine writers seem to burn themselves out after a decade or so of brilliance, what has kept Fritz Leiber producing fresh, evolving, major work down through the decades?

In major part, of course, this secret must remain hidden in the mysterious workings of Leiber's gray matter, in that private spaceless time where the seat of the pants meets the hard surface of a chair and the writer's eyes confront that blank page in the typewriter. No doubt Fritz Leiber too has had his writer's blocks, whether for days, weeks, months, or years, and his own eldritch ways of breaking them. There have of course been periods of silence. But not only have they been relatively short and relatively few, the new work that keeps emerging has never devolved into formula reworkings of past glories; rather it continues to evolve, to grow, to change, and to remain perpetually youthful in the best sense of the word.

Aside from the secret writerly magics involved in such a process hidden to all but the man himself, certain clues to this rare untimebound success are evident in the work itself, and many of them are present in *Destiny Times Three,* a relatively early work, written in the closing years of World War II, and heavily inspired by the atmosphere and mood of that dark, yet somehow also optimistic period.

Personal karma and the games writers play with themselves aside, one of the keys to long-term success as a writer, and especially a science fiction writer, is scope and depth of interests and psychic involvement with the total universe outside both the shoptalk world of writers and the narrow continuum of the science fiction genre itself. Many science fiction writers have come out of the little world of science fiction fandom, or have been sucked into it at early stages of their careers. After a decade or so, they find themselves writing, reading, thinking, dreaming, living, and loving within this pocket universe. They are influenced not so much by the total universe around them as by *other science fiction*. Since all writing, and fiction in particular, is strictly the output of the writer's mind, the openness of that mind, the depth, the scope, and the quality of the *input* it gathers unto itself are critical for the ongoing dynamic evolution of a writer's work. Small wonder, then, that so many science fiction writers who allow their heads to feed only on the genre itself end up derivative of other writers, then of their own earlier work, and then fall silent.

But, as clearly evident in *Destiny Times Three,* Fritz Leiber, though he has certainly always been a part of the extended world of the science fiction genre, never allowed himself to be trapped in this cul-de-sac.

That *Destiny Times Three* derives not from other science fiction but from the deep well of the space-time continuum of the period in which Leiber wrote it is evident even from the quotes used as chapter headings. Lovecraft. *The Eddas*. Shakespeare. *The Rubaiyat*. Keats. More minor works by more minor writers in several languages. And all of it germane, all of it adding to the mythic dimension of the story, which in turn both draws upon and transmogrifies the archetypal conflict enveloping the world outside Leiber's workroom at the time he wrote it.

This is, of course, a self-proclaimed story about destiny, or rather destinies, branching off as alternate realities from nexuses on the timeline of history, interpenetrating, interweaving, interfering, and interrelating with each other; the whole, meanwhile, being tampered with by cosmic forces transcending any individual alternative reality, any branch of the Tree Yggdrasil, the tree of ultimate reality, who "great evil suffers far more than men do know."

Though one-to-one analogies might be difficult to draw, how like the overall universe and story of *Destiny Times Three* the realities of World War II were at the time Leiber was writing the story! At least three mutually exclusive world-views, alternate realities if you will, were vying for control of the main line of human destiny—the Faustian nightmare of Nazi Germany, the twisted utopia of the Soviet Union, and the fragile ambiguity of the democratic forces. The clear total victory of either of the three would have altered human destiny forever by expunging the competing world-views, as, indeed, the Nazi reality was in fact expunged. Whether the West and the Communist world can coexist in the same reality over the long term is a question still very much with us today; indeed, in a certain sense, one might argue that these two world-views have *already* created alternate realities on either side of the Iron Curtain.

And, as in *Destiny Times Three*, it is the very conflict between mutually exclusive realities that gnaws at the roots of Yggdrasil, at the commonality of human destiny, at the cohesion of total reality itself—in the time of the Nazi *Götterdämmerung* and in our time as well.

Indeed, eerily enough, the world-destroying potential of "subtronic power," benign in the hands of Leiber's utopians, but capable of smashing the fabric of reality itself in the service of darker or less sane visions, hovers threateningly over the worlds of *Destiny Times Three* even as the Promethean power of the atom hovers like a final storm cloud over the conflicting realities of our own time.

Other science fiction writers were writing "hard science fiction" about the power of the atom at the time—the basic knowledge was in the air, and science fictional antennae were attuned to it—but in *Destiny Times Three*, Leiber, immersed in both timeless legend and imagery and in the forces converging on the nexus of the time, caught some kind of precognitive flash of what such life-and-death power in human hands would mean in the post-War world. Not the science or technology of it, but the essence. The Yggdrasil-eroding powers of conflicting realities armed with potential world-destroying power.

Destiny Times Three, like most of Leiber's work, is

not "hard science fiction." It does not create clear, hard-edged imaginary realities based on a wealth of minute technical, scientific, or even cultural details. Its sense of verisimilitude does not come from the detailed creation of a self-contained fictional universe. Rather, its power comes from its extensions beyond its own fictional bounds—into the human cultural past, into timeless image and archetype, and into the interplay of forces at work at the moment of historical time in which Leiber wrote it.

It is, if you will, a mythologization of the karmic moment of World War II, which draws upon not merely the instantaneous historical parallels but upon the shared Jungian roots of Yggdrasil, relating this new human drama to the timeless and bottomless well of human experience expressed in the total mythic heritage of the species.

Most of Leiber's science fiction shares this quality; it is perhaps no accident that he has had a parallel career in heroic fantasy. Indeed, just as this mythopoetic impulse passes over from his heroic fantasy into his science fiction, so is his heroic fantasy marked by an unusual sense of irony and detail which crosses over the other way.

In fact, the interplay between the dark murky forces of destiny and myth and the hard-edged clarity of more positivistic "scientific" realities is a dominant theme in much of Leiber's work. So too the multiplexity and mutability of ultimate reality, expressed here in *Destiny Times Three* and in an even more fully developed form in *The Big Time*. Science and magic, technology and myth, all interpenetrate in the body of Leiber's work.

This, I would submit, is a sign of a writer whose mind has remained open to past and future, to the mythic roots of literary imagery, to the realities and unrealities of the timestream that passes through him.

And perhaps this is why Fritz Leiber has produced so much science fiction of so much merit so steadily for such a long time. The man doesn't live in a constricted little world bounded by the conventional confines of his chosen genre. He is *connected*—to myth and history, to his time and to times past and future, to ongoing science and the timeless Jungian unconscious, to literature, to poetry, to magics light and dark, to the dance of destiny itself.

To the wellsprings of creativity itself.

RIDING THE TORCH

BY NORMAN SPINRAD

Flashing rainbows from his skintight mirror suit, flourishing a swirl of black cape, Jofe D'mahl burst through the shimmer screen that formed the shipside wall of his grand salon to the opening bars of Beethoven's *Fifth Symphony*. The shimmer rippled through the spectrum as his flesh passed through it, visually announcing his presence with quicksilver strobes of dopplering light. Heads turned, bodies froze, and the party stopped for a good long beat as he greeted his guests with an ironic half-bow. The party resumed its rhythm as he walked across the misty floor toward a floating tray of flashers. He had made his entrance.

D'mahl selected a purple sphere, popped the flasher into his mouth, and bit through an exquisite brittle sponginess into an overwhelming surge of velvet, a gustatory orgasm. A first collection by one Lina Wolder, Jiz had said, and as usual she had picked a winner. He tapped the name into his memory banks, keying it to the sensorium track of the last ten seconds, and filed it in his current party listing. Yes indeed, a rising star to remember.

Tapping the floater to follow him, he strode through the knee-high multicolored fog, nodding, turning, bestowing glances of his deep green eyes, savoring the ambience he had brought into being.

D'mahl had wheedled Hiro Korakin himself into designing the grand salon as his interpretation of D'mahl's own personality. Korakin had hung an immense semicircular slab of simmed emerald out from the hull of the ship itself and had blistered this huge balcony in transparent plex, giving D'mahl's guests a breathtaking and uncompromising view of humanity's universe. As *Excelsior* was near the center of the Trek, the great concourse of ships tiaraed the salon's horizon line, a triumphant jeweled city of coruscating light. Ten kilometers bow-ward, the hydrogen interface was an auroral skin stretched across the unseemly nakedness of interstellar space.

But to look over the edge of the balcony, down the sleek and brilliantly lit precipice of *Excelsior*'s cylindrical hull, was to be confronted by a vista that sucked slobbering at the soul: the bottomless interstellar abyss, an infinite black pit in which the myriad stars were but iridescent motes of unimportant dust, a nothingness that went on forever in space and time. At some indefinable point down there in the blackness, the invisible output of *Excelsior*'s torch merged with those of two thousand and thirty-nine other ships to form an ethereal comet's tail of all-but-invisible purplish fire that dwindled off into a frail thread which seemed to go on forever down into the abyss: the wake of the Trek, reeling backward in space and time for hundreds of light-years and nearly ten centuries, a visible track that the eye might seemingly follow backward through the ages to the lost garden, Earth.

Jofe D'mahl knew full well that many of his guests found this prime reality visualization of their basic existential position unsettling, frightening, perhaps even in bad taste. But that was *their* problem; D'mahl himself found the view bracing, which, of course, justifiably elevated his own already high opinion of himself. Korakin wasn't considered the best psychetect on the Trek for nothing.

But D'mahl himself had decorated the salon, with the inevitable assistance of Jiz Rumoku. On the translucent emerald floor he had planted a tinkling forest of ruby, sapphire, diamond, and amethyst trees—cunningly detailed sims of the ancient life-forms that waved flashing crystal leaves with every subtle current of air. He had topped off the effect with the scented fog that picked up blue, red, and lavender tints from the internally incandescent trees, and customarily kept the gravity at .8 g to sync with the faerie mood. To soften the crystal edges, Jiz had gotten

him a collection of forty fuzzballs: downy globs in sub-
dued green, brown, mustard, and gray that floated
about randomly at floor level until someone sat in
them. If Korakin had captured D'mahl's clear-eyed
core, Jofe had expressed the neobaroque style of his
recent sensos, and to D'mahl, the combined work of art
sang of the paradox that was the Trek. To his guests,
it sang of the paradox that was Jofe D'mahl. Egowise,
D'mahl himself did not deign to make this distinction.

The guest list was also a work of art in D'mahl's
neobaroque style: a constellation of people designed to
rub purringly here, jangle like broken glass there, gen-
erate cross-fertilization someplace else, keep the old
karmic kettle boiling. Jans Ryn was displaying herself
as usual to a mixed bag that included *Excelsior*'s chief
torchtender, two dirtdiggers from *Kantuck,* and Tanya
Daivis, the velvet asp. A heated discussion between
Dalta Reed and Trombleau, the astrophysicist from
Glade, was drawing another conspicuous crowd. Less
conspicuous guests were floating about doing less conspicuous things. The party needed a catalyst to really
start torching up lights.

And at 24.00 that catalyst would zap itself right into
their sweet little taps—the premiere tapping of Jofe
D'mahl's new senso, *Wandering Dutchmen.* D'mahl
had carved something prime out of the void, and he
knew it.

"—by backbreeding beyond the point of original radiation, and then up the line to the elm—"

"—like a thousand suns, as they said at Alamagordo,
Jans, and it's only a bulkhead and a fluxfield away—"

"—how Promethean you must feel—"

"Jof, this nova claims he's isolated a spectral pattern
synced to organic life," Dalta called out, momentarily
drawing D'mahl into her orbit.

"In a starscan tape?" D'mahl asked dubiously.

"In theory," Trombleau admitted.

"Where've I heard that one before?" D'mahl said,
popping another of the Wolder flashers. It wriggled
through his teeth, then exploded in a burst of bitter-

sweet that almost immediately faded into a lingering smoky aftertaste. Not bad, D'mahl thought, dancing away from Trombleau's open mouth before he could get sucked into the argument.

D'mahl flitted through the mists, goosed Arni Simkov, slapped Darius Warner on the behind, came upon a group of guests surrounding John Benina, who had viewpointed the Dutchman. They were trying to pump him about the senso, but John knew that if he blatted before the premiere, his chances of working with Jofe D'mahl again were exactly zip.

"Come on, Jofe, tell us something about *Wandering Dutchmen*," begged a woman wearing a cloud of bright-yellow mist. D'mahl couldn't remember her with his flesh, but didn't bother tapping for it. Instead, he bit into a cubical flasher that atomized at the touch of his teeth, whiting out every synapse in his mouth for a mad micropulse. Feh.

"Two hints," D'mahl said. "John Benina played one of the two major viewpoints, and it's a mythmash."

A great collective groan went up, under cover of which D'mahl ricocheted away in the direction of Jiz Rumoku, who was standing in a green mist with someone he couldn't make out.

Jiz Rumoku was the only person privileged to bring her own guests to D'mahl's parties, and just about the only person not involved in the production who had any idea of what *Wandering Dutchmen* was about. If Jofe D'mahl could be said to have a souler (a dubious assumption), she was it.

She was dressed, as usual, in tomorrow's latest fashion: a pants suit of iridescent, rigid-seeming green-and-purple material, a mosaic of planar geometric forms that approximated the curves of her body like a medieval suit of armor. But the facets of her suit articulated subtly with her tiniest motion—a fantastic insectile effect set off by a tall plumelike crest into which her long black hair had been static-molded.

But D'mahl's attention was drawn to her companion, for he was obviously a voidsucker. He wore noth-

ing but blue briefs and thin brown slippers; there was
not a speck of hair on his body, and his bald head was
tinted silver. But persona aside, his eyes alone would
have instantly marked him: windows of blue plex into
an infinite universe of utter blackness confined by
some topological legerdemain inside his gleaming
skull.

D'mahl tapped the voidsucker's visual image to the
banks. "I.D.," he subvoced. The name "Haris Bandoora" appeared in his mind. "Data brief," D'mahl
subvoced.

"Haris Bandoora, fifty standard years, currently
commanding Scoutship Bela-37, returned to Trek
4.987 last Tuesday. Report unavailable at this realtime."

Jiz had certainly come up with something tasty this
time, a voidsucker so fresh from the great zilch that
the Council of Pilots hadn't yet released his report.

"Welcome back to civilization, such as it is, Commander Bandoora," D'mahl said.

Bandoora turned the vacuum of his eyes on D'mahl.
"Such as it is," he said, in a cold clear voice that
seemed to sum up, judge, and dismiss all of human
history in four dead syllables.

D'mahl looked away from those black pits, looked
into Jiz's almond eyes, and they cross-tapped each other's sensoriums for a moment in private greeting. Jofe
saw his own mirrored body, felt the warmth it evoked in
her. He kissed his lips with Jiz's, tasting the electric
smokiness of the flashers he had eaten. As their lips
parted, they broke their taps simultaneously.

"What's in that report of yours that the Pilots haven't
released to the banks yet, Bandoora?" D'mahl asked
conversationally. (How else could you make small talk
with a voidsucker?)

Bandoora's thin lips parted in what might have
been a smile, or just as easily a grimace of pain.
D'mahl sensed that the man's emotional parameters
were truly alien to his experience, prime or simmed.
He had never paid attention to the voidsuckers before,

and he wondered why. There was one beyond senso to be made on the subject!

"They've found a planet," Jiz said. "There's going to be a blanket bulletin at 23.80."

"Drool," D'mahl said, nuancing the word with most of the feelings that this flash stirred up. The voidsuckers were always reporting back with some hot new solar system, turning the Trek for a few months while they high-geed for a telltale peek, then turning the Trek again for the next Ultima Thule just as the flash hit that the last one was the usual slokyard of rock and puke-gas. The voidsuckers had been leading the Trek in a zigzag stagger through space from one vain hope to another for the better part of a millennium; the latest zig was therefore hardly a cosmic flash in Jofe D'mahl's estimation. But it *would* be a three-month wonder at least, and tapping out a blanket bulletin just before the premiere was a prime piece of up-staging, a real boot in the ego. Drool.

"The probabilities look good on this one," Bandoora said.

"They always do, don't they?" D'mahl said snidely. "And it always turns out the same. If there's a rock in the habitable zone, it's got gravity that'd pull your head off, or the atmosphere is a tasty mixture of hydrogen cyanide and fluorine. Bandoora, don't you ever get the feeling that some nonexistent cosmic personage is trying to tell you something you don't want to hear?"

Bandoora's inner expression seemed to crinkle behind his impassive flesh. A tic made his lower lip tremble. What did I do *this* time? D'mahl wondered. These voidsuckers must be far beyond along some pretty strange vectors.

Jiz forced a laugh. "The torch Jof is riding is all ego," she said. "He's just singed because the bulletin is going to bleed some H from his premiere. Isn't that right, Jof, you egomonster, you?"

"Don't knock ego," D'mahl said. "It's all that stands between us and the lamer universe we have the bad taste to be stuck in. Since my opinion of myself is the only thing I know of higher in the karmic pecking order than my own magnificent being, my ego is the only thing I've found worth worshiping. Know what that makes me?"

"Insufferable?" Jiz suggested.

"A human being," D'mahl said. "I'm stuck with it, so I might as well enjoy it."

"A bulletin from the Council of Pilots." The words intruded themselves into D'mahl's mind with a reasonable degree of gentleness, an improvement over the days when the Pilots had felt they had the right to snap you into full sensory fugue on the spot whenever the spirit moved them. "Ten . . . nine . . . eight . . . seven . . ." D'mahl pulled over a green fuzzball and anchored the floating cloud of particles by planting his posterior in it. Jiz and Bandoora sat down flanking him. "Six . . . five . . . four . . ."

Whichever guests were standing found themselves seats; there was no telling how long one of these bulletins would last. The Pilots have a grossly exaggerated sense of their own importance, D'mahl thought. And what does that make them?

". . . three . . . two . . . one . . ."

Human beings.

D'mahl sat on a bench at the focus of a small amphitheater. Tiered around him were two thousand and forty people wearing the archaic blue military tunics, dating back to the time when Ship's Pilot was a paramilitary rank rather than an elective office. D'mahl found the uniformity of dress stultifying and the overhead holo of the day sky of an Earthlike planet banal and oppressive, but then he found most Pilots, with their naïve notion of the Trek's existential position, somewhat simpleminded and more than a little pathetic.

Ryan Nakamura, a white-haired man who had been Chairman of the Council of Pilots longer than anyone cared to remember, walked slowly toward him, clapped him on the shoulder with both hands, and sat down beside him. Nakamura smelled of some noxious perfume designed to sim wisdom-odors of moldy parchment and decayed sweetness. As an artist, D'mahl found the effect competent if painfully obvious; as a citizen, he found it patronizing and offensive.

Nakamura leaned toward him, and as he did, the amphitheater vanished and they sat cozily alone on an abstract surface entirely surrounded by a firmament of tightly packed stars.

"Jofe, Scoutship Bela-37 has returned to the Trek and reported that a solar system containing a potentially habitable planet is located within a light-year and a half of our present position," Nakamura said solemnly.

D'mahl wanted to yawn in the old bore's face, but of course the viewpoint player hunched him intently toward Nakamura instead as the Chairman blatted on. "The Council has voted 1,839 to 201 to alter the vector of the Trek toward this system, designated 997-Beta, pending the report of the telltale."

D'mahl sat midway up in the amphitheater as Nakamura continued formally from a podium on the floor below. "It is our earnest hope that our long trek is at last nearing its successful completion, that in our own lifetimes men will once more stand on the verdant hills of a living planet, with a sky overhead and the smells of living things in our nostrils. We conclude this bulletin with brief excerpts from the report of Haris Bandoora, commander of Bela-37."

Behind the podium, Nakamura faded into Haris Bandoora. "Bela-37 was following a course thirty degrees from the forward vector of the Trek," Bandoora said tonelessly. "Torching at point nine . . ."

D'mahl stood on the bridge of Bela-37—a small round chamber rimmed with impressive-looking gadgetry, domed in somewhat bluish plex to compensate for the doppler shift, but otherwise visually open to the terrifying glory of the deep void. However, one of the four voidsuckers on the bridge was a woman who easily upstaged the stellar spectacle as far as D'mahl was concerned. She wore briefs and slippers and was totally bald, like the others, and her skull was tinted silver, but her preternaturally conical breasts and shining, tightly muscled flesh made what ordinarily would have been an ugly effect into an abstract paradigm of feminine beauty. Whether the warmth he felt was his alone, or his reaction plus that of the viewpoint player, apparently Bandoora himself, was entirely beside the point.

"Ready to scan and record system 997-Beta," the stunning creature said. D'mahl walked closer to her, wanting to dive into those bottomless voidsucker eyes. Instead, he found his lips saying, with Bandoora's voice: "Display it, Sidi."

Sidi did something to the control panel before her (how archaic!) and the holo of a yellow star about the diameter of a human head appeared in the geometric center of the bridge. D'mahl exchanged tense glances with his crew, somatically felt his expectation rise.

"The planets . . ." he said.

Five small round particles appeared, rotating in compressed time around the yellow sun.

"The habitable zone . . ."

A transparent green torus appeared around the holo of 997-Beta. The second planet lay within its boundaries.

There was an audible intake of breath, and D'mahl felt his own body tremble. "The second planet," Bandoora's voice ordered. "At max."

The holo of the star vanished, replaced by a pale, fuzzy holo of the second planet, about four times its diameter. The planet seemed to be mottled with areas of brown, green, blue, yellow, and purple, but the holo was washed out and wavered as if seen through miles of heat-haze.

A neuter voice recited instrument readings. "Estimated gravity 1.2 gs plus or minus ten percent . . . estimated mean temperature thirty-three degrees centigrade plus or minus six degrees . . . estimated atmospheric composition: helium, nitrogen, oxygen as major constituents . . . percentages indeterminate from present data . . . traces of carbon dioxide, argon, ammonia, water vapor . . . estimated ratio of liquid area to solid surface 60–40 . . . composition of oceans indeterminate from present data. . . ."

D'mahl felt the tension in his body release itself through his vocal cords in a wordless shout that merged with the whoops of his companions. He heard his lips say, with Bandoora's voice: "That's the best prospect any scoutship's turned up within my lifetime."

D'mahl was seated in the amphitheater as Bandoora addressed the Council. "A probe was immediately dispatched to 997-Beta-II. Bela-37 will leave within twenty days to monitor the probe data wavefront. We estimate that we will be able to bring back conclusive data within half a standard year."

D'mahl was an abstract viewpoint in black space. A huge hazy holo of 997-Beta-II hovered before him like a ghostly forbidden fruit as the words in his mind announced: "This concludes the bulletin from the Council of Pilots."

Everyone in Jofe D'mahl's grand salon immediately began babbling, gesticulating, milling about excitedly. Head after head turned in the direction of D'mahl, Jiz, and Bandoora. D'mahl felt a slow burn rising, knowing to whom the fascinated glances were directed.

"Well, what do you think of *that,* Jof!" Jiz said, with a sly knife edge in her voice.

"Not badly done," D'mahl said coolly. "Hardly art, but effective propaganda, I must admit."

Once again, Bandoora seemed strangely stricken, as if D'mahl's words had probed some inner wound.

"The planet, Jof, the *planet!*"

Fighting to control a building wave of anger, D'mahl managed an arch smile. "I was paying more attention to Sidi," he said. "Voidsuckers come up with planets that look that good from a distance much more often than you see bodies that look that good that close."

"You think the future of the human race is a rather humorous subject," Bandoora said loudly, betraying annoyance for the first time.

D'mahl tapped the time at 23.981. His guests were all blatting about the prospects of at last finding a viable mudball, and *Wandering Dutchmen* was about to begin! Leaping to his feet, he shouted: "Bandoora, you've been out in the big zilch too long!" The sheer volume of his voice focused the attention of every guest on his person. "If *I* were confined in a scoutship with Sidi, I'd have something better than slok planets on my mind!"

"You're a degenerate and an egomaniac, D'mahl!" Bandoora blatted piously, drawing the laughter D'mahl had hoped for.

"Guilty on both counts," D'mahl said. "Sure I'm an egomaniac—like everyone else, I'm the only god there is. Of course I'm a degenerate, and so is everyone else—soft protoplasmic machines that begin to degenerate from day one!"

All at once D'mahl had penetrated the serious mood that the bulletin had imposed on his party, and by donning it and taking it one step beyond, had recaptured the core. "We're stuck where we are and with what we are. We're Flying Dutchmen on an endless sea of space, we're Wandering Jews remembering what we killed for all eternity—"

A great groan went up, undertoned with laughter at the crude bridge to the impending premiere, overtoned with sullenness at the reminder of just who and what they were. D'mahl had blown it—or at least failed to entirely recover—and he knew it, and the knowledge was a red nova inside his skull. At this moment of foul karma, 24.000 passed into realtime, and on tap frequency E-6—

You are standing at the base of a gentle verdant hill on whose tree-dotted summit a man in a loincloth is being nailed to a cross. Each time the mallet descends, you feel piercing pains in your wrists. You stand in an

alleyway in ancient Jerusalem holding a jug of water
to your breast as Jesus is dragged to his doom, and you
feel his terrible hopeless thirst parching your throat.
You are back at Calvary listening to the beat of the
mallet, feeling the lightnings of pain in your wrists,
the taste of burning sands in your mouth.

You are on the quarterdeck of an ancient wooden
sailing ship tasting the salt wind of an ocean storm.
The sky roils and howls under an evil green moon.
Your crew scurries about the deck and rigging, shouting and moaning in thin spectral voices, creatures of
tattered rags and ghostly transparent flesh. Foam flies
into your face, and you wipe it off with the back of
your hand, seeing through your own flesh as it passes
before your eyes. You feel laughter at the back of
your throat, and it bubbles out of you—too loud, too
hearty, a maniac's howl. You raise your foglike fist
and brandish it at the heavens. Lightning bolts crackle. You shake your fist harder and inhale the storm
wind like the breath of a lover.

You look up the slope of Calvary as the final
stroke of the mallet is driven home and you feel the
wooden handle and the iron spike in your own hands.
The cross is erected, and it is you who hang from it,
and the sky is dissolved in a deafening blast of light
brighter than a thousand suns. And you are trudging
on an endless plain of blowing gray ash under a sky
the color of rusting steel. The jagged ruins of broken
buildings protrude from the swirling dust, and the
world is full of maimed and skeletal people marching
from horizon to horizon without hope. But your body
has the plodding leaden strength of a thing that knows
it cannot die. Pain in your wrists, and ashes in your
mouth. The people around you begin to rot on their
feet, to melt like Dali watches, and then only you remain, custodian of a planetary corpse. A ghostly sailing ship approaches you, luffing and pitching on the
storm-whipped ash.

The quarterdeck pitches under your feet and skies
howl. Then the storm clouds around the moon melt

away to reveal a cool utter blackness punctuated by myriad hard points of light, and the quarterdeck becomes a steel bulkhead under your feet and you are standing in an observation bubble of a primitive first-generation torchship. Around your starry horizon are dozens of other converted asteroid freighters, little more than fusion torchtubes with makeshift domes, blisters, and toroid decks cobbled to their surfaces—the distant solar ancestors of the Trek.

You turn to see an ancient horror standing beside you: an old, old man, his face scarred by radiation, his soul scarred by bottomless guilt, and his black eyes burning coldly with eternal ice.

You are standing in an observation bubble of a first-generation torchship. Below, the Earth is a brownish, singed, cancerous ball still stewing in the radiation of the Slow Motion War. Somewhere a bell is tolling, and you can feel the tug of the bellrope in your hands. Turning, you see a lean, sinister man with a face all flat planes and eyes like blue coals. His face fades into fog for a moment, and only those mad eyes remain solid and real.

"Hello, Dutchman," you say.

"Hello, Refugee."

"I'm usually called Wanderer."

"That's no longer much of a distinction," the Dutchman says. "All men are wanderers now."

"We're all refugees too. We've killed the living world that gave us birth. Even you and I may never live to see another." The bite of the nails into your wrists, the weight of the mallet in your hand. Thirst, and the tolling of a far-off bell.

You are the Dutchman, looking out into the universal night; a generation to the nearest star, a century to the nearest hope of a living world, forever to the other side. Thunder rolls inside your head and lightnings flash behind your eyes. "We've got these decks under our feet, the interstellar wind to ride, and fusion torches to ride it with," you say. "Don't whine to me,

I've never had more." You laugh a wild maniac howl. "And I've got plenty of company, now."

You are the Wanderer, looking down at the slain Earth, listening to the bell toll, feeling the dead weight of the mallet in your hand. "So do I, Dutchman, so do I."

The globe of the Earth transforms itself into another world: a brown-and-purple planetary continent marbled with veins and lakes of watery blue. Clad in a heavy spacesuit, you are standing on the surface of the planet: naked rock on the shore of a clear blue lake, under a violet sky laced with thin gray clouds like jet contrails. A dozen other suited men are fanned out across the plain of fractured rock, like ants crawling on a bone pile.

"Dead," you say. "A corpse-world."

Maniac laughter beside you. "Don't be morbid, Wanderer. Nothing is dead that was never alive."

You kneel on a patch of furrowed soil cupping a wilted pine seedling in your hands. The sky above you is steel plating studded with overhead floodlights, and the massive cylindrical body of the torchtube skewers the watertank universe of this dirtdigger deck. The whole layout is primitive, strictly first-generation Trek. Beside you, a young girl in green dirtdigger shorts and shirt is sitting disconsolately on the synthetic loam, staring at the curved outer bulkhead of the farm deck.

"I'm going to live and die without ever seeing a sky or walking in a forest," she says. "What am I doing here? What's all this for?"

"You're keeping the embers of Earth alive," you say in your ancient's voice. "You're preserving the last surviving forms of organic life. Some day your children or your children's children will plant these seeds in the living soil of a new Earth."

"Do you really believe that?" she says earnestly, turning her youthful strength on you like a sun. "That we'll find a living planet some day?"

"You must believe. If you stop believing, you'll be

with us here in this hell of our own creation. We Earthborn were life's destroyers. Our children must be life's preservers."

She looks at you with the Wanderer's cold eternal eyes, and her face withers to a parchment of ancient despair. "For the sake of our bloodstained souls?" she says, then becomes a young girl once more.

"For the sake of your own, girl, for the sake of your own."

You float weightless inside the huddled circle of the Trek. The circular formation of ships is a lagoon of light in an endless sea of black nothingness. Bow-ward of the Trek, the interstellar abyss is hidden behind a curtain of gauzy brilliance: the hydrogen interface, where the combined scoopfields of the Trek's fusion torches form a permanent shock wave against the attenuated interstellar atmosphere. Although the Trek's ships have already been modified and aligned to form the hydrogen interface, the ships are still the same converted asteroid freighters that left Sol; this is no later than Trek Year 150.

But inside the circle of ships, the future is being launched. The *Flying Dutchman*, the first torchship to be built entirely on the Trek out of matter winnowed and transmuted from the interstellar medium, floats in the space before you, surrounded by a gnat swarm of intership shuttles and men and women in voidsuits. A clean, smooth cylinder ringed with windowed decks, it seems out of place among the messy jury-rigging of the first-generation torchships, an intrusion from the future.

Then an all-but-invisible purple flame issues from the *Dutchman*'s torchtube and the first Trekborn ship is drawing its breath of life.

Another new torchship appears beside the *Flying Dutchman*, and another and another and another, until the new Trekborn ships outnumber the converted asteroid freighters and the hydrogen interface has more than doubled in diameter. Now the area inside the Trek is a vast concourse of torchships, shuttles, suited people, and the dancing lights of civilized life.

You are standing on a bulkhead catwalk overlooking the floor of a dirtdigger deck: a sparse forest of small pines and oaks, patches of green grass, a few rows of flowers. Above is a holo of a blue Earth sky with fleecy white clouds. Dirtdiggers in their traditional green move about solemnly, tending the fragile life-forms, measuring their growth. Your nostrils are filled with the incense odor of holiness.

And you sit at a round simmed marble table on a balcony café halfway up the outer bulkhead of an amusement deck sipping a glass of simmed burgundy. A circle of shops and restaurants rings the floor below, connected by radial paths to an inner ring of shops around the central torchtube shaft. Each resulting wedge of floor is a different bright color, each is given over to a different amusement: a swimming pool, a bandstand, a zero-g dance-plate, carnival rides, a shimmer maze. Noise rises. Music plays.

Across from you sits the Wanderer, wearing dirtdigger green and an expression of bitter contempt. "Look at them," he says. "We're about to approach another planet, and they don't even know where they are."

"And where is that, Refugee?"

"Who should know better than you, Dutchman?" he says. And the people below turn transparent, and the bulkheads disappear, and you are watching zombies dancing on a platform floating in the interstellar abyss. Nothing else lives, nothing else moves, in all that endless immensity.

Manic laughter tickles your throat.

A planet appears as a pinpoint, then a green-and-brown mottled sphere with fleecy white clouds, and then you are standing on its surface among a party of suited men trudging heavily back to their shuttleship. Hard brown rock veined with greenish mineral streakings under a blue-black sky dotted with pastel-green clouds. You are back on your balcony watching specters dance in the endless galactic night.

"Great admiral, what shall you say when hope is gone?" the Wanderer says.

And you are down among the specters, grown ten feet tall, a giant shaking your fist against the blackness, at the dead planet, howling your defiance against the everlasting night. "Sail on! Sail on! Sail on and on!"

"No more ships! No more ships! Soil or death!" You are marching at the head of a small army of men and women in dirtdigger green as it bursts into the amusement deck from the deck below, bearing crosses wrapped with simmed grape leaves. Each chanted shout sends nails through your wrists.

And you are leading your carnival of ghosts on a mad dance through a dirtdigger deck, carelessly trampling on the fragile life-forms, strewing gold and silver confetti, flashers, handfuls of jewels—the bounty of the fusion torch's passage through the interstellar plankton.

You are in a droptube falling through the decks of a ship. Amusement decks, residential decks, manufacturing decks, sifting decks—all but the control and torchtender decks—have been rudely covered over with synthetic loam and turned into makeshift dirtdigger decks. The growth is sparse, the air has a chemical foulness, metal surfaces are beginning to corrode, and the green-clad people have the hunched shoulders and sunken eyes of the unwholesomely obsessed. The vine-covered cross is everywhere.

You are rising through a lift-tube on another ship. Here the machinery is in good repair, the air is clean, the bulkheads shiny, and the decks of the ship glory in light and sound and surfaces of simmed ruby, emerald, sapphire, and diamond. The people are birds-of-paradise in mirror suits, simmed velvets and silks in luxurious shades and patterns, feathers and leathers, gold, silver, and brass. But they seem to be moving to an unnatural rhythm, dancing a mad jig to a phantom fiddler, and their flesh is as transparent as unpolarized plex.

You are floating in space in the center of the Trek; behind you, the Trekborn ships are a half-circle diadem of jeweled brilliance. In front of you floats the Wanderer, and behind him the old converted asteroid freighters, tacky and decayed, pale greenery showing behind every blister and viewport.

"Your gardens are dying, Wanderer."

"Yours never had life, Dutchman," he says, and you can see stars and void through your glassy flesh, through the ghost-ships behind you.

Two silvery headbands appear in the space between you in a fanfare of music and a golden halo of light. Large, crude, designed for temporary external wear, they are the first full sensory transceivers, ancestors of the surgically implanted tap. They glow and pulse like live things, like the gift of the nonexistent gods.

You pick one of the headbands, laugh, place it on the Wanderer's head. "With this ring, I thee wed."

Unblinkingly, he places the other band on yours. "Bear my crown of thorns," he says.

You stand on the bridge of a torchship, the spectral Dutchman at your side. Beyond the plex, the stars are a million live jewels, a glory mirrored in the lights of the Trek.

You kneel among tiny pine trees in a dirtdigger deck beside the Wanderer, and they become a redwood forest towering into the blue skies of lost Earth, and you can feel the pain of the nails in your ghostly wrists, hearing the tolling of a far-off bell, feel the body's sadness, smell the incense of irredeemable loss.

You rise through a lift-tube, the Dutchman's hand in yours, and you hear the hum of energy as you pass through deck after jeweled and gleaming deck, hear the sounds of human laughter and joy, see crystal trees sprouting and rising from the metal deckplates. The flesh of the spectral people solidifies and the Dutchman's hand becomes pink and solid. When you look at his face, your own Wanderer's eyes look back, pain muted by a wild joy.

You float in the center of the Trek with the Wanderer as the ships around you rearrange themselves in an intricate ballet: Trekborn and converted asteroid freighters in hundreds of magical *pas de deux*, reintegrating the Trek.

You are droptubing down through the decks of a dirtdigger ship, watching green uniforms transform themselves into the bird-of-paradise plumage of the Trekborn ships, watching the corrosion disappear from the metal, watching crystal gazebos, shimmer mazes, and bubbling brooks appear, as shrines to sadness become gardens of joy.

And you are sitting across a round simmed marble table from the Dutchman on a balcony café halfway up the bulkhead of an amusement deck. The central torchtube shaft is overgrown with ivy. The pool, bandstand, shimmer mazes, dance-plates, and carnival rides are laid out in a meadow of green grass shaded by pines and oaks. The bulkheads and upper decking dissolve, and this garden square stands revealed as a tiny circle of life lost in the immensity of the eternal void.

"We're Wanderers in the midnight of the soul," the Dutchman says. "Perhaps we're guardians of the only living things that ever were."

"Flying Dutchmen on an endless sea, perhaps the only gods there be."

And you are a detached viewpoint watching this circle of life drift away into the immensity of space, watching the Trek dwindle away until it is nothing more than one more abstract pinpoint of light against the galactic darkness. Words of pale fire appear across the endless starfield:

WANDERING DUTCHMEN

by Jofe D'mahl

There was an unmistakable note of politeness in the clicking of tongues in Jofe D'mahl's grand salon. The applause went on for an appropriate interval (*just* appropriate), and then the guests were up and talking, a brightly colored flock of birds flitting and jabbering about the jeweled forest.

". . . you could see that it had well-defined continents, and the green areas *must* be vegetation . . ."

". . . oxygen, sure, but can we breathe all that helium?"

Standing between Jiz Rumoku and Bandoora, Jofe D'mahl found himself in the infuriating position of being a vacuum beside the focus of attention. Eyes constantly glanced in their direction for a glimpse of Bandoora, but no gaze dared linger long, for at the side of the voidsucker, D'mahl was sizzling toward nova, his eyes putting out enough hard radiation to melt plex.

But Bandoora himself was looking straight at him, and D'mahl sensed some unguessable focus of alien warmth pulsing up at him from the depths of those unfathomable eyes. "I'm sorry the Pilots' bulletin ruined your premiere," he said.

"Really?" D'mahl snarled. "What makes you think your precious blatt has so much importance?" he continued loudly. There was no reason for the guests not to stare now; D'mahl was shouting for it. "You dreeks expect us to slaver like Pavlov's dogs every time you turn up some reeking mudball that looks habitable until you get close enough to get a good whiff of the dead stink of poison gas and naked rock. Your blatt will be a six-month nova, Bandoora. Art is forever."

"Forever may be a longer time than you realize, D'mahl," Bandoora said calmly. "Other than that, I agree with you entirely. I found *Wandering Dutchmen* quite moving." Were those actually *tears* forming in his eyes? "Perhaps more moving than even you can imagine."

Silence reigned now as the attention of the guests became totally focused on this small psychodrama. Some of the bolder ones began to inch closer. D'mahl found that he could not make out Bandoora's vector; in this little ego contest, there seemed to be no common set of rules.

"I'd like to atone for interfering with the premiere of a great work of art," Bandoora said. "I'll give you a chance to make the greatest senso of your career, D'mahl." There was a thin smile on his lips, but his eyes were so earnest as to appear almost comical.

"What makes you think *you* can teach *me* anything about sensos?" D'mahl said. "Next thing, you'll be asking me for a lesson in voidsucking." A titter of laughter danced around the salon.

"Perhaps I've already gotten it, D'mahl," Bandoora said. He turned, began walking through the colored mists and crystal trees toward the transparent plex that blistered the great balcony, focusing his eyes on D'mahl through the crowd, back over his shoulder. "I don't know anything about sensos, but I can show you a reality that will make anything you've experienced pale into nothingness. Capture it on tape if you dare." A massed intake of breath.

"*If I dare!*" D'mahl shouted, exploding into nova. "Who do you think you're scaring with your cheap theatrics, Bandoora? I'm Jofe D'mahl, I'm the greatest artist of my time, I'm riding the torch of my own ego, and I know it. *If I dare!* What do you think any of us have to do *but* dare, you poor dreek? Didn't you understand *anything* of what you just experienced?"

Bandoora reached the plex blister, turned, stood outlined against the starry darkness, the blaze of the concourse of ships. His eyes seemed to draw a baleful energy from the blackness. "No theatrics, D'mahl," Bandoora said. "No computer taps, no sensos, no illusions. None of the things all you people live by. *Reality*, D'mahl, the real thing. Out there. The naked void."

He half turned, stretched out his right arm as if to embrace the darkness. "Come with us on Bela-37, D'mahl," he said. "Out there in your naked mind where nothing exists but you and the everlasting void. *Wandering Dutchmen* speaks well of such things—for a senso by a man who was simming it. What might you do with your own sensorium tape of the void itself—if you dared record it through your own living flesh? Do you dare, D'mahl, do you dare face the truth of it with your naked soul?"

"Jof—"

D'mahl brushed Jiz aside. *"Simming it!"* he bellowed in red rage. "Do I dare!" The reality of the grand salon, even the ego challenge hurled at him before his guests, burned away in the white-hot fire of the deeper challenge, the gauntlet Bandoora had flung at the feet of his soul. *I can face this thing, can you? Can you truly carve living art out of the dead void, not metaphorically, but out of the nothingness itself, in the flesh, in realtime? Or are you simming it? Are you a fraud?*

"I told you, Bandoora," he said, hissing through his rage, "I've got nothing to do *but* dare."

The guests oohed, Jiz shook her head, Bandoora nodded and smiled. Jofe D'mahl felt waves of change ripple through his grand salon, through himself, but their nature and vector eluded the grasp of his mind.

As he flitted from *Excelsior* to *Brigadoon* across a crowded sector of the central Trek, it seemed to Jofe D'mahl that the bubble of excitement in which he had been moving since the premiere party had more tangibility than the transparent shimmer screen of his void-bubble. The shimmer was visible only as the interface between the hard vacuum of space and the sphere of air it contained, but the enhancement of his persona was visible on the face of every person he saw. He was being tapped so frequently by people he had never met in senso or flesh that he had finally had to do something 180 degrees from his normal vector: tap a screening program into his banks that rejected calls from all people not on a manageable approved list. He was definitely the Trek's current nova.

Even here, among the bubbled throngs flitting from ship to ship or just space-jaunting, D'mahl felt as if he were outshining the brilliance of the concourse of torchships, even the hydrogen interface itself, as most of the people whose trajectories came within visible range of his own saluted him with nods of their heads or subtle sidelong glances.

It almost made up for the fact that it wasn't *Wandering Dutchmen* that had triggered his nova but his public decision to dare six standard months with the void-suckers—away from the Trek, out of tap contact with the banks, alone in his mind and body like a primitive pre-tap man. Waller Nan Pei had achieved the same effect by announcing his public suicide a month in advance, but blew out his torch forever by failing to go through with it. D'mahl knew there could be no backing out now.

He flitted past *Paradisio*, accepted the salutations of the passengers on a passing shuttle, rounded *Ginza*, throttled back his g-polarizer, and landed lightly on his toes on *Brigadoon*'s main entrance stage. He walked quickly across the ruby ledge, passed through the shimmer, collapsed his bubble, and took the nearest droptube for Jiz Rumoku's gallery on twelvedeck, wondering what the place would look like this time.

Thanks to Jiz's aura, *Brigadoon* was the chameleon-ship of the Trek; whole decks were completely done over about as often as the average Trekker redid his private quarters. Fashions and flashes tended to spread from *Brigadoon* to the rest of the Trek much as they spread from Jiz's gallery to the decks of her ship. Recently, a motion to change the ship's name to *Quicksilver* had come within fifty votes of passage.

Dropping through the decks, D'mahl saw more changes than he could identify without tapping for the previous layouts, and he had been on *Brigadoon* about a standard month ago. Threedeck had been living quarters tiered around a formalized rock garden; now it was a lagoon with floating houseboats. Sixdeck had been a sim of the ancient Tivoli; now the amusements were arranged on multileveled g-plates over a huge slow-motion whirlpool of syrupy rainbow-colored liquid. Ninedeck had been a ziggurat-maze of living quarters festooned with ivy; now it was a miniature desert of static-molded gold and silver dust-dunes, latticed into a faerie filigree of cavelike apartments. Fluidity seemed to be the theme of the month.

Twelvedeck was now a confection of multicolored energy. The walls of the shops and restaurants were tinted shimmer screens in scores of subtle hues, and the central plaza around the torchtube shaft was an ever-changing meadow of slowly moving miniature fuzzballs in blue, green, purple, yellow, and magenta. The torchtube itself was a cylindrical mirror, and most of the people were wearing tinted mirror suits, fogrobes, or lightcloaks. It was like being inside a rainbow, and D'mahl felt out of sync in his comparatively severe blue pants, bare chest, and cloth-of-gold cloak.

Jiz Rumoku's gallery was behind a sapphire-blue

waterfall that cascaded from halfway up the curved bulkhead to a pool of mist spilling out across the floor of the deck. D'mahl stepped through it, half expecting to be soaked. Mercifully, the waterfall proved to be a holo, but with Jiz, you never knew.

"You who are about to die salute us," Jiz said. She was lying in a blushing-pink fuzzball, naked except for blinding auroras of broad-spectrum light coyly hiding her breasts and loins. The pink fuzzball floated in a lazy ellipse near the center of the gallery, which was now a circular area contained by a shimmer screen around its circumference that rippled endless spectral changes. The ceiling was a holo of roiling orange fire, the floor a mirror of some soft substance.

"Better in fire than in ice," D'mahl said. "My motto." They cross-tapped, and D'mahl lay in the fuzzball feeling an electric glow as his body walked across the gallery and kissed Jiz's lips.

"Voidsucking isn't exactly my idea of fire, Jof," Jiz said as they simultaneously broke their taps.

"This is?" D'mahl said, sweeping his arm in an arc. Dozens of floaters in sizes ranging from a few square centimeters to a good three meters square drifted in seemingly random trajectories around the gallery, displaying objects and energy-effects ranging from tiny pieces of static-molded gemdust jewelry to boxes of flashers, fogrobes, clingers, holopanes that were mostly abstract, and several large and very striking fire-sculptures. The floaters themselves were all transparent plex, and very few of the "objects" on them were pure matter.

"I cog that people are going to be bored with matter for a while," Jiz said, rising from the fuzzball. "After all, it's nothing but frozen energy. Flux is the coming nova, energy-matter interface stuff. It expresses the spirit of the torch, don't you think? Energy, protons, electrons, neutrons, and heavy element dust from the interstellar medium transmuted into whatever we please. This current collection expresses the transmutational state itself."

"I like to have a few things with hard surfaces around," D'mahl said somewhat dubiously.

"You'll see, even your place will be primarily interface for the next standard month or so. You'll put it in sync."

"No I won't, Oh creator of tomorrow's flash," D'mahl said, kissing her teasingly on the lips. "While everyone else is going transmutational, I'll be out there in the cold hard void, where energy and matter know their places and stick to them."

Jiz frowned, touched his cheek. "You're really going through with it, aren't you?" she said. "Months of being cooped up in some awful scoutship, sans tap, sans lovers, sans change. . . ."

"Perhaps at least not sans lovers," D'mahl said lightly, thinking of Sidi. But Jiz, he saw, was seriously worried. "What's the matter, Jiz?"

"What do you actually know about the voidsuckers?"

"What's to know? They man the scoutships. They look for habitable planets. They live the simplest lives imaginable."

"Have you tapped anything on them?"

"No. I'm taking a senso recorder along, of course, and I'll have to use myself as major viewpoint, so I don't want any sensory preconceptions."

"I've tapped the basic sensohistory of the voidsuckers, Jof. There's nothing else in the banks. Doesn't that bother you?"

"Should it?"

"Tap it, Jof."

"I told you—"

"I know, no sensory preconceptions. But I'm asking you to tap it anyway. I have, and I think you should." Her eyes were hard and unblinking, and her mouth was hardened into an ideogram of resolve. When Jiz got that look, D'mahl usually found it advisable to follow her vector, for the sake of parsimony, if nothing else.

"All right," he said. "For you, I'll sully my pristine

consciousness with sordid facts. Voidsuckers, basic history," he subvoced.

He stood in an observation blister watching a scoutship head for the hydrogen interface. The scout was basically a torchship-size fusion tube with a single small toroid deck amidship and a bridge bubble up near the intake. "Trek Year 301," a neuter voice said. "The first scoutship is launched by the Trek. Crewed by five volunteers, it is powered by a full-size fusion torch though its mass is only one-tenth that of a conventional torchship. Combined with its utilization of the Trek's momentum, this enables it rapidly to reach a terminal velocity approaching .87 lights."

D'mahl was a detached observer far out in space watching the scoutship torch ahead of the Trek. Another scoutship, then another, and another, and finally others too numerous to count easily, torched through the hydrogen interface and ahead of the Trek, veering off at angles ranging from ten to thirty degrees, forming a conical formation. The area of space enclosed by the cone turned bright green as the voice said: "By 402, the scoutships numbered forty-seven, and the still-current search pattern had been regularized. Ranging up to a full light-year from the Trek and remote-surveying solar systems from this expanded cone of vision, the scoutship system maximized the number of potential habitable planets surveyed in a given unit of time."

Now D'mahl sat on the bridge of a scoutship looking out the plex at space. Around him, two men and a woman in blue voidsucker shorts were puttering about with instrument consoles. "In 508, a new innovation was introduced." A small drone missile shot slightly ahead of the scoutship, which then began to veer off. "Scoutships now dispatched telltale probes to potentially habitable planets, returning at once to the Trek."

D'mahl was a viewpoint in space watching a stylized diorama of the Trek, a scoutship, a telltale, and a solar system. The scout was torching back to the Trek while the telltale orbited a planet, broadcasting a red wavefront of information Trekward. The scout reached the Trek, which altered its vector toward the telltale's solar system. The scout then left the Trek to monitor the oncoming telltale wavefront. "By turning the Trek toward a prospective system, then returning to monitor the telltale wavefront by scoutship, our fully evolved planetary reconnaissance system now maximizes the number of solar systems investigated in a given time period and also minimizes the reporting time for each high-probability solar system investigated."

D'mahl was aboard a scoutship, playing null-g tennis with an attractive female voidsucker. He was in a simple commissary punching out a meal. He was lying on a grav-plate set at about .25 g in small private sleeping quarters. He was a female voidsucker making love to a tall powerful man in null-g. "The scout's quarters, though comfortable and adequate to maintain physical and mental health, impose some hardship on the crew owing to space limitations," the neuter voice said. "Tap banks are very limited and access to the central Trek banks impossible. Scout crews must content themselves with simple in-flesh amusements. All Trekkers owe these selfless volunteers a debt of gratitude."

Jofe D'mahl looked into Jiz Rumoku's eyes. He shrugged. "So?" he said. "What does that tell me that I didn't already know?"

"Nothing, Jof, not one damned thing! The void-suckers have been out there in the flesh for over half a millennium, spending most of their lives with no tap connection to the Trek, to everything that makes the only human civilization there is what it is. What's their karmic vector? What's inside their skulls? Why are they called voidsuckers, anyway? Why isn't there anything in the banks except that basic history tape?"

"Obviously because no one's gone out there with them to make a real senso," D'mahl said. "They're certainly not the types to produce one themselves. That's why I'm going, Jiz. I think Bandoora was right—

there's a beyond senso to be made on the voidsuckers, and it may be the only virgin subject matter left."

A little of the intensity went out of Jiz's expression. "Ego, of course, has nothing to do with it," she said.

"Ego, of course, has everything to do with it," D'mahl replied.

She touched a hand to his cheek. "Be careful, Jof," she said quite softly.

Moved, D'mahl put his hand over hers, kissed her lightly on the lips, feeling, somehow, like an Earth-bound primitive. "What's there to be afraid of?" he said with equal tenderness.

"I don't know, Jof, and I don't know how to find out. That's what scares me."

Jofe D'mahl felt a rising sense of vectorless anticipation as the shuttle bore him bow-ward toward Bela-37, a silvery cylinder glinting against the auroral background of the hydrogen interface as it hung like a Damoclean sword above him. Below, the ships of the Trek were receding, becoming first a horizon-filling landscape of light and flash, then a disk of human warmth sharply outlined against the cold black night. It occurred to him that Trekkers seldom ventured up here where the scoutships parked, close by the interface separating the Trek from the true void. It was not hard to see why.

"Long way up, isn't it?" he muttered.

The shuttle pilot nodded. "Not many people come up here," he said. "Voidsuckers and maintenance crews mostly. I come up here by myself sometimes to feel the pressure of the void behind the interface and look down on it all like a god on Olympus." He laughed dryly. "Maybe I've ferried one voidsucker too many."

Something made D'mahl shudder, then yearn for the communion of the tap—the overwhelmingly rich inter-meshing of time, space, bodies, and realities from which he was about to isolate himself for the first time in his life. The tap is what we live by, he thought, and who so more than I?

"Jiz Rumoku," he subvoced, and he was in her body, standing beside a fire-sculpture in her gallery with a chunky black man in a severe green velvet suit. "Hello, Jiz," he said with her vocal cords. "Hello and good-bye."

He withdrew his tap from her body, and she followed into his, high above the Trek. "Hello, Jof. It's sure a long way up." She kissed his hand with his lips. "Take care," his voice said. Then she broke the tap, and D'mahl was alone in his flesh as the shuttle decelerated, easing up alongside Bela-37's toroid main deck.

"This is it," the shuttle pilot said. "You board through the main shimmer." D'mahl gave the pilot an ironic salute, erected his voidbubble, grabbed his kit and senso recorder, and flitted across a few meters of space to Bela-37's main entrance stage.

Stepping through the shimmer, he was surprised to find himself in a small closetlike room with no droptube shaft in evidence. A round door in the far bulkhead opened and a tall, pale voidsucker stepped inside. "I'm Ban Nyborg, D'mahl," he said. He laughed rather humorlessly. "This is an airlock," he said. "Safety feature."

Automatically, D'mahl tapped for a definition of the new word: *double-doored chamber designed to facilitate ship entry and exit, obsoleted by the shimmer screen.* "How quaint," he said, following Nyborg through the open door.

"Lose power, lose your shimmer, this way you keep your air," Nyborg said, leading D'mahl down a dismal blue pastel corridor. "Radial passageway," Nyborg said. "Leads to circular corridor around the torchtube. Five other radials, tubes to the bridge and back, that's the ship." They reached the circumtorchtube corridor, done in washed-out blue and yellow, walked sixty degrees around it past some instrument consoles and an orange radial corridor, then another sixty degrees and halfway up a green radial to a plain matter door.

Nyborg opened the door and D'mahl stepped into a grim little room. There was a g-plate, a blue pneumatic chair, a tall simmed walnut chest, a shaggy red rug, and, beyond an open door, toilet facilities. The ceiling was deep gray, and three of the walls were grayish tan. The fourth was a holo of the interstellar abyss itself—pinpoint stars and yawning blackness—and it faced the g-plate.

"Bandoora's quarters," Nyborg said. "He's doubling with Sidi."

"Charming," D'mahl grunted. "I'm touched."

"Ship's got three tap frequencies: library, communications, external visual. Bridge is off limits now. You can tap our departure on external." Nyborg turned, walked unceremoniously out of the little cell, and closed the door behind him.

D'mahl shuddered. The walls and ceiling seemed to be closing in on him as if to squeeze him into the reality of the holo. He found himself staring into the starfield, leaning toward it as if it were pulling him down into it.

He blinked, feeling the strangeness of the sensation, which drew his attention away from the holo and to his senso recorder. Ought to get all this down. He turned the recorder on, dropped in a hundred-hour pod of microtape, keyed it to his own sensorium. But the initial moment of vertigo had passed; now he was just in an excruciatingly dull little room with a big starfield holo on one wall.

D'mahl set the g-plate for .1 g, just enough to hold him in place, and lay down on the padding. He found himself staring into the starfield holo again from this position. Did Bandoora actually like being sucked at by that thing?

Bandoora tapped him, audio only: "Welcome to Bela-37, D'mahl. We're about to torch through the interface. Perhaps you'd care to tap it."

"Thanks," D'mahl tapped back through the scout's com frequency, "but I'd rather record it in the flesh from the bridge."

"Sorry, but the bridge is off limits to you now," Bandoora said, and broke the tap.

"Drool!" D'mahl snarled to no one, and irritably tapped the scout's external visual frequency.

He was a disembodied viewpoint moving through the silent frictionless darkness of space. It was like being in a voidbubble and yet not like being in a voidbubble, for here he was disconnected from all internal and external senses save vision. He found that he could tap subfrequencies that gave him choice of visual direction, something like being able to turn his non-existent head. Below, the Trek was a jewel of infinitely subtle light slowly shrinking in the velvet blackness. All other vectors were dominated by the hydrogen interface, a sky of rainbow brilliance that seemed to all but surround him.

It was a moving visual spectacle, and yet the lack of the subtleties of full sense also made it pathetic, filled D'mahl with an elusive sadness. As the rainbow sheen of the hydrogen interface moved visibly closer, that sadness resolved along a nostalgia vector as D'mahl realized that he was about to lose tap contact with the Trek's banks. The interface energies would block out the banks long before time-lag or signal attenuation even became a factor. It was his last chance to say good-bye to the multiplex Trek reality before being committed to the unknown and invariant void beyond.

He broke his tap with the scout's visual frequency, and zip-tapped through the multiplicity of the Trek's frequencies like a dying man flashing through his life's sensorium track before committing it to the limbo banks.

He stood among the crystal trees of his own grand salon. He was Dalta Reed punting across Blood Lake on *Lothlorien* and he was Erna Ramblieu making love to John Benina on his balcony overlooking Sundance Corridor of *Magic Mountain*. He watched *Excelsior* being built from the body of a welder working on the hull, and he flashed through the final sequence of *Wandering Dutchmen.* He riffled through his own sensorium track—making love to Jiz five years ago in a dirtdigger deck, moments of ten parties, dancing above a null-g plate as a boy, cutting *Wandering Dutchmen* at his editor—realizing suddenly that he was leaving the world of his own stored memories behind with everything else. Finally, he flashed through Jiz Rumoku's body as she led the man in the green velvet suit past a holoframe of the Far Look Ballet dancing *Swan Lake* in null-g, and then his tap was broken, and he was lying on his g-plate in Bela-37, unable to reestablish it.

He tapped the scout's visual frequency and found himself moving into the world-filling brilliance of the hydrogen interface behind the auroral bubble of Bela-37's own torch intake field. The lesser rainbow touched the greater, and D'mahl rapidly became sheathed in glory as Bela-37's field formed a bulge in the Trek's combined field, a bulge that enveloped the scoutship and D'mahl, became a closed sphere of full-spectrum fire for an instant, then burst through the hydrogen interface with a rush that sent D'mahl's being soaring, gasping, and reeling into the cold hard blackness of the open void beyond.

D'mahl shook, grunted, and broke the tap. For a panicked moment he thought he had somehow been trapped in the abyss as his vision snapped back into his flesh staring at the holo of the void that filled the wall facing him.

The lift-tube ended and Jofe D'mahl floated up out of it and onto the circular bridge of Bela-37. The bridge was a plex blister up near the bow of the torchtube encircled by consoles and controls to waist level but otherwise visually naked to the interstellar void. Bow-ward, the ship's intake field formed a miniature hydrogen interface; sternward, the Trek was visible as a scintillating disk behind a curtain of ethereal fire, but otherwise nothing seemed to live or move in all that eternal immensity.

"Isn't there any getting away from it?" D'mahl muttered, half to himself, half to Haris Bandoora, who had watched him emerge from the lift-tube with those unfathomable eyes and an ironic, enigmatic grin.

"You people spend your lives trying to get away from it," Bandoora said, "and we spend our lives drenching ourselves in it because we know there *is* no real escape from it. One way or the other, our lives are dominated by the void."

"Speak for yourself, Bandoora," D'mahl said. "Out there is only one reality." He touched a forefinger to his temple. "In here are an infinity more."

"Illusion," said a woman's voice behind him. D'mahl turned and saw Sidi—conical bare breasts, hairless silvered skull, tightly muscled body, opaque voidsucker eyes—a vision of cold and abstract feminine beauty.

D'mahl smiled at her. "What is," he said, "is real."

"Where you come from," Sidi said, "no one knows what's real."

"*Réalité c'est moi,*" D'mahl said in ancient French. When both Sidi and Bandoora stared at him blankly, failing to tap for the reference, *unable* to tap for the reference, he had a sharp flash of loneliness. An adult among children. A civilized man among primitives. And out there . . . out there . . .

He forced his attention away from such thoughts, forced his vision away from the all-enveloping void, and walked toward one of the instrument consoles where a slim woman with a shaven untinted skull sat in a pedestal chair adjusting some controls.

"This is Areth Lorenzi," Bandoora said. "She's setting the sweep-sequence of our extreme-range grav-scan. We automatically scan a twenty light-year sphere for new planeted stars even on a mission like this. We can pick up an Earth-massed body that far away."

The woman turned, and D'mahl saw a face steeped in age. There were wrinkles around her eyes, at the corners of her mouth, even a hint of them on her cheeks; extraordinary enough in itself, but it was her deep, deep pale-blue eyes that spoke most eloquently of her years, of the sheer volume of the things they had seen.

"How often have you detected such bodies?" D'mahl asked conversationally, to keep from obviously staring.

Something seemed to flare in those limpid depths. She glanced over D'mahl's shoulder at Bandoora for a moment. "It's . . . a common enough occurrence," she said, and turned back to her work.

"And finally, this is Raj Doru," Bandoora said with a peculiar hastiness, indicating the other voidsucker on the bridge: a squat, dark, powerful-looking man with a fierce mouth, a sweeping curve of a nose, and bright brown eyes glowering under his shaven brows. He was standing, hands on hips, regarding D'mahl scornfully.

"What is, is real," Doru said acidly. "What do you know about real, Jofe D'mahl? You've never confronted the reality of the universe in your whole life! Cowering behind your hydrogen interface and your tap and your mental masturbation fantasies! The void would shrivel your soul to a pinpoint and then snuff it out of existence."

"Raj!" Bandoora snapped. Psychic energy crackled and clashed as the two voidsuckers glared at each other for a silent moment.

"Let's see the great D'mahl suck some void, Haris, let's—"

"Everything in its time," Bandoora said. "This isn't it."

"Raj is an impatient man," Sidi said.

"A peculiar trait for a voidsucker," D'mahl replied dryly. These people were beginning to grate on his consciousness. They seemed humorless, obsessive, out of sync with their own cores, as if the nothingness in which they continuously and monomaniacally wallowed had emptied out their centers and filled them with itself.

D'mahl found himself looking up and out into the starry blackness of the abyss, wondering if that eternal coldness might in time seep into his core too, if the mind simply could not encompass that much nothingness and still remain in command of its own vector.

"Patience is an indifferent virtue out here," Areth said. It did not seem a comforting thought.

What do these people *do* with themselves? Jofe D'mahl wondered as he paced idly and nervously around the circumtorchtube corridor for what seemed like the thousandth time. A week aboard Bela-37 and he was woozy with boredom. There was a limit to how much chess and null-g tennis you could play, and the ship's library banks were pathetic—a few hundred standard reference tapes, fifty lamer pornos, a hundred classic sensos (four of his own included, he was wanly pleased to note), and an endless log of dull-as-death scoutship reports.

"Patience is an indifferent virtue out here," Areth Lorenzi had said. To D'mahl, it seemed the only virtue possible under the circumstances, and his supply of it was rapidly running out.

Up ahead, he heard footfalls coming down a radial corridor, and a moment later his vector intersected that of Sidi, striding beautifully and coldly toward him like a robot simmed in flesh. Even his initial attraction to her was beginning to fade. Inside that carapace of abstract beauty she seemed as disconnected from any reality he cared to share as the others.

"Hello, D'mahl," she said distantly. "Have you been getting good material for your senso?"

D'mahl snorted. "If you can call a pod and a quarter of boredom footage interesting material," he said. "Bandoora promised me something transcendent. Where is it?"

"Have you not looked around you?"

D'mahl nodded upward, at the ceiling, at space beyond. "Out there? I can see that from my own grand salon."

"Wait."

"For what?"

"For the call."

"What call?"

"When it comes, you will know it," Sidi said, and walked past him up the corridor. D'mahl shook his head. From Doru, hostility; from Bandoora, lamer metaphysics; from Nyborg, a grunt now and then; from Areth Lorenzi, a few games of nearly silent chess. Now brain-teases from Sidi. Can it be that that's all these people have? A few lamer quirks around a core of inner vacuum? Nothing but their own obsessiveness between them and eternal boredom? It might make a reasonably interesting senso, if I could figure out a way to dramatize vacuity. He sighed. At least it gave him a valid artistic problem to play with.

"*All* routine here," Ban Nyborg said, bending his tall frame over the readout screen, across which two columns of letters and numbers slowly crawled. "Star catalog numbers on the left, masses of any dark bodies around them on the right."

"A simple program could monitor this," D'mahl said. "Why are you doing it?"

"Computer *does* screen it, I'm just backing up. Something to do."

D'mahl shook his head. He had wandered into this comp center by accident—none of the voidsuckers had even bothered to mention it to him. Yet here was much of the equipment at the heart of the scoutship's mission: the ship's computer and banks, the gravscan readout, and a whole series of other instrument consoles he would have had to tap for to identify. But the dull gray room had a strange air of neglect about it.

"You sound almost as bored as I am, Nyborg," he said.

Nyborg nodded without looking up. "All waiting, till you get the call."

"*The call?* What call?"

Nyborg turned, and for the first time in nearly two standard weeks, D'mahl saw animation on his long face; fire, perhaps even remembered ecstasy in his pale eyes. "When the void calls you to it," he said. "You'll see. No use talking about it. It calls, and you go, and that's what it's all about. That's why we're all here."

"That's why you're here? What about all this?" D'mahl said, sweeping his hand in a circle to indicate the roomful of instruments.

He could visibly see the life go out of Nyborg's face; curtains came down over the fire in his eyes, and he was once again Nyborg the cyborg.

"All this is the mission," Nyborg grunted, turning back to the readout screen. "What gets us out here. But the call is why we come. Why do you think we're called voidsuckers?"

"Why?"

"We suck void," Nyborg said.

"You mean you don't care about the mission? You're not dedicated to finding us a new living world?"

"Drool," Nyborg muttered. "Scoutships don't need us, can run themselves. *We* need *them*. To get us to the void." He deliberately began to feign intense interest in what he was doing, and D'mahl could not extract a syllable more.

"Just how long have you been on scoutships, Areth?" Jofe D'mahl said, looking up from his hopeless position on the chessboard.

"About a century and a half," Areth Lorenzi said, still studying her next move. As always, she volunteered nothing.

"You must really be dedicated to the mission to have spent such a long life out here in nowhere," D'mahl said, trying to get something out of her. Those eyes hinted of so much and that mouth said so little.

"I've always heard the call."

"What's this call I keep hearing about?"

"The void calls, and for those who are called, there is nothing but the void. You think our lives are sacrifices for the common good of humanity?"

"Well, aren't they?"

Areth Lorenzi looked up at him with her ancient

crystalline eyes. "We man the scoutships to reach the void, we don't brave the void to man the scoutships," she said. "We sacrifice nothing but illusion. We live with the truth. We live for the truth."

"And the truth shall set you free?" D'mahl said archly. But the reference blew by her since she had no way to tap for it.

Areth dropped her gaze. A note of bitterness came into her voice. "The truth is: No man is free." She moved her rook to double-check D'mahl's king and queen. "Checkmate in three moves, D'mahl," she said.

D'mahl found Haris Bandoora alone on the bridge looking sternward, back toward where the Trek had been visible until recently as a tiny bright disk among the pinpoint stars. Now the Trek, if it was visible at all, was nothing more than one point of light lost in a million others. Bela-37 seemed frozen in a black crystal vastness speckled with immobile motes of sparkling dust, an abstract universe of dubious reality.

A tremor of dread went through D'mahl, a twinge of the most utter aloneness. Even the presence of the enigmatic and aloof Bandoora seemed a beacon of human warmth in the dead uncaring night.

"Overwhelming, isn't it?" Bandoora said, turning at the sound of D'mahl's footfalls. "A hundred million stars, perhaps as many planets, and this one galaxy is a speck of matter floating in an endless nothingness." There was a strange overlay of softness in those dark and bottomless eyes, almost a misting of tears. "What are we, D'mahl? Once we were bits of some insignificant anomaly called life contaminating a dust-mote circling a speck of matter lost in a tiny cloud of specks, itself a minor contaminant of the universal void. Now we're not even that. . . ."

"We're the part that counts, Bandoora," D'mahl said.

"To whom?" Bandoora said, nodding toward the abyss. "To *that?*"

"To ourselves. To whatever other beings share con-

sciousness on planets around whichever of those stars.
Sentience is what counts, Bandoora. The rest of it is
just backdrop." D'mahl laughed hollowly. "If this be
solipsism, let us make the most of it."

"If only you knew . . ."

"If only I knew what?"

Bandoora smiled an ironic smile. "You *will* know,"
he said. "That's why you're here. We can't be alone
with it forever."

"What—"

"I've heard the call, Haris." Raj Doru had risen to
the bridge, and now he walked rapidly to Bandoora's
side, his brown eyes feverish, and uncharacteristic lan-
guor in his posture.

"When?" Bandoora asked crisply.

"Now."

"How long?"

"Twenty-four hours."

Bandoora turned and followed Doru toward the
droptube. "What's going on?" D'mahl asked, trailing
after them.

"Raj is going to suck void," Bandoora said. "He's
heard the call. Care to help me see him off?"

At the round airlock door, Raj Doru took a
voidbubble-and-flitter harness from the rack, donned
it, took a flask of water and a cassette of ration out of
a locker, and clipped them to the belt of his shorts.
His eyes looked off into some unguessable reality that
D'mahl could not begin to sync with.

"What are you doing, Doru?" he asked.

Doru didn't answer; he didn't even seem to notice
D'mahl's presence. "Put on a voidbubble and see,"
Bandoora said, taking two harnesses off the rack and
handing one to him.

D'mahl and Bandoora donned their harnesses, then
Bandoora opened the airlock door and the three men
stepped inside. They erected their bubbles, Bandoora
sealed the door behind them, then the three of them

walked through the shimmer screen onto the scoutship's entrance stage.

Out on the narrow metal shelf, D'mahl found himself utterly overwhelmed by the black immensities, the
infinite hole in which the scoutship hung precariously
suspended. This was utterly unlike the view from his
grand salon, for here there was no concourse of ships
or even torchtube wake to ease the impact of the abyss
upon the soul. Here there was only a tiny ship, the
abstract stars, three small men—and an infinity of
nothing. D'mahl reeled and quaked with a vertigo that
pierced the core of his being.

"Twenty-four hours, Haris," Doru tapped on the
com frequency. He spread his arms, turned on his g-
polarizer, and leaped up and out into the blackness of
the interstellar abyss.

"What's he doing?" D'mahl shouted vocally. He
caught himself, tapped the question to Bandoora as
Doru began to pick up velocity and dwindle into the
blackness along a vector at right angles to the ship's
trajectory.

"He's going to suck void for twenty-four hours,"
Bandoora tapped. "He's answering the call. He'll go
out far enough to lose sight of the ship and stay there
for a standard day."

Doru was already just a vague shape moving against
the backdrop of the starfield. As D'mahl watched, the
shape fuzzed to a formless point. "What will he do out
there?" he asked Bandoora quietly, a shudder racking
his body.

"What happens between a man and the void is between a man and the void."

"Is it . . . safe?"

"Safe? We have a fix on him, and he's still inside the
cone of our interface. His body is safe. His mind . . .
that's between Raj and the void."

Now D'mahl could no longer make Doru out at all.
The voidsucker had vanished . . . into the void.
D'mahl began to catch his mental breath, realizing
that he was missing the only prime senso footage that

had yet presented itself to him. He tried to tap Doru through the ship's com frequency, but all he got was a reject signal.

"I've got to get this on tape, Bandoora! But he's rejecting my tap."

"I told you, what happens between a man and the void is between that man and the void. The only way you'll ever bring back a senso of *this* reality, D'mahl, is to experience it in your own flesh and tap yourself."

D'mahl looked into Bandoora's cool even eyes; then his gaze was drawn out into the black and starry depths into which Doru had disappeared. To which Doru had willingly, even ecstatically, given himself. Fear and fascination mingled inside him. Here was an experience the contemplation of which caused his knees to tremble, his heart to pound, and a cold wind to blow through his soul. Yet here too was an experience whose parameters he could not predict or fathom, a thing he had never done nor dreamed of doing, the thing that lay at the core of what the voidsuckers were. The thing, therefore, that was the core of the senso for which he was enduring these endless months of boredom. A thing, therefore, that he must inevitably confront.

"Why do you do it?" he tapped, turning from the abyss to face Bandoora.

"Each man has his own reason," the voidsucker tapped. "The call has many voices." He smiled a knowing smile. "You're beginning to hear it in your own language, D'mahl," he said.

D'mahl shivered, for somewhere deep inside him, the opening notes of that siren-song were indeed chiming, faraway music from the depths of the beyond within.

Standing on the bridge watching Bandoora disappear into the void, Jofe D'mahl felt like a hollow stringed instrument vibrating to yet another strumming of the same endless chord. Doru, Nyborg, Areth, Sidi, and now finally Bandoora had committed themselves to the abyss in these past three weeks, Areth and

Nyborg twice apiece. Each of them had refused to let him tap them or even to discuss the experience afterward, and each of them had come back subtly changed. Doru seemed to have much of the hostility leached out of him; Nyborg had become even less talkative, almost catatonic; Areth seemed somehow slightly younger, perhaps a bit less distant; and Sidi had begun to ignore him almost completely. He could find no common denominator, except that each succeeding voidsuck had made him feel that much more isolated on Bela-37, that much more alone, that much more curious about what transpired between the human mind and the void. Now that the last of them was out there, D'mahl felt the process nearing completion, the monotonous chord filling his being with its standing-wave harmonics.

"Are you hearing it, Jofe D'mahl?" the quiet voice of Areth Lorenzi said beside him. "Do you finally hear the call?"

"I'm not sure what I'm hearing," D'mahl said, without looking away from the immensities outside the plex. "Maybe what I'm hearing is my own ego calling. I've got to get a voidsuck on tape, or I've wasted all this time out here."

"It's the call," Areth said. "I've seen it often enough. It comes to each along his own natural vector."

With an effort, D'mahl turned to face her. "There's something you people aren't telling me," he said. "I can feel it. I know it."

Now it was Areth who spoke without looking at him, whose eyes were transfixed by the overwhelming void. "There is," she said. "The void at the center of all. The truth we live with that you deny."

"Drool on all this crypticism!" D'mahl snapped. "What is this cosmic truth you keep teasing me with?"

"To know, you must first taste the void."

"*Why?*"

"To know that, you must first answer the call."

A wordless grunt of anger and frustration exploded from D'mahl's throat. "You think I don't know the

game you people are playing?" he said. "You think I
don't know what you're doing? But why? Why are you
so anxious for me to suck void? Why did you want me
here in the first place?"

"Because of who you are, Jofe D'mahl," Areth said.
"Because of *Wandering Dutchmen*. Because you may
be the one we have sought. The one who can share the
truth and lift this burden from our souls."

"Now it's flattery, is it?"

Areth turned to face him, and he almost winced at
the pain, the despair, the pleading in her eyes. "Not
flattery," she said. "Hope. I ask you, one human being
to another, to help us. Bandoora would not ask, but I
do. Lift our burden, D'mahl, heed the call and lift our
burden."

Unable to face those eyes, D'mahl looked off into
the star-speckled blackness. Bandoora could no longer
be seen, but something out there was indeed beckoning to him with an unseen hand, calling to him with
an unheard voice. Even his fear seemed to be a part of
it, challenging him to face the void within and the
void without and to carve something out of it if he
had the greatness of soul to dare.

"All right," he said softly—to Areth, to Bandoora, to
all of them, and to that which waited beyond the plex
blister of the bridge. "You've won. When Bandoora
comes back, I'll answer your damned call. As I once
said, I've got nothing to do but dare."

But the man who had said it seemed long ago and
far away.

They were all out on the entrance stage in voidbubbles to see him off. "Eighteen standard hours,
D'mahl," Bandoora tapped over the com frequency.
"Remember, we've got a fix on you, and we can come
right out and get you if it becomes too much. Just
tap."

Inside his own bubble, D'mahl nodded, silently. He
fingered his water flask and his ration cassette. He
tapped the time at 4.346. He could not for a moment

draw his eyes away from the endless black sea into which he was about to plunge. Millions of pinpoint stars pulsed and throbbed in the darkness like needles pricking his retinas. A silent roaring pulsed up at him from out of the abyss, the howl of the eternal silences themselves. His body seemed to end at the knees. The void appeared to be a tangible substance reaching out to enfold him in its cold and oceanic embrace. He knew that he must commit himself to it *now,* or in the next moment flee gibbering and sweating into the psychic refuge of Bela-37.

"See you at 22.000," he tapped inanely, activating his g-polarizer. Then he flexed his knees and dived off the little metal shelf into the vast unknown.

The act of leaping into the abyss seemed to free him of the worst of his fears, as if he had physically jumped out of them, and for a while he felt no different than he had at times when, flitting from one Trek ship to another, he had temporarily lost sight of all. Then he looked back.

Bela-37 was a small metal cylinder slowly dwindling into the starry darkness. The five tiny figures standing on the entrance stage hovered on the edge of visibility and then melted into the formless outline of the scout-ship. Nothing else existed that seemed real. Only the shrinking cylinder of metal, one single work of man in all that nothing. D'mahl shuddered and turned his head away. Somehow the sight of the pure void itself was less terrifying than that of his last connection with the things of man disappearing from view into its depths.

He did not look back again for a long time. When he did, his universe had neither back nor front nor sides nor top nor bottom. All around him was an infinite black hole dusted with meaningless stars, and every direction seemed to be down. His mind staggered, reeled, and rejected this impossible sensory data. Polarities reversed, so that the entire universe of stars and nothingness seemed to be collapsing in on him, crushing the breath out of him. He screamed, closed

his eyes, and was lost in the four-dimensional whirlpool of his own vertigo.

By feel, he turned off the g-polarizer, whirling inside the vacuum of his own mind, sucked spiraling
downward into meaningless mazes of total disorientation. Half whimpering, he opened his eyes again to a
new transformation.

It was as if he were imbedded in a clear, motionless,
crystalline substance englobed by a seamless black wall
onto which the stars had been painted. Nothing
moved, no event transpired, time could not be said to
be passing. It was the very essence of tranquillity: calm-
ing, eternal, serene.

D'mahl sighed, felt his constricted muscles relax and
his mind drift free. He floated in the void like an immortal embryo in everlasting amnion, waiting for he
knew not what. Nor cared.

Time did not pass, but there was duration. D'mahl
floated in the void, and waited. Thirst came and was
slaked, and he waited. Hunger came; he nibbled ration, and waited. He grew aware of the beating of his
own heart, the pulsing of blood through his veins, and
he waited. The kinesthetic awareness of his own bodily functions faded, and he still waited.

Nothing moved. Nothing lived. Nothing changed.
Silence was eternal. Gradually, slowly, and with infinite subtlety, D'mahl's perception of his environment
began to change again. The comforting illusion of
being held in crystalline suspension in a finite reality
enclosed by a painted backdrop of stars and blackness
began to fade under the inexorable pressure of dura-
tionless time and forced contemplation. The clear crystal substance of space dissolved into the nothingness
whence his mind had conjured it, and as it did, the
stars became not points of paint on distant walls but
motes of incandescent matter an infinity away across
vast gulfs of absolute nothingness. The overwhelming
blackness was not the painted walls of a pocket reality
but an utter absence of everything—light, warmth,

sound, motion, color, life—that went on and on without boundaries to give it shape or span to give it meaning.

This was the void and he was in it.

Strangely, D'mahl now found that his mind could encompass this mercilessly true perception of reality, however awesome, however terrifying, without the shield of perceptual illusions. Endless duration had stripped him of the ability to maintain these illusions, and between gibbering terror and a cool, detached acceptance of the only reality he could maintain, his mind chose detachment.

He was, and he was in the void. That was reality. He moved, and all else was static. That was real. He could hear the sound of his own breath, and all else was silence. That was inescapable truth. He could perceive his body's shape as the interface between his internal reality and the nothingness outside, and all else was formless forever in space and time. That was the void. That was the universe. That was prime reality. That was the reality from which men fled—into religion, dream, art, poetry, philosophy, metaphysics, literature, film, music, war, love, hate, paranoia, the senso, and the tap. Into the infinity of realities within.

Outside the realities of the mind there was nothingness without form or end, minutely contaminated with flecks of matter. And man was but the chance end-product of a chain of random and improbable collisions between these insignificant contaminants. The void neither knew nor cared. The void did not exist. It was the eternal and infinite nonexistence that dwarfed and encompassed that which did.

D'mahl floated in this abyss of nonbeing, duration continued, and the void began to insinuate tendrils of its nonself into his being, into his pith and core, until it was reflected by a void within.

Jofe D'mahl experienced himself as a thin shell of being around a core of nothingness floating in more nonbeing that went on timelessly and formlessly for-

ever. He was the atom-thin interface between the void
without and the void within. He was an anomaly in
all that nothingness, a chance trick knot whereby
nothingness redoubled upon itself had produced somethingness—consciousness, being, life itself. He was
nothing and he was everything there was. He was the
interface. He did not exist. He was all.

For more timeless duration, Jofe D'mahl existed as a
bubble of consciousness in a sea of nonbeing, a chance
bit of matter recomplicated into a state it was then
pleased to call life, a locus of feeling in a nothingness
that knew neither feeling nor knowing itself. He had
passed beyond terror, beyond pride, beyond humility,
into a reality where they had no meaning, where nothing had meaning, not even meaning itself.

He tried to imagine other bubbles of consciousness
bobbing in the everlasting void—on Bela-37, on the
ships of the Trek, on unknown planets circling those
abstract points of light contaminating the sterile per-
fection of the abyss. But out here in the true void, in
this endless matrix of nonbeing, the notion that consciousness, or even life itself, was anything but the improbable product of a unique and delicate chain of
random interactions between bits of recomplicated
nothingness called "matter" seemed hopelessly jejune
and pathetically anthropocentric. One possible chain
of unlikely events led to life and all others led back to
nothingness. One misstep on the part of nonexistent
fate, and the unlikely spell was broken.

The wonder was not that life had arisen so sparsely,
but that it had arisen at all.

D'mahl floated in the blackness of the abyss, in the
sea of timeless nonbeing, clinging to the life-preserver
of one incontrovertible truth. I am, he thought. I exist, and every thought I've ever had, every reality that
ever existed in my mind, also exists. This may be
prime reality, but everything that is, is real.

Coldly, calmly, almost serenely, Jofe D'mahl waited
in the silent immobile darkness for the recall signal

from Bela-37, the call to return from the nonbeing of
the void to the frail multiplexity of the worlds of man.

They were all out on the entrance stage in voidbubbles to greet him. Silently, they conveyed him inside
the scoutship, their eyes speaking of the new bond between them. With a strange ceremoniousness, they es-
corted D'mahl into the ship's commissary. Bandoora
seated him at a short side of one of the rectangular
tables, then sat down across its length from him. The
others arranged themselves on either long side of the
table. It would have been a moot point as to who was
at the foot and who the head were it not for another
of the scoutship's endless holos of space forming the
wall behind Bandoora. This one was a view of the galaxy as seen from far out in the intergalactic emptiness,
and it haloed Bandoora's head in stardust and blackness.

"Now that you have confronted the void, Jofe
D'mahl," Bandoora said solemnly, "you are ready to
share the truth."

Petty annoyance began to fade the reality of
D'mahl's so recent experience from the forefront of his
consciousness. This was beginning to seem like some
kind of ridiculous ceremony. Were they going to treat
his experience out there as an initiation into some ludicrous *religion*? Replete with incantations, tribal secrets, and Bandoora as high priest?

"Say what you have to say, Bandoora," he said. "But
please spare me the formalities."

"As you wish, D'mahl," Bandoora said. His eyes
hardened, seemed to pick up black flashes of void
from the holo of space behind him. "What happened
between you and the void is between you and the
void," he said. "But you felt it. And for half a millennium our instruments have been confirming it."

"Confirming what?" D'mahl muttered. But the qua-
ver in his voice would not let him hide from that awful foretaste that bubbled up into his consciousness
from the void inside.

"We have instruments far beyond what we've let you people believe," Bandoora said, "and we've had them for a long time. We've gravscanned tens of thousands of stars, not thousands. We've found thousands of planets, not hundreds. We've found hundreds of Earth-parameter planets orbiting in habitable zones, not dozens. We've been lying, D'mahl. We've been lying to you for centuries."

"Why?" D'mahl whispered, knowing the answer, feeling it screaming at him from the holo behind Bandoora's head, from the voidsucker's opaque eyes, from the void beyond.

"You know why," Doru said harshly. "Because they're nothing but dead rock and gas. Over seven hundred of them, D'mahl."

"All of them should have been teeming with life by any parameters our scientists can construct," Areth Lorenzi said. "For centuries, we hoped that the next one or the one after that would disprove the only possible conclusion. But we've not found so much as a microbe on any of them. We have no hope left."

"Gets as far as protein molecules sometimes," Nyborg grunted. "Maybe one in eighty."

"But the telltale probes can't—"

"Telltales!" Doru snorted. "The telltale probes are more illusion to protect you people! We've got microspectrographs that could pick up a DNA molecule ten light-years away, and we've had them for centuries."

"We already know that 997-Beta-II is dead," Sidi said. "We knew it before we reported to the Council of Pilots. This whole mission, like hundreds before it, is an empty gesture."

"*But why have you been lying to us like this?*" D'mahl shouted. "What right did you have? What—"

"What were we supposed to say?" Bandoora shouted back. "That it's all dead? That life on Earth was a unique accident? That nothing exists but emptiness and dead matter and the murderers of the only life there ever was? What are we supposed to say, D'mahl? What are we supposed to do?"

"For over two centuries we have lived with the conviction that our mission is hopeless," Areth said softly. "For over two centuries we have been leading the Trek from one false hope to the next, knowing that hope was false. Don't judge us too harshly. What else could we have done?"

"You could have told us," D'mahl croaked. "You could have told us the truth."

"Could we?" Areth said. "Could we have told you before you yourself confronted the void?"

Anger and despair chased each other in a yin-yang mandala at Jofe D'mahl's core. Anger at the smug arrogance of these narrow lamer people who dared treat all of human civilization as retarded children who could not be told the truth. Despair at the awful nature of that truth. Anger at the thought that perhaps the voidsuckers were hiding their true reason for silence, that they had kept the Trek in ignorance so that they wouldn't risk the termination of the scout-ship program and with it the one act that gave their lamer lives meaning. Despair at the treacherous thought that the voidsuckers might be right after all, that the truth would shatter the Trek like radiation-rotted plex. Anger at himself for even thinking of joining the voidsuckers and sitting in such arrogant judgment.

"You lamer drool-ridden dreeks!" D'mahl finally snarled. "How dare you judge us like that! Who do you think you are, gods on Olympus? Living your narrow little lives, cutting yourselves off from the worlds inside, and then presuming to decide what *we* can face!"

His flesh trembled, his muscles twanged like steel wire tensed to the snapping point, and adrenaline's fire pounded through his arteries as his hands ground into the edge of the table.

But the voidsuckers sat there looking up at him quietly, and what he saw in their eyes was relief, not anger, or reaction to anger.

"Then you'll do it, D'mahl?" Bandoora said softly.

"Do what?"

"Tell them in your own way," Areth said. "Lift the burden from us."

"*What?*"

"When I tapped *Wandering Dutchmen,* I felt you might be the one," Bandoora said. "You sensed the edges of the truth. You seemed to be looking at the void and yet beyond. You know your people, D'mahl, as we do not. You've just said it yourself. Tell them. Make a senso that tells them."

"All this . . . this whole trip . . . it was all a trick to get me out here . . . to tell me this . . . to drop your load of slok on me. . . ."

"I promised you the chance to make the greatest senso of your career," Bandoora said. "Did I lie?"

D'mahl subsided into his chair. "But you didn't tell me I was going to have to succeed," he said.

IV

The scoutship came in tail-first on a long shallow arc over the hydrogen interface, still decelerating. Tapping Bela-37's visual frequency, Jofe D'mahl saw the ships of the Trek suddenly appear in all their glory as the scoutship passed the auroral wavefront, as if the interface were a rainbow curtain going up on a vast ballet of motion and light.

Thousands of shining cylinders hung in the blackness, their surfaces jeweled with multicolored lights. The space between them coruscated and shone with shuttle exhausts and a haze of subtle reflections off thousands of moving voidbubbles. The thin purple wake of the Trek cut an ethereal swath of manifested motion and time through the eternal immobile nothingness.

The Trek seemed larger and lovelier than even D'mahl's memory had made it during the long sullen trip back. Its light drove back the everlasting darkness, its complexity shattered the infinite sameness of the void; it danced in the spotlight of its own brilliance. It was alive. It was beautiful. It was home.

Bandoora had calculated well; as Bela-37 passed sternward of the Trek, its relative velocity dwindled away to zero and it hung in space about twenty kilometers behind the great concourse of ships. Bandoora turned the scoutship end-for-end and began to ease it toward the Trek, toward its eventual parking slot just behind the hydrogen interface. D'mahl broke his tap with the scout's visual frequency and lay on the g-plate in his room for a long moment staring into the starfield holo before him for the last time.

Then, like a lover reaching for remembered flesh after a long parting, like a man rising out of a long

coma toward the dawning light, he tapped Jiz Rumoku.

He was sitting at a clear glass table sipping an icy
blue beverage out of a pewter mug, washing down a
swallow of lavender sponge. Across the table, Varn Ka-
menev was pouring himself another mugful from a
matching pitcher. The table was on a disk of clear
plex, floating, like dozens of others, through what
seemed like a topless and bottomless forest of ivy. He
didn't recognize the restaurant, but didn't bother to
tap for it.

"Home is the hero," he said with Jiz's throat and
lips, feeling her body warm to his presence.

"Jof! Where are you, what happened, let me tap—"

"Wait for the flesh, Jiz," he told her. "I'll be in
your gallery within two hours. I wanted you to be the
first, but I've got to zip-tap my way back to realities
before I die of thirst."

"But what was it like—"

"Miles and miles of miles and miles," he said, feeling a surge of exhilaration at the thought that he was
with someone who could and would tap for the reference. "Next year in Jerusalem," he said with her
mouth. He kissed her hand with her lips and broke
the tap.

And zip-tapped through the changes like a random
search program for the phantom tapper.

He was Para Bunning, soaring naked in a low-g dive
into a pool of fragrant rose-colored water heated to
body temperature. He watched Bela-37 pop through
the hydrogen interface with himself aboard from the
sensorium track of the shuttle pilot, then watched it
arrive back at the Trek on the news-summary frequency. He stood in his own grand salon glaring
through the party's mists at Haris Bandoora, then
tapped it in realtime—the bare emerald floor, the darkened crystal trees, and, beyond the plex, the great concourse of ships shining in the galactic night.

He was in John Benina's body, looking down on
Sundance Corridor. Vines crawled up and down the

sheer glass faces of the apartments now, and pines grew around the faceted mirror in the center of the square, subduing the usual brilliance. He tapped a fragment of *Let a Thousand Flowers Bloom,* a senso by Iran Capabula that had been premiered during his absence: bent over under a yellow sun in a clear blue sky, he was weeding an endless field of fantastically colorful flowers, soaked in their incenselike perfume. He danced a few measures of *Starburst* as male lead for the Far Look Ballet. He made love for the first time on a hill of blue fur in *Samarkand,* for the last time at Jiz's, and a dozen times in between. He edited *Blackout,* his first senso, and *Wandering Dutchmen,* his latest. He dined amidst colored clouds on *Ariel* and at the shore of Blood Lake on *Lothlorien* and a dozen other meals between. He tapped random sequences of every senso he had ever made.

And when he was through, he was one with the D'mahl that had been, he was back in the universe of infinite realities that he had left; he was whole, and he was home.

Brigadoon, as D'mahl had expected, was totally transformed. But the nature of the current flash was hardly anything that he would have expected, and something about it chilled him at the core.

Twodeck was a sim of an ancient Alpine Earth village—simmed wooden houses, grass growing on synthetic loam, pine trees; even the bulkheads were hidden by a 360-degree holo of snowcapped mountains under a blue sky. The amusements of sixdeck had been cut down and ludicrously simplified to fit into an American county fair motif: Ferris wheel, merry-go-round, dart-and-balloon games, a baseball diamond, even mechanical sims of prize cattle, sheep, dogs, and pigs. Once again, the deck was enclosed in a 360-degree holo, this one of fields of corn waving in a breeze. Eightdeck, a residential deck, was a simmed African village—thatched huts in a circle, a kraal containing mechanical cattle and antelope, lions and hyenas slink-

ing about the holoed veldt that enclosed it. Tendeck
had actually been made over into a functional dirtdigger deck: row after row of pine tree seedlings, thickly
packed vine trellises, beds of flowers, people in dirtdigger green bustling about everywhere.

It wasn't so much the theme of the flash that appalled D'mahl—*Brigadoon* had gone through nature
flashes before—but the monomania of its application,
the humorlessness of it all, the sheer lack of brio. This
latest transformation of *Brigadoon* seemed so deadly
earnest, an attempt to accurately sim old Earth envi-
ronments rather than to use them to ring artistic
changes.

Twelvedeck, Jiz's deck, the epicenter of all of *Brigadoon*'s waves of transformation, appalled him most of
all. Everything was wood and trees. The shops and restaurants were constructed of simmed logs with rough
bark on them; the windows were small square panes of
plex set in wooden grillworks. The furniture in them
was of simmed rough-hewn wood. The paths were flag-
stone. Huge simmed chestnut and eucalyptus trees
were everywhere, towering to the ceiling of the deck to
form an almost seamless forest canopy, and dwarfing
and almost crowding out the modest neoprimitive
cabins. The air had been made redolent with the odors
of burning leaves and moldering loam; birdcalls and
vague animal rustlings burbled continually in the ear.

Jiz Rumoku's gallery was a single large room carved
out of the simmed stump of what would have been an
enormous redwood tree, with her living quarters a
rude lean-to atop it. Inside, the walls and floor were
simmed redwood planking, the ceiling was ribbed by
heavy wooden beams, and an orange fire flickered and
roared in a red-brick fireplace. Elegant simmed oak
tables and chests in the clean, severe Shaker style
served to display representational woodcarvings, clay
pottery, blue-and-white ceramic dishes, simple gold
and silver jewelry, wickerwork baskets and animals,
neohomespun clothing. Cast iron stoves, scythes,

tools, and plowshares were scattered around the gallery.

Jiz stood behind a low table wearing a clinging, form-fitting dress of red-and-white checked gingham, cut in bare-breasted Minoan style. She was drinking something out of a clay mug.

"Jof!" she shouted, and they cross-tapped. D'mahl felt the scratchiness of the dress against her skin as his body kissed her lips and his arms hugged her to him. He tasted the remnants of the drink in her mouth—something sweet, slightly acrid, and vaguely alcoholic. His own lips tasted hard and electric by comparison.

"I don't know where to begin!" she said, as they broke the tap. "Let me tap your sensorium track of the trip!"

"Not in the banks yet," D'mahl said. "Remember, I was cut off."

"That's right! How bizarre! Are you actually going to have to *tell* me about it?"

"I'll tap the recordings into the banks soon enough," D'mahl mumbled, wondering whether he was lying. "But in the meantime, what's all *this*, talking about bizarre?"

"That's right," Jiz said, "you *have* been out of touch. How strange! The transmutational flash didn't last quite as long as I had expected, mostly because it began to seem so artificial, so out of sync with our future vector."

"Future vector?"

"Eden."

"*Eden?*"

"Our coming new home, Jof. We couldn't keep calling it 997-Beta-II, could we? We had a referendum and 'Eden' won, though I preferred Olympia. I've always found the Greek mythos more simpatico."

Chimes of nausea rolled through D'mahl's being from a center of nothingness below his sternum. "Don't you think all this is a bit premature, Jiz?" he said.

"That's the nature of my game, Jof, you know

that," Jiz said, touching the tip of his nose with a playful fingertip. "But this time, I'm doing more than creating flash. I'm helping to prepare us for the transformation."

"Transformation?"

She flitted around the gallery, touching wood, brick, clay, wicker, iron. "Oh Jof, you said it yourself in *Wandering Dutchmen!* Flying Dutchmen on an endless sea, that's what we've been too long. Eternal adolescents low-riding our faerie ships through the night. And now that we've got a chance to grow up, to sink new roots in fresh soil, we've got to sync our minds with the coming reality, we've got to climb off the torch we're riding and get closer to the ground. Wood, brick, iron, clay, growing things! *Planetary* things! We're preparing ourselves to pioneer a virgin world."

"Slok," D'mahl muttered under his breath. "Dirtdigger slok," he said aloud. Something like anger began simmering toward nova inside him.

Jiz paused, a butterfly frozen in mid-dance. "What?"

D'mahl looked at her, bare breasts held high over red-and-white gingham, proudly presiding over the synthetic primitivism she had created, over the vain and pathetic dream that would never be, and for a long moment she seemed to be made of thin clear glass that would shatter at the merest sound of his voice. The gallery, twelvedeck, *Brigadoon*, the Trek were clouds of smoke that would dissipate at a careless wave of his hand. Beyond and within, the void gibbered and laughed at poor wraiths who tried so hard to be real. How can I tell her? D'mahl thought. And to what end? To what damned end?

"Nothing," he said lamely. "I guess I just don't like the idea of growing up. I've got too much pan in my peter."

Jiz giggled as she tapped the triple-reference pun, and it enabled the moment to slide by. But D'mahl felt a distancing opening up between himself and Jiz, between himself and the Trek, between reality and illusion. Is this what it feels like to be a voidsucker? he wondered. If it is, you can torch it to plasma and feed it to the converter!

"But you've been out there, Jof," Jiz said, moving back across the gallery toward him. "You've read the telltale wavefront, you've looked inside the gates of Eden." Her eyes sparkled, but beyond that sugarplum glow D'mahl saw only the lurking void. "Are there oceans with fish and skies full of birds? Is the grass green? Do the plants flower?"

"A gentleman never tells," D'mahl muttered. What do I say, that the green grass is copper salts and the oceans are blue with cyanide and the skies full of poison? He began to feel more sympathy for the voidsuckers now. How could you make a life out of telling people these things? How do *you* like being the angel of death?

"*Jof!*"

"I can't say anything, Jiz. I promised not to."

"Oh come on, how could the voidsuckers or the Council squeeze a promise like that out of you?"

With enormous effort, D'mahl painted a smug smile across his face; the creases in his skin felt like stress-cracks in a mask of glass. "Because that's the quid I'm paying for their pro quo, ducks," he said.

"You mean . . . ?"

"That's right. You didn't think I'd spend all that time out there and let some dry-as-Luna bulletin from the Council upstage me, did you? No bulletin—997-Beta-II—Eden—is my next senso."

Jiz bounced up, then down, and kissed him on the lips. "I cog it'll be your greatest," she said.

D'mahl hugged her briefly to him, his eyes looking through her mane of hair to a set of plain clay dishes on an oaken chest beside the brick fireplace. He shuddered, feeling the void inside every atom of every molecule of matter in those simmed projections of a past that was dead forever into a future that would never be. He was committed to doing it now, the way through was the only way out, and he had taken it upon himself to find it.

"It had better be," he said. "It had damned well better be."

D'mahl stood in Aric Moreau's body amidst solemn people in their loathsome homespun wandering drool-eyed through tightly packed rows of pine seedlings jamming a dirtdigger deck on *Glade.* There was no attempt to sim anything here; the dirtdiggers were force-growing a forest for transplantation to the non-existent fertile soil of Eden, and, as with the other dirtdigger decks he had tapped, aesthetics had been gobbled up by function. Angrily, he made excrement rain from the sky, turned the fashionable neohome-spun garments to filthy denim rags, and threw in a few wrathful lightning bolts for good measure.

He ran the segment of Bela-37's report where the holo of 997-Beta-II hung like an overripe fruit in the center of the scoutship's bridge and made a tongue and mouth appear at the equator, giving a big juicy raspberry. He floated in the void, falling, falling, eter-nally falling into an infinite black hole dusted with meaningless stars. He caused the stars to become crudely painted dots on black paper, and punched his way out of the paper-bag continuum and into—the abyss.

He tapped a newstape from 708, the year 557-Gamma-IV had been the light that failed, and watched Trekkers in Biblical-style robes moping about a dirt-digger deck crammed with overgrown flower beds and the reek of rotting vegetation. He exaggerated the sour expressions into ludicrous clown caricatures of them-selves that melted slowly into pumpkins, and Big Ben chimed midnight. He stood poised on the entrance stage of Bela-37, reeling and quaking, utterly over-whelmed by the black immensities in which the scout-ship hung precariously suspended.

He snorted, took the effects ring off his head like a discarded crown, and sat in the cocoon chair staring moodily at the microtape pod turning futilely on the output spindle of his editor. He pressed a blue button and wiped the pod. The slok I've been laying down these three days just isn't worth saving, he thought. I'm just diddling with the banks and the effects ring; it doesn't add up to anything.

And time was growing short. Everyone knew that Bela-37 had returned, and everyone knew that the reason there had been no bulletin was that Jofe D'mahl was going to release the news in the form of a senso. Jiz in her innocence and Bandoora in his cowardly cunning had seen to that. The longer it took for the senso to appear, the more cosmic import it took on, and the more certain people became that the only possible reason for releasing the scoutship report in this bizarre manner was to do karmic justice to the greatest and most joyous event in the history of the Trek, to write a triumphant finis to man's long torchship ride.

So the longer he sat here dead in space like a ship with its torch blown out, the farther people would travel along hope's false vector, the worse the crash would be when it came, the harder it became to conceive of a senso that could overcome all that dynamic inertia, and on into the next turning of the terrible screw. Now D'mahl understood only too well why the voidsuckers had chosen to lie for half a millennium. The longer the lie went on, the more impossible it became to dare to tell the truth.

And what was the way out that the voidsuckers took? They ignored the asymptotic nature of the Frankenstein Monster they had created and gave themselves over to the void! For them, the ultimate reality was the greatest escape illusion of them all.

D'mahl slammed both hands angrily down on the edge of the editor console. All right, damn it, if the void is where all vectors lead, then the void has to be the core! It's the best footage I've got anyway. I'll go to the center, and I won't come back till I've got the heart of this senso beating in the palm of my hand.

He fitted the pod of his voidsuck onto the

editor's auxiliary playback spindle and programmed continuous-loop replay. He started to program a twenty-four-standard-hour limit, then changed his mind. No, he thought, I want the power in my hand, and I want this to be open-ended. He programmed a cutoff command into the effects ring bank, threw blocks across all other effects programming, and put the ring on his head.

Now he would confront his void footage as if it were the original naked reality, with only the power to break the loop, without the reality-altering powers of the editor. And I won't use the cutoff until I can come back with what I need, he promised himself as he opened his tap to the voidsuck pod. I won't come back until I can come back riding my own torch again.

He was an immortal embryo floating free in the eternal amnion of the universal abyss, and the millions of stars were motes of incandescent matter an infinity away across vast gulfs of absolute nothingness. The overwhelming blackness was an utter absence of everything—light, warmth, sound, color, life—that went on and on without boundaries to give it shape or span to give it meaning. This was the void and he was in it.

But to his surprise, D'mahl found that his mind now immediately grasped this mercilessly true perception of reality without illusion, and with only the residual somatic vertigo and terror recorded on the sensorium tape. Even this soon faded as the tape's memory caught up with the cool clarity of mind it had taken him an unknown duration of disorientation and terror to achieve in realtime.

He was, and he was in the void. He moved, and all else was static. He could perceive his body's shape, the interface between his internal reality and the nothingness outside, and all else was without edge or interface forever in space and time. Outside the realities of his own mind was void without form or end, minutely contaminated with flecks of matter, and man was but the chance end-product of a chain of random and improbable collisions between these insignificant contaminants. The void neither knew nor cared. The void did not exist. It was the eternal and infinite nonexistence that dwarfed and encompassed that which did. D'mahl experienced himself as a thin shell of being around a core of nothingness floating in more nonbeing, a trick anomaly of somethingness lost in timeless and formless forever. Nothing had meaning, not even meaning itself. The wonder was not that life had arisen but once in this endless matrix of nonbeing, but that it had arisen at all.

Black void, meaninglessly dusted with untouchable stars, the internal churnings of his own flesh, the utter knowledge of the utter emptiness that surrounded him, and timeless duration. Once you have reached this place, D'mahl thought, then what? Once asked, the question became ridiculous, for here in the void there was nothing to address any question to but himself. There was nothing to perceive but the absence of perception. There was nothing to perceive. There was nothing. There wasn't.

D'mahl floated in physical nothingness and mental void waiting for the transcendent revelation he had sought. Waiting for the revelation. Waiting for. Waiting. Waiting. Waiting.

Games chased themselves through his mind as he waited in the absence of event, in the absence of meaningful perception, in the absence of measurable time, in the total absence. He counted his own pulsebeats trying to reestablish time, but soon lost count and forgot even what he had been doing. He tried to imagine the nature of what it was he sought, but that immediately tangled itself up in tautological feedback loops: if he knew what he sought, he would not have to seek it. He tried to speculate on what lay beyond the infinite nothingness that surrounded him in order to establish some frame of metaphysical reference, but any such concept hovered forever in unreachable realms of mathematical gobbledygook. He tried to immerse himself in the nothingness itself and found he was there already.

Games evaporated from his consciousness, and then the possibility of games, and he became nothing but a viewpoint trapped in a vacuum of nondata. The blackness of space could no longer be perceived as anything like a color, and the stars became no more than mere flecks of retinal static. Vision and hearing were becoming forgotten concepts in this utter nonreality where the only sensory data seemed to be the noise in the sensory systems themselves.

Thought itself began to follow the senses into oblivion, and finally there was nothing left but a focus of ache in the vast and endless nothing, a bonging mantra of boredom so total, so complete, so without contrast that it became a world of universal pain.

No, not even pain, for pain would have been welcome relief here.

Something somewhere whimpered. Something nowhere whimpered. Nothing nowhere whimpered. Why? Why? Why? it cried. Why? Why? Why? Why is this happening to me? Why is this not happening to me? Why doesn't something happen? Happen . . . happen . . . happen . . . happen . . . happen . . . happen . . .

A mental shout shattered the void. "Why am I doing this to myself?"

And there was mind, chastising itself. And there was mind, chastising itself for its own stupidity. There was mental event, there was content, there was form.

There was the mind of Jofe D'mahl floating forever in eternal boredom. And laughing at itself.

You *are* doing this to yourself, you silly dreek! D'mahl realized. And with that realization, the meaningless patterns on his retinas resolved themselves into a vision of the galactic abyss, speckled with stars. And in his mind, that vision further resolved itself into microtape unreeling endlessly on a pod in his editor in his living quarters on *Excelsior* near the center of the Trek.

You're doing it *all* to yourself, cretin! *You* control this reality, but you forgot you control it. There isn't any problem. There was a problem. The only problem is that we refused to see it.

"Cut," D'mahl tapped, and he was sitting in his co-coon chair bathed in his own sweat, staring at the console of his editor, laughing, feeling the power of his own torch coursing through him, crackling from his fingertips, enlivening his exhausted flesh.

Laughing, he cleared the blocks from his effects banks. Who needs planets? Who needs life beyond the germ we carry? Who needs prime reality at all?

"*Réalité, c'est moi,*" D'mahl muttered. He had said it before, but hadn't savored its full meaning. For on his brow he wore not a crown of thorns but the crown of creation.

He ran back a few feet of the tape and floated once more in the empty stardusted blackness. He laughed. "Let there be light," he tapped. And behold, the firmament shattered, and there was light.

"Cut," Jofe D'mahl tapped. And sat hovering over his editor. And began to carve another segment of his own meaning out of the void.

A bright golden light fills your vision and a delicious warm glow suffuses your body. The light recedes until it becomes something no naked human eye could bear: the plasma heart of a torchtube, which seems to beat and throb like a living thing. And now you are straddling this phoenix-flame; it grows between your legs and yet you are riding it through a galaxy preternaturally filled with stars, a blazing firmament of glory. As you ride faster and faster, as the warm glow in your body builds and builds with every throb of the torchtube, letters of fire light-years high appear across the starfield:

RIDING THE TORCH

by Jofe D'mahl

And you scream in ecstasy and the universe explodes into crystal shards of light.

An old man with long white hair, a matted white beard, dressed in an ancient grimy robe, sits on a fluffy white cloud picking his red, beaklike nose. He has wild-looking pop eyes under bushy white brows and a shock of lightning bolts in his right hand. On the cloud next to him sits Satan in a natty red tuxedo, black cape, and bow tie, with apple-green skin and a spiffy black Vandyke. He is puffing on the end of his long sinuous tail, exhaling occasional whiffs of lavender smoke that smells of brimstone. You are watching this scene from slightly above, inhaling stray Satanic vapors. They are mildly euphoric.

"Job, Job," Satan says. "Aren't you ever going to get tired of bragging about that caper? What did it prove, anyway?"

"That my creatures love me no matter how much crap I dump on them," the old man says. "I don't see them building no Sistine Chapels to *you*, Snake-eyes."

"You really are a sadistic old goat, aren't you? You ought to audition for *my* part."

"You think I couldn't do it? You think you're such a red-hot badass?" The old man stands up, scowling thunders, brandishing his lightning bolts. "By the time I got through with those yucks, they'd be drooling to *you* for mercy. Either way, I am the greatest. Remember how I creamed those Egyptians?"

Satan blows lavender smoke at him. "Ten crummy plagues and a drowning scene. Strictly amateur stuff."

"*Oh yeah? Oh yeah?*" the old man shouts, flinging random lightning bolts, his eyes rolling like pinwheels. "I'll show you who's the tail-torcher around here! I'll show you who's Lord God Allah Jehovah, King of the Universe!"

"Oh, really?" Satan drawls. "Tell you what, you want to make it double or nothing on the Job bet?"

"Anytime, Snake-eyes, anytime!"

"Okay, Mr. I Am, you dumped all you had on Job and he still crawled on his hands and knees to kiss your toes. If you're such a hotshot, let's see you break them. All of them. Let's see you make the whole human race curl up into fetal balls, stick their thumbs in their mouths, and give up. That's the bet, Mr. In the Beginning. I'll take them against you."

"You gotta be kidding! I run this whole show! I'm omniscient, omnipotent, and I can deal marked cards off the bottom of the deck."

"I'll give you even money anyway."

The old man breaks into maniacal laughter. Satan looks up into your face, shrugs, and twirls his finger around his right temple. "You got a bet, sonny!" the old man says. "How's *this* for openers?" And with a mad whoop, he starts flinging lightning bolts down from his cloud onto the world below.

You are standing in a crowded street in Paris as the sky explodes and the buildings melt and run and the Eiffel Tower crumbles and falls and your flesh begins to slough off your bones. You are a great bird, feathers aflame in a burning sky, falling toward a wasteland of blowing ash and burning buildings. You are a dolphin leaping out of a choking bitter sea into sandpaper air. You stand beside your orange orchard watching the trees ignite like torches under a sky-filling fireball as your hair bursts into flame. You lie, unable to breathe, on an endless plain of rubble and gray ash, and the sky is a smear of cancerous purples and browns.

You are watching Satan and the wild-eyed old man drifting above the ruined ball of the Earth on their fleecy clouds. Satan looks a bit greener than before, and he sucks nervously on the end of his tail. The old man, grinning, flings occasional lightning bolts at small islands of green below, turning them to more gray ash and purplish-brown wasteland.

"Zap!" the old man giggles, flinging a bolt. "How's *that*, Snake-eyes? I *told* you I was omnipotent. They never had a chance. Fork over, Charley!" He holds out the palm of his left hand.

"I've got to admit that tops your Land of Egypt number," Satan says. "However . . ." He takes his tail out of his mouth and blows a pointed arrow of lavender smoke upward past your nose. Following it, you see dozens of distant silvery cylinders moving outward into the starry blackness of the galactic night.

"Oh, yeah?" the old man says, cocking a lightning bolt at the fleet of converted asteroid freighters. "I'll take care of *that!*"

"Hold on, Grandpa!" Satan drawls. "You can't win your bet that way! If there are none of them left to give up, then I win and you lose."

Trembling with rage, the old man uncocks his throwing arm. His eyes whirl like runaway galaxies, his teeth grind into each other, and black smoke steams out of his ears. "You think you're so damned smart, do you? You think you can get the best of the old Voice from the Whirlwind, do you? You think those shaved apes have a chance of making it to the next green island in their lousy tin-can outrigger canoes?"

"There's a sweet little world circling Tau Ceti, and they've got what it takes to get that far," Satan says, throwing you a little wink on the side.

"Don't tell me about Tau Ceti!" the old man roars. "I'm omnipotent, I'm omniscient, and I can lick any being in this bar!" He snaps his fingers and you, he, and Satan are standing on a rolling meadow of chartreuse grass under a royal-blue sky scudded with faerie traceries of white cloud. Huge golden fernlike trees sway gently in a sweet fragrant breeze, swarms of tiny neon-bright birds drift among beds of huge orange-, emerald-, ruby-, and sapphire-colored flowers, filling the air with eldritch music. Red velvety kangaroolike creatures with soulful lavender eyes graze contentedly, leap about, and nuzzle each other with long mobile snouts.

"Here's your sweet little world circling Tau Ceti," the old man snarls. "Here's the new Eden those monkeys are making for, and it's as good a job as I did on Earth, if I do say so myself."

"Maybe better," Satan admits.

"Is it?" the old man howls with a voice of thunder. And his eyes rumble and he flings a handful of lightning bolts into the air, and his face turns bright red with rage as he screams: "Turn to slok!"

And the sky becomes a sickly chemical violet veined with ugly gray clouds. And the chartreuse grass, the golden fern trees, and the bright flowers dissolve into a slimy brown muck as the birds and red velvet kangaroos evaporate into foul purple mists. And the brown muck and purple mists mingle and solidify. . . .

And you are clad in a heavy spacesuit, standing on an endless plain of purplish-brown rock under a cruel dead sky, one of a dozen suited men crawling over the planetary corpse like ants on a bone pile.

You are watching Satan and the old man hovering over the converted asteroid freighters of the Trek as they slink away from Tau Ceti V into the galactic night. A gray pall seems to exude from the ships, as if the plex of their ports and blisters were grimed with a million years of despair's filth.

"Take a look at them now!" the old man crows. He snaps his fingers and the three of you are looking down into a primitive dirtdigger deck from a catwalk. The scudding of green is like an unwholesome fungus on the synthetic loam, the air smells of ozone, and the dirtdiggers below are gray hunchbacked gnomes shuffling about as if under 4 gs. "It won't be long now," the old man says. "It's a century to the next live world I've put out here. None of them are going to live to see it, and boy oh boy, do they know it!"

He snaps his fingers again and the three of you are standing by the torchtube in a first-generation residence deck: grim blue corridors, leaden overheads, ugly steel plating, row after row of identical gray doors. The people plodding aimlessly up and down seem as leached of color and life as their surroundings.

"And before their children can get there, they're going to start running out of things," the old man says. "Carbon for their flesh. Calcium for their bones. Phosphorus for their life's juices. Iron for their blood." The light begins to get dim, the walls begin to get misty. The people begin to slump and melt, and you can feel your own bones begin to soften, your blood thinning to water; your whole body feels like a decomposing pudding. "They're going to turn slowly to slok themselves," the old man says, leering.

He snaps his fingers once more, and you are an abstract viewpoint beside the old man and Satan as they hang over the dimming lights of the Trek.

"Well, Snake-eyes, are you ready to pay up now?" the old man says smugly, holding out his palm.

"They haven't given up yet," Satan says, dragging on the tip of his tail.

"You're a stubborn dreek!" the old man snaps irritably.

Satan blows out a plume of lavender smoke that seems endless. It billows and grows and expands into a great cloud of mist that completely envelops the fleet of converted asteroid freighters. "So are they," he says.

And when the lavender mist clears, the Trek has been transformed. Where there had been scores of converted asteroid freighters slinking through space in their own pall of gloom, there are now hundreds of new Trekborn torchships coruscating like a pirate's treasure of jewels against the black velvet of the night, promenading through the abyss behind their own triumphant rainbow shield, the hydrogen interface.

Satan laughs, he cracks his long sinuous tail like a whip, and the three of you are standing beside the great circumtorchtube coils of a sifting deck, amid recovery canisters, control consoles, and a Medusa's head of transfer coils. You can feel the immense power of the torch in your bones, through the soles of your feet. Satan points grandly from canister to canister with the tip of his tail. "Carbon for their flesh," he mimics in a croaking parody of the old man's voice. "Calcium for their bones. Phosphorus for their life's juices. Iron for their blood. And all of it from the interstellar medium itself, which you can't get rid of without shutting down your whole set, Mr. Burning Bush! They're not turning to slok, they're turning slok to themselves."

He breaks into wild laughter, snaps his tail again, and the three of you are standing in a small pine forest in a dirtdigger deck beneath a holoed blue sky inhaling the odors of growing things. "Lo, they have created a garden in your wilderness," Satan says, doubling over with laughter as the old man's face purples with rage. Another crack of the tail and you are floating above a grand promenade in a particularly brilliant amusement deck: restaurants in gold, sapphire, and silver, diamond tables drifting on null-g plates, gypsy dancers twirling weightless in the air, rosy fountains, sparkling music, and the smell of carnival. "And a city of light in your everlasting darkness."

Yet another snap of the tail and the three of you are drifting in the center of the Trek, surrounded by the great concourse of bright ships, under the aurora of the hydrogen interface. Satan holds out his palm to the old man. "Does this look as if they're going to give up, Mr. Have No Others Before Me? All they'll ever need, and all from pure slok! They can go on forever. Cross my palm with silver, Mr. Creator of All He Surveys. Your sons and your daughters are beyond your command."

The old man's face turns from purple to black. Fire shoots out of his nostrils. The hairs of his beard curl and uncurl with a furious electrical crackle. "For I am a god of vengeance and wrath," he roars, "and I am going to smite them hip and thigh."

"You're wasting your dingo act on *me*, cobber," Satan drawls, puffing out lavender smoke rings. "They've got you by the short hairs."

"Oh, have they, sonny? Wait till they get to their next Ultima Thule!" The old man snaps his fingers with a peal of thunder and the three of you are stand-

ing in a forest of immensely tall and stately trees with
iridescent green bark and huge sail-like leaves at their
crown that roll and snap ponderously in the wind. A
thick carpet of brownish mosslike grass covers the cool
forest floor, punctuated with red, blue, yellow, and
purple fans of flowery fungi. Feathered yellow and orange monkey-size bipeds leap from leaf to leaf high
overhead, and fat little purplish balls of fur roll about
the brownish grass nibbling on the fungi. The air
smells of cinnamon and apples, and the slight over-
richness of oxygen makes you pleasantly lightheaded.

"Let me guess," Satan sighs, sucking languidly on
the tip of his tail.

"Turn to slok!" the old man bellows, and his shout
is thunder that rends the sky and the forest crystallizes
and shatters to dust and the brownish grass hardens to
rock and the feathered bipeds and purplish furballs
decompress and explode and you are standing on a
plain of mean brown rock streaked with green under a
blue-black sky soiled with green clouds, and the air
reeks of chlorine.

"You're slipping, Mr. You Were," Satan says. "They
don't need your gardens anymore, for theirs is the
power and the glory forever, amen."

"Oh, is it?" the old man says, grinning. "They don't
need the old Master of the Universe anymore, do they?
You've been the Prince of Liars too long, sonny. You
don't understand how these jerks have been programmed. For thus have I set them one against the
other and each against himself. It's the oldest trick in
the book."

He snaps his fingers and the three of you are pressed
up against the outer bulkhead of an amusement deck
as a wild-eyed mob of dirtdiggers surges through it,
smashing crystal tables, toppling fire-sculptures, brandishing crosses wrapped with simmed grape leaves, and
chanting: "No more ships! No more ships! Soil or
death!"

"They don't need my gardens anymore, do they?"
the old man gloats. "I can play their minds like harp-

sichords, because *I* created their universe, outer *and* inner." He snaps his fingers. "Look at your masters of energy and matter now!"

And you are standing in a corroding dirtdigger deck breathing sour air. The pine trees are stunted, the grass is sickly, and the dirtdiggers' eyes are feverish and shiny as they bow down to the vine-covered cross. "Groveling on their hands and knees where they belong," the old man says. "The old guilt routine, it gets 'em every time." He snaps his fingers again, and you are falling through a droptube through the decks of a well-maintained ship. The air is sweet, the lights clear and bright, the metallic and jeweled surfaces clean and sparkling, but the peacock crowds seem ridden with fear, whirling at nothing, jumping at shadows. "And if the right don't get them, the left hand will," the old man says. "Each man is an island, each man stands alone. What profiteth them if they gain the universe as long as I hold the mortgage on their souls?"

"Ah, but what profiteth them if they *forsake* your cheapjack housing development and *gain* their souls?" Satan says, blowing chains of smoke rings into each passing deck. The rings of lavender smoke alight on the brows of the people and turn into silvery bands—the first full sensory transceivers, ancestors of the tap. "Behold the tap!" Satan says as the transceiver bands melt into the skulls of their wearers, becoming the surgically implanted tap. "The Declaration of Independence from your stage set, O Producer of Biblical Epics! The bridge between the islands! The door to realities into which you may not follow! The crown of creation!"

Satan turns to you as the three of you leave the droptube in a quiet residential deck: walkways of golden bricks wandering among gingerbread houses of amethyst, quartz, topaz. He blows a smoke ring at you which settles on your head and then sinks into your skull. "What about it, man?" he asks you with a cock of his head at the old man. "Is Merlin the Magnificent here the Be-All and End-All, or just another circus act?"

Satan breaks into mad laughter, and then you are snapping your tail, laughing madly, and blowing lavender puffs of smoke at the old man, who stares at you with bugging pop eyes.

"Where did he go?" the old man says.

"Allow me to introduce myself," you say.

"The Lord is not mocked!" the old man shouts.

"Behold the master of space beyond spaces and times beyond time," you say, sucking on the tip of your tail.

You bounce one of the purplish furballs on your hand under huge iridescent green trees. You stand on the Champs Elysées in fair Paris on lost Earth. You dance in Jofe D'mahl's grand salon and pop a flasher into your mouth which explodes in a flash of pink velvet that transforms you into a woman making love to a golden man on black sands on the shore of a silver lake under blue and orange moons. You ride a surfboard of emerald light in the curl of a wave a mile high that rolls across an endless turquoise sea. You soar singing into the heart of a blue-white sun, burning yet unconsumed.

You are a viewpoint beside Satan and the old man rising through a lift-tube in a torchship transformed. Somber dirtdigger shorts turn to cloaks of many colors. Trees, ivy, and flowers sprout from metal deckplates. Corrosion melts from the bulkheads of dirtdigger decks, the vine-colored crosses evaporate, and sour-smelling gloomings become fragrant gardens of delight.

Anger boils through the old man. His red face dopplers through purple into ultraviolet black as sparks fly from his gnashing teeth and tiny lightning bolts crackle from his fingertips. "They've . . . they've . . . they've . . ." He stammers in blind rage, his eyes rolling thunders.

"They've eaten from the Tree of Creation this

time," Satan says with a grin. "How do you like *them* apples?"

"For eating of the Tree of Good and Evil I drove these drool-headed dreeks from Eden with fire and the sword!" the old man roars with the voice of a thousand novas. "For *this* will I wreak such vengeance as will make all that seem like a cakewalk through paradise!"

And he explodes in a blinding flash of light, and now you can see nothing but the starry firmament and an enormous mushroom pillar cloud of nuclear fire light-years high, roiling, immense, static, and eternal. "For now I am become the Lord of Hosts, Breaker of Worlds! Look upon my works, ye mortals, and despair!"

And you are watching Jofe D'mahl flitting from a shuttle to the entrance stage of Bela-37. You watch him emerge from a lift-tube onto the bridge of the scoutship. And you are Jofe D'mahl, staring back through the plex at the Trek, a disk of diamond brilliance behind the rainbow gauze of its hydrogen interface. As you watch, it dwindles slowly to a point of light, one more abstract star lost in the black immensities of the boundless void.

"Overwhelming, isn't it?" Haris Bandoora says, moving partially into your field of vision. "A hundred million stars, perhaps as many planets, and this one galaxy is a speck of matter floating in an endless nothing. Once we were bits of some insignificant anomaly called life contaminating a dust-mote circling a dot of matter lost in the universal void. Now we're not even that."

"We're the part that counts," you say.

"If only you knew."

"Knew what?"

"I've heard the call, Haris." Raj Doru, fever in his fierce brown eyes, has risen to the bridge and walked to Bandoora's side.

You are standing in a voidbubble on Bela-37's entrance stage with Haris Bandoora and Raj Doru. Your field of vision contains nothing but the tiny ship, the abstract stars, the two men, and an infinity of nothing. You reel with vertigo and nausea before that awful abyss.

Doru spreads his arms, turns on his g-polarizer, and leaps up and out into the blackness of the void.

"What's he doing?" you shout.

"Sucking void," Bandoora says. "Answering the call. He'll go out far enough to lose sight of the ship and stay there for a standard day."

"What will he do out there?" you ask softly as Doru disappears into the everlasting night.

"What happens between a man and the void is between a man and the void."

"Why do you do it?"

"Each man has his own reason, D'mahl. The call has many voices. Soon you will hear it in your own language."

And you are standing on the scoutship's bridge watching Haris Bandoora himself disappear into that terrible oceanic immensity.

"Are you hearing the call, Jofe D'mahl?" says the quiet voice of Areth Lorenzi, the ancient voidsucker now standing beside you like a fleshly ghost.

"I'm not sure what I'm hearing," you say. "Maybe just my own ego. I've got to get a voidsuck on tape, or I've wasted my time out here."

"It's the call," she says. "It comes to each of us along his own natural vector."

"There's something you people aren't telling me."

"There is, but to know, you must first taste the void."

You stand in your voidbubble on Bela-37's entrance stage, knees flexed, looking out into the endless abyss into which you are about to leap; millions of needle-point stars prick at your retinas, and the black silences howl in your ears. You inhale and dive up and out into the unknown.

And you float in clear black nothingness where the stars are motes of incandescent matter infinities away across the empty purity of the abyss. Nothing moves. Nothing changes. No event transpires. Silence is eternal. Time does not exist.

"What is it that the voidsuckers know?" you finally say, if only to hear the sound of your own voice. "What is it that they hear out here in this endless nowhere?"

And an immense and horrid laughter rends the fabric of space, and the firmament is rent asunder by an enormous mushroom pillar cloud light-years high that billows and roils and yet remains changeless, outside of time. "You would know what the voidsuckers know, would you, vile mortal?" says the voice from the pillar of nuclear fire. "You would know a truth that would shrivel your soul to a cinder of slok?"

And the mushroom cloud becomes an old man in a tattered robe, with long white hair and beard, parsecs tall, so that his toenails blot out stars and his hands are nebulae. Novas blaze in his eyes, comets flash from his fingertips, and his visage is wrath, utter and eternal. "Behold your universe, upright monkey, all that I now give unto thee, spawn of Adam, and all that shall ever be!"

You stand on a cliff of black rock under a cruel actinic sun choking on vacuum. You tread water in an oily yellow sea that sears your flesh while blue lightnings rend a pale-green sky. Icy-blue snow swirls around you as you crawl across an endless fractured plain of ice under a wan red sun. Your bones creak under 4 gs as you try to stand beneath a craggy overhang while the sky beyond is filthy gray smeared with ugly bands of brown and purple.

"Behold your latest futile hope, wretched creature!" the voice roars. "Behold Eden, 997-Beta-II!" And you stand on a crumbling shelf of striated green rock overlooking a chemically blue sea. The purplish sky is mottled with blue and greenish clouds and the air sears your lungs as your knees begin to buckle, your consciousness to fade.

And once more you float in a void sundered by a

galactic mushroom pillar cloud that becomes a ghastly vision of an old man light-years tall. The utter emptiness of the interstellar abyss burns with X-ray fire from the black holes of his eyes, his hair and beard are manes of white-hot flame that sear the firmament, his hands are claws crushing star clusters, his mouth is a scar of death across the face of the galaxy, and his rage is absolute.

"Slok, stinking microbe!" he howls with a voice that blasts ten thousand planets from their orbits. "It's all slok! That's what the voidsuckers know. Lo, I have created a universe for you that goes on forever, time and space without end. And in all that creation, one garden where life abounded, one Earth, one Eden, and that you have destroyed forever. And all else is slok— empty void, poison gas, and dead matter, worlds without end, time without mercy! Behold my works, mortals, behold your prison, and despair!"

And his laughter shakes the galaxy and his eyes are like unto the nether pits of hell.

You shake your head, and you smile. You point your right forefinger at the ravening colossus. "You're forgetting something, you lamer," you say. "*I* created this reality. You're not real. Evaporate, you drool-headed dreek!"

And the monstrous old man begins to dissolve into a huge lavender mist. "I may not be real," he says, "but the situation you find yourself in sure is. Talk your way out of that one!" He disappears, thumbing his nose.

And you are watching Jofe D'mahl, a small figure in a shiny mirror suit standing alone in the eternal abyss. He turns to you, begins to grow, speaks.

> Have thou and I not against fate conspired,
> And seized this sorry scheme of things entire?
> And shaped it closer to the heart's desire?

D'mahl's mirror suit begins to flash endlessly through the colors of the spectrum. Lightnings crackle from his fingertips and auroras halo his body like waves of hydrogen interfaces. "Let there be light, we have said on the first day, and there is light."

You are D'mahl as the entire jeweled glory of two thousand and forty torchships springs into being around you. "Let there be heavens, we have said on the second day," you say, and you are standing on a meadow of rolling purple hills under a rainbow sky in a dancing multitude of Trekkers. "And Earth." And the multitude is transported to *Erewhon*, where the dirtdiggers have combined three whole decks and created a forest of towering pines and lordly oaks under an azure sky.

"Let there be matter and energy without end, we have said on the third day," you say, and you feel the power flowing through your body as you straddle a naked torchtube, as you become the torch you are riding. "And there is matter and energy everlasting."

"And now on the fourth day, we have rested," you say, floating in the void. "And contemplated that which we have not made. And found it devoid of life or meaning, and hopelessly lame."

"And on the fifth day," D'mahl says as you watch him standing in the blackness in his suit of many lights, "we shall give up the things of childhood—gods and demons, planets and suns, guilts and regrets."

D'mahl is standing in front of a huge shimmer screen overlooking the grass and forest of a dirtdigger deck. "And on the sixth day, shall we not say, let there be life? And shall there not be life?"

Bears, cows, unicorns, horses, dogs, lions, giraffes, red velvety kangaroolike creatures, hippos, elephants, tigers, buffalo, mice, hummingbirds, shrews, rabbits, geese, zebras, goats, monkeys, winged dragons, tapirs, eagles come tumbling, soaring, and gamboling out of the shimmer screen to fill the forest and meadow with their music.

And you are D'mahl, feeling the power of the torch pour through your body, flash from your fingertips, as you stand in the center of the Trek, awash in light and life and motion, saying: "And on the seventh day, shall we not say, let us be fruitful and multiply and fill the dead and infinite reaches of the void with ships and life and meaning?"

And you stretch out your arms and torchships explode into being around you as the Trek opens like an enormous blossoming mandala, filling the blackness of the abyss with itself, immense, forever unfolding, and eternal. "And shall not that day be without end?"

Afterword by Fritz Leiber

When I was first getting into *Torch* I couldn't help thinking of Henry Kuttner's early science-fiction series of Hollywood on the Moon—because Norm Spinrad does the frenetic, murderously competitive Hollywood-Broadway opening night atmosphere so very well. I found myself casting Liz Taylor as Jiz Rumoku, Erich Von Stroheim (or Max von Sydow?) as Bandoora, with the director himself (Peter Bogdanovich?) playing D'mahl. And when you get down to it, it's really not at all farfetched to think of doing *Torch* as a film, remembering *2001, Star Wars, Zardoz, The Man Who Fell to Earth,* and the living forests loaded aboard giant spaceships in *Silent Running.* And the film-within-a-film form would actually help.

Of course as I got into the story I realized that the colossal sensos were more in the nature of vast species-experiences, like the acts of mass telepathic communion of all mature intelligences in Olaf Stapledon's *Starmaker,* and indeed this is the way that Norm ultimately brings them off. Still, the theatric element is always there. My father played a Bible-quoting Dutch sailor in David Belasco's production of *Vanderdecken* back around 1920 with David Warfield as the Flying Dutchman himself, and so I early became acquainted with the legend of the Hollandish skipper doomed to spend eternity trying to round Cape Horn in the face of God's unending storms—"And I'll double the Cape if it takes till Judgment Day. And a curse on the wind and waves. And a curse on Him who made them!"

It is artful of Norm to have given shape to his book by joining this legend to that of Job, who, when directed to "Curse God and Die," elects to endure instead and praise the cosmic creativity which gave the horse strength and "clothed his neck with thunder. The glory of his nostrils is terrible"—and formed that leviathan who "maketh the deep to boil like a pot," and "maketh a path to shine after him; one would think the deep to be hoary. Upon earth is not his like, who is made without fear." Truly, in legend there is strength.

Torch is of course a trek novel, taking the form of a quest across the galaxy and beyond, one of a long line including the Grey Lensman's search through the galaxy for weapons and allies against the Eich, the cosmos-spanning quest of *Starmaker*, the treks in Heinlein's books—*Have Spacesuit—Will Travel*, *Citizen of the Galaxy*, the long, long treks of the *Children of Methuselah* and Lazarus Long—and *Star Trek* itself. With this difference, that in *Torch* the trek's discovery that what it is searching for is itself provides the denouement. Norm was early—prophetic—in pointing out that man does not need planets, he can live in space without them.

In D'mahl's last and maturer senso, we find God and the Devil played naturally enough for comedy—in the film they'd be animations. I particularly like the way the comically wrathful Old Testament Jehovah dissolves into a huge lavender mist while saying, "I may not be real, but the situation you find yourself in sure is. Talk your way out of that one!" (He disappears, thumbing his nose.)

It somehow reminds me of Charles Fort's story of the dog who said "Good morning" and vanished in a cloud of green gas. ("You can't fool me with that dog story," Fort said.)

Will it all work out as well as D'mahl envisages and appears to hope it will? Will man be able to face the void bravely without his supernatural security blanket and in the absence of any intelligence in the cosmos other than his own? Will the telepathy of tap and the communion of the sensos be sufficient to allow him to take up the task of the *Last Men* of Stapledon of creating intelligences greater and more diverse than his own? I wish I knew.

I don't know why *Torch* is such a short novel, but I sure know why *Destiny Times Three* is. I wrote it during World War II, while I was a precision inspector at Douglas Aircraft, Santa Monica plant, and in the months immediately thereafter. I'd been successful with my three-part serial, *Gather Darkness!* in the magazine *Astounding Stories,* and this new one, originally titled *Roots of Yggdrasil* after the Norse legend of the three worlds of the Gods, the Frost Giants, and Man, was going to be my masterpiece, a four- or five-parter at least—a big canvas to fit a big subject.

But before I began writing it I sent my plans and outline to *Astounding*'s editor, John W. Campbell, Jr., for his approval and any helpful advice he might be able to give me. (I'd profited greatly from his astute suggestions on my earlier novel and also on *Conjure Wife,* which had sold to his *Unknown.*)

If I'd asked my question a few months earlier or later, it would have been all right, but at that particular time many of *Astounding*'s readers were among the American servicemen fanned out across the world, and some of them had been writing him asking him not to publish any serials, because they could never be sure of getting the next issue. So he told me, "Make it a two-parter, at most."

And so in the course of one feverish, miserable, long castrating night, I spread my vast outline on the cleared dining-room table and ruthlessly pared it down. (I and my wife needed the money!) My God, I even cut out all the female characters—something had to go and they were a shade less central to the plot.

You see, in the threefold world of that story each major character *had* to exist in triplicate (amount to *three* major characters) ; otherwise the whole different-destinies point would be lost. At only 40,000 words or so, I couldn't handle over a dozen major characters. A drastic simplification to a manageable six was required, though I'm sure now it was a mistake to sacrifice the women. As a result, the diminished novel has a ghostly, cold, lonely male quality to me, peopled by the resentful, unseen feminine presences of all those cut characters. I don't think my Anima ever forgave me.

I'm sorry about that, for at the time I greatly loved that world of giant skyscrapers known by their colors and cross sections—the Black Star, the Scarlet T, the Mauve H, and so on. It's not good to pull in your sights, scale down your concepts. For the next five years I had a lot of trouble writing anything at all. My vengeful Anima, perhaps.

I'm not the only one to have suffered that way. In the early days of science-fiction paperbacks (the late 1940s and 1950s), publishers considered a science-fiction novel over 60,000 words to be unthinkable, out of the question. James Blish, for instance, had to pare down *A Case of Conscience* to get Ballantine to publish it.

I'm glad that my 125,000-word *The Wanderer* (happily with the aid of Ballantine) was one of the books that helped break that straitjacket.

The Latest Science Fiction And Fantasy From Dell

☐ WOLFLING by Gordon R. Dickson $1.50 (19633-7)

☐ A PLACE BEYOND MAN
   by Cary Neeper $1.50 (16931-3)

☐ INTERWORLD by Isidore Haiblum $1.50 (12285-6)

☐ THE RETURN by Isidore Haiblum $1.50 (17395-7)

☐ FADE OUT by Patrick Tilley $1.95 (12232-5)

☐ HEALER by F. Paul Wilson $1.50 (13569-9)

☐ THE SILVER WARRIORS
   by Michael Moorcock $1.50 (17994-7)

☐ DEUS IRAE by Philip K. Dick and
   Roger Zelazny $1.75 (11838-7)

☐ YLANA OF CALLISTO by Lin Carter...$1.50 (14244-X)

☐ JANDAR OF CALLISTO
   by Lin Carter $1.50 (14182-6)

☐ FLASHING SWORDS! #4:
   BARBARIANS AND BLACK
   MAGICIANS edited by Lin Carter $1.50 (12627-4)

At your local bookstore or use this handy coupon for ordering:

Dell DELL BOOKS
P.O. BOX 1000, PINEBROOK, N.J. 07058

Please send me the books I have checked above. I am enclosing $_____
(please add 35¢ per copy to cover postage and handling). Send check or money
order—no cash or C.O.D.'s. Please allow up to 8 weeks for shipment.

Mr/Mrs/Miss_____

Address_____

City_____ State/Zip_____

They came to Hudson City
offering so much.
And all of it was evil.

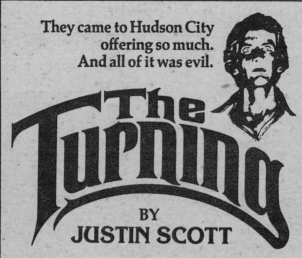

The Turning

BY
JUSTIN SCOTT

Hudson City was a sleepy upstate New York
town, until They came. The Revelationists.
Healthy, fresh-faced young people from the West
Coast filled with a raging fervor. One by one they
came to Hudson City. Like a black shadow, they
moved across the country to fulfill their mission.

Someone would have to be ready to resist.

A Dell Book $1.95

At your local bookstore or use this handy coupon for ordering:

Dell	**DELL BOOKS** **P.O. BOX 1000, PINEBROOK, N.J. 07058**	THE TURNING $1.95 (17472-4)

Please send me the above title. I am enclosing $_____
(please add 35¢ per copy to cover postage and handling). Send check or money
order—no cash or C.O.D.'s. Please allow up to 8 weeks for shipment.

Mr/Mrs/Miss_____

Address_____

City_____ State/Zip_____

AT LAST!
TEN YEARS IN THE MAKING!
Richard A. Lupoff's

The most outrageous, audacious, daring,
romantic, poignant, touching, biting, satiric,
violent space adventure you've ever read!

"There has never been a thing like this one
before. It will raise one hell of a noise!"
—Harlan Ellison

A Dell Book $1.95

At your local bookstore or use this handy coupon for ordering:

Dell | **DELL BOOKS**
P.O. BOX 1000, PINEBROOK, N.J. 07058

SPACE WAR BLUES $1.95 (16292-0)

Please send me the above title. I am enclosing $_____
(please add 35¢ per copy to cover postage and handling). Send check or money
order—no cash or C.O.D.'s. Please allow up to 8 weeks for shipment.

Mr/Mrs/Miss_____

Address_____

City_____ State/Zip_____

Dell Bestsellers

☐ **THE PROMISE** a novel by Danielle Steel
  based on a screenplay by
  Garry Michael White $1.95 (17079-6)
☐ **PUNISH THE SINNERS** by John Saul $1.95 (17084-2)
☐ **FLAMES OF DESIRE** by Vanessa Royall $1.95 (14637-2)
☐ **THE HOUSE OF CHRISTINA** by Ben Haas....$2.25 (13793-4)
☐ **CONVOY** by B.W.L. Norton $1.95 (11298-2)
☐ **F.I.S.T.** by Joe Eszterhas $2.25 (12650-9)
☐ **HIDDEN FIRES** by Janette Radcliffe $1.95 (10657-5)
☐ **SARGASSO** by Edwin Corley $1.95 (17575-5)
☐ **CLOSE ENCOUNTERS OF THE THIRD KIND**
  by Steven Spielberg..$1.95 (11433-0)
☐ **THE TURNING** by Justin Scott $1.95 (17472-4)
☐ **NO RIVER SO WIDE** by Pierre Danton $1.95 (10215-4)
☐ **ROOTS** by Alex Haley $2.75 (17464-3)
☐ **THE CHOIRBOYS** by Joseph Wambaugh $2.25 (11188-9)
☐ **CLOSING TIME** by Lacey Fosburgh $1.95 (11302-4)
☐ **THIN AIR** by George E. Simpson and
  Neal R. Burger $1.95 (18709-5)
☐ **PROUD BLOOD** by Joy Carroll $1.95 (11562-0)
☐ **NOW AND FOREVER** by Danielle Steel $1.95 (11743-7)
☐ **A PLACE TO COME TO**
  by Robert Penn Warren $2.25 (15999-7)
☐ **STAR FIRE** by Ingo Swann $1.95 (18219-0)

At your local bookstore or use this handy coupon for ordering:

Dell | **DELL BOOKS**
P.O. BOX 1000, PINEBROOK, N.J. 07058

Please send me the books I have checked above. I am enclosing $_____
(please add 35¢ per copy to cover postage and handling). Send check or money
order—no cash or C.O.D.'s. Please allow up to 8 weeks for shipment.

Mr/Mrs/Miss_____

Address_____

City_____State/Zip_____

A MAJOR SCIENCE FICTION EVENT!

DEUS IRAE

Two Award-Winning Giants Together for the First Time!
PHILIP K. DICK & ROGER ZELAZNY

PHILIP K. DICK: Hugo Award winning author of *The Man in the High Castle* and *A Scanner Darkly*.

ROGER ZELAZNY: Hugo and Nebula Award winning author of *Lord of Light* and *Nine Princes in Amber*.

Together they have created a powerful and wondrous vision of the future, an amazing journey of imagination and wonder, in search of the Great God of Wrath.

"The most successful collaboration in years!" —Library Journal

A Dell Book $1.75

At your local bookstore or use this handy coupon for ordering:

| Dell | **DELL BOOKS**
P.O. BOX 1000, PINEBROOK, N.J. 07058 | DEUS IRAE $1.75   (11838-7) |

Please send me the above title. I am enclosing $_____
(please add 35¢ per copy to cover postage and handling). Send check or money order—no cash or C.O.D.'s. Please allow up to 8 weeks for shipment.

Mr/Mrs/Miss_____

Address_____

City_____ State/Zip_____